USA Today, and *Wall Street Journal* bestselling author, Nina Levine, lives in Brisbane, Australia, and is the author of more than thirty romantic suspense and contemporary romance novels, including the international bestselling Escape With a Billionaire and Storm MC series.

CONNECT ONLINE

ninalevineromance.com

authorninalevine

AuthorNinaLevine

RECKLESSLY, WILDLY YOURS

USA *TODAY* BESTSELLING AUTHOR
NINA LEVINE

DEDICATION

To my readers.
I am so grateful for you.
I've been doing this for ten years now and this is the book that
made me fall in love with writing all over again and get
excited for another ten years.
I hope you love Ethan & Maddie as much as I do.
N x

GLOSSARY OF SLANG

BMS: broke my scale i.e. in reference to someone's attractiveness where on a scale of 1-10, they broke the scale, and their attractiveness is off the charts.

MFW: my face when, used to indicate someone's reaction in a scenario.

OOMF: one of my followers.

TFW: that feeling when, references a particular feeling in a specific situation.

Ate that: used to indicate someone doing a good job at something.

It's giving: used to reference something giving off a certain vibe.

Main character energy: you're acting as if you're the star of your own show. Used in a positive light.

Unalive: used as an alternative for kill.

Credit card slam: used in the same context as "shut up and take my money".

Say sike rn: translates to "please tell me you're joking right now".

We stan a ___ queen/king: it means you're a fan of that person and support them i.e. if a certain singer was focused on asking for permission before touching people while shooting a music video for one of their songs, you'd say, "We stan a consent king."

Moots: short for "mutuals" i.e. when you follow someone on social media, and they follow you back.

Ick: something that someone does that is an instant turn-off for you, making you hate the idea of being romantically involved with them.

Beige flag: something that's neither good nor bad but that makes you pause when you notice it and then just continue on. Something odd. Similar to red flags (bad) and green flags (good).

Sheesh: daaaamn!

Heather: a beautiful, popular "desirable person" that everyone is in love or like with.

rn: right now.

RedZone: subscription service for football games.

ILY: I love you.

1

MADELINE

BESTIE, giddyap! Strap on your riding boots, we're in our cowgirl era now! Ya'll know that the country music scene isn't really for us, but then there's country superstar @madelinemontana and we adore that girl so we're always on #MaddieWatch and today is her wedding day! We've loved having front row seats for the magical love story between Maddie and Country King @tuckerbrandt over the last three years and can't wait to see them get hitched and start making beautiful babies together. Tucker has talked openly about his desire to see Maddie with his baby in her belly and we are here for all of this. I mean, the #daddysigh is a real thing and he always makes us sigh when he talks about wanting to be a daddy. Stay tuned for all the updates on this celebrity wedding. We're all over it!

· · ·

I PACE my hotel room and take a deep breath as I read the Instagram post from The Tea, my anxiety over today spiking to all new levels. I've never suffered high anxiety until this past year. Planning my wedding to Tucker has been one anxious journey and here I am today feeling it in every bone of my body.

Your wedding day is supposed to be one of the best days of your life but I've already vomited once and I think I could spend the rest of the day being sick. Reading social media posts like the one I just read only makes everything worse.

Since the day three years ago that Tucker released a duet he recorded with me, his rabid fan base has been all over us. Tucker is the reigning King of Country and has been for five years. I was a nobody songwriter sent to write a song with him and our instant connection helped us write a song that debuted at No. 1 on the Top 100 chart and stayed there for twenty weeks. Tucker took me under his wing and literally propelled me to instant country superstardom. His fans also took me under their wing, especially since he started a relationship with me and moved me into his home five weeks after we met.

Our whirlwind love story has been a story both our fan bases have been heavily invested in for years which has me all twisted up because what I'm contemplating doing is something that would shock them all and likely harm my career.

I can't marry Tucker and I really wish I hadn't spent the last six months burying my head in the sand on this decision because now I have two hours before I'll be saying "I do" and joining our lives together in ways I know deep down I don't want them to be joined.

I'm lost in these thoughts when my phone rings, my manager's name appearing on the screen.

"Shit." The word barely whispers from my lips as my thoughts and feelings crash their way around my head and heart. My voice seems too soft. It comes nowhere close to conveying the confusion and conflict consuming me.

The call ends but starts up again almost immediately. Darren is nothing if not persistent. And resourceful. If I don't answer his call, he'll find another way to get what he wants from me.

I put the phone to my ear. "Darren."

His voice comes on the line clipped as usual. "Tucker is on his way and I'll be there in about twenty minutes. Make sure you're ready for the wedding then because there won't be any free time after we arrive."

God, I hate this man. With a burning passion.

"No, I've got two hours and I'm not giving up even a second of them. Whatever you have planned for me can wait until after the ceremony."

"Today isn't the day to dig your heels in on whatever rebellion you've been waging with me for the past month, Madeline. We've got problems with the tour that can't wait to be fixed. Just be ready by the time Tucker and I get there."

I open my mouth to argue with him but the call ends and I'm left staring at my phone like I always am when this man manipulates me into doing what he wants. Which, if I'm honest, is also what my fiancé has been doing for three years. Manipulating me.

"Shit, shit, shit." Still a whisper. Still not loud enough. But then, I've always stayed quiet, smiled, and gotten on with it. Neither of these men have heard me get loud. *The world* has never heard me get loud.

I draw a long breath in and eye myself in the full-length mirror. Placing my hands to my stomach, I attempt to calm my nerves and the anger that's gathering.

My long blonde hair falls in beautiful curls down over my white mermaid wedding dress that's made of antique lace crotchet. The dress has a low back and plunging neckline, revealing more skin than I've ever shown in public. It hugs every curve of my body and I hate it. But Tucker and Darren agreed it was perfect. For our fans, that is. Darren especially wants to give them something they've never seen from me. He wants to cultivate a whole new level of interest in us and is convinced a new sexy look will achieve that.

I've wanted to scream at him that a wedding is about love not commerce.

I've wanted to scream that I didn't say yes to Tucker so I could put myself on display for the world on the day that's supposed to be just about us.

I've wanted to scream that I'm done.

Because I *am* done.

And I'm so angry at myself right now for ignoring that fact for six months.

I pull in more air trying to find my center. The problem with trying to do that when you've given your center away for so long is that you have no clue where to even begin finding it.

Grab your purse and your phone. That's all you need. And then get the hell out of here.

My mind is a mess but I know these thoughts are right.

I need to leave before Tucker or Darren arrive. It's the only way I have a shot at figuring out what I truly want to do because I need space and that's not something either of them have ever given me.

I'm halfway out of the hotel suite when a text comes through from Tucker.

TUCKER

Babe. Darren's on his way to go over some tour bullshit before the wedding. I was gonna make it there before him but I've been held up so just start without me.

This text slows me down for two reasons. Firstly, it's not the kind of text I ever imagined a man would send his soon-to-be wife on their wedding day. It's certainly not what I would have hoped to receive from my fiancé. Second, I know why he's been held up and the fact that I'm relieved rather than furious tells me everything I need to know right now.

My fiancé is going to be late because he's fucking another woman and he's just inadvertently given me the go-ahead to skip our wedding.

I gather up the short train of my dress and keep hold of it while I run even though running in a mermaid dress is almost impossible. I have no idea where I'm heading but for the first time in my life, I don't care. Anywhere would be better than where I am.

2

ETHAN

GAGE

Are you nearly here?

ME

Almost.

HAYDEN

Almost to you means something very different to us. How far away are you exactly?

ME

Traffic is ridiculous today.

GAGE

Jesus, Ethan, how far?

BRADFORD

You have the rings, right?

ME

Yes, I have the rings.

I START TAPPING out a text to my brothers with my ETA but am distracted midway when a blonde woman runs into the hectic Manhattan traffic I'm sitting in, causing a near accident. Taxis and cars swerve to miss her and George, my driver, slams on the brakes. He lets out a string of curse words while I wonder what's made her put herself in harm's way.

The sound of horns blaring and people yelling doesn't seem to deter her. She continues running through the traffic as I watch in interest. I wish I had my camera here so I could capture the escape she appears to be making. Or perhaps it's not an escape but rather she's late. For her wedding, that is, because she's wearing a wedding dress of all things.

She disappears across the street and when I lose sight of her, I go back to my phone.

ME

I'm less than ten minutes away. Maybe fifteen.

GAGE

Fuck me. I should have just gotten the rings myself.

ME

This was unavoidable. My flight was late and I don't know what's going on in Manhattan today but something has the traffic jammed up.

BRADFORD

See you soon.

The car starts moving but then jerks to a halt almost immediately. I glance up to find the bride again, this time darting back through the traffic in the direction she came from. She's got the train of her dress hiked up so she can hold it high enough to not trip on it. When she's halfway across the street, she abruptly stops and jerks her head to look in all directions, panic etched across her delicate features. Like a gazelle trapped in the concrete jungle.

A text comes in as I'm contemplating what the hell is going on in her life to cause this kind of behavior.

> GAGE
>
> Don't be late. Callan's counting on you being here on time.

Fuck.

I haven't seen my family in fifteen months and the last thing I want is to be late to my brother's wedding. I eye the blonde who has managed to singlehandedly cause traffic chaos on a busy Saturday in the middle of Manhattan. She appears to be frozen and unsure of what to do and all I can think is if she doesn't get herself together soon, my best man duties are at risk. And if that happens, my strained relationship with Callan will also be at risk. Not to mention the fact I promised his fiancée, Olivia, one of my oldest friends, that nothing will stop me from being by my brother's side while he marries her.

As George rants about the holdup, I exit the car and stride toward the blonde. Her eyes meet mine as I draw nearer, and up close, I see just how alarmed she is. Big, blue, almond-shaped eyes with long lashes that aren't that fake shit I hate stare back at me, and if I'm not mistaken, they're screaming for help.

"Have you got a death wish today?" I ask, horns

loudly blaring all around us. "Because these drivers aren't far from anarchy if you keep them waiting."

She's a living statue adorned in white lace. Barely breathing. "No." Her answer whispers out of her on a rush of anxiety.

If there's one thing I understand the fuck out of, it's anxiety. This causes me to momentarily forget the fact I'm in a hurry and that she's the one stalling my journey. I soften my voice and ask, "Do you need help?"

Her eyes flare a fraction and she nods. The fact there's no hesitation in that nod propels me into action.

I gently but firmly take hold of her arm, and usher her to the car. There's no uncertainty in her steps, which reassures me that she really does want my help.

I help settle her in the car, noting the frantic edge to her movements as she secures her seatbelt. "Are you running to your wedding or from it?" I figure we may be able to drop her somewhere on our way.

Her breath catches as she looks at me. "From it." She shifts her gaze to the window, scanning the busy street while the car restarts the slow crawl to the church where Callan is getting married. She then quickly inspects the back seat of the car like she's looking for something. When she spots my backpack, she asks, "Do you have a jacket?" Her question feels urgent.

"No." I frown. "Are you cold?" She shouldn't be. It's a warm eighty degrees today.

She ignores my question, her fingers shaking as she removes her earrings. "What about a T-shirt?"

I watch as she drops her earrings into her purse before running her fingers through her long hair, quickly tousling the perfect waves like she's trying to mess them up. "No T-shirt I'm afraid. I do have cash though if you want to go buy yourself some clothes."

"A hat maybe?" Her voice wavers.

"I'm sure there's a store that sells hats close by," I offer, trying to calm her nerves.

"No, do you have one in your backpack?"

I lean in close toward her and whisper conspiratorially, "Are you trying to disguise yourself so your fiancé doesn't find you?" I'm joking, still trying to help her shift her anxiousness, but the look in her eyes tells me I'm not wrong. "Fuck, okay." I grab my backpack and pass her my cap. "Are you in danger? Has he hurt you? Do you need —"

"No, nothing like that." She secures my well-worn baseball cap in place and hell if it doesn't look good on her. "Let's just say that being unrecognizable would make my life easier right now."

"Right. Here then, put these on." I retrieve my sunglasses and hand them to her.

She smiles as she takes them. It's soft, tentative, more a delicate curve of her lips than a real smile but there's a subtle easing of her tension in it. A hint that her frayed nerves have found a temporary respite. "Thank you," she says with quiet sincerity.

I return her smile. "That dress really is going to be a problem though. I'm not sure why you thought it a good idea to stage an escape in such an outfit."

She regards me for a long beat. Her shoulders relax and her eyes flicker with amusement. "Believe me, it seemed like a better plan in my head."

"Well, you certainly made an impression on New York."

She peers out of the car again when it comes to a stop at the lights. "Not really the kind of impression I ever hope for." Then, her eyes widen as she spots something through the window. "Shit," she mutters before diving face first into my lap and burying herself there like her life depends on it.

In the space between her face meeting my crotch and my brain catching up to this, I share a moment with my driver in the rearview mirror. George gives me a look. *What the fuck have we walked into here?* I shoot him back: *Just go with me here.*

I glance down at the blonde. "Do we have a problem?"

She doesn't lift her head. Instead, her answer is muffled as she talks into my lap. "Can you see those two guys in suits across the street?"

I locate the men she's referencing. Two brick walls of muscle surveying the crowd like they're looking for someone. "Tell me you're not supposed to be marrying into the mafia today."

"That's not a bad comparison." She lifts her head a little to glance up at me. "What are they doing?"

I take another look. "One is on his phone. The other is searching for you, I presume."

"Right, but what *exactly* is he doing?"

"Well, right now he's reaching his hand into his trouser pocket—"

"No, is he coming this way?"

I shake my head. "They're both still on the sidewalk."

She exhales her relief.

"Who are they?" I ask, intrigued as fuck over what's happening. So much so that I'm ignoring my phone that's vibrating in my pocket with what I guess are texts from my brothers. It's not every day a man's sitting in traffic minding his own business when a beautiful bride crashes into his life.

"My security guys."

"And you need security because?"

"Are they still on the sidewalk?"

"I note your skill of avoiding questions."

"We don't really have time for all these questions right now."

"But we have time for you to get up close and personal with my lap?"

"Are they still on the sidewalk?"

"Yes, still there. Still on the phone and...no, now they're walking through the traffic."

"Shit."

"They're coming our way." My eyes flick down to hers. "Are we going to have a problem if they find you with your face where it is?"

Before I see it coming, she reaches for my neck and pulls me down while shifting positions so she's lying across the back seat with me on top of her.

She grips my neck tightly while staring up into my eyes with determination. "Cover me with your body so they can't see my dress if they look in the car."

"I'll take that as a yes to my question about the kind of trouble we're in."

She makes eyes at me that blaze with *just do as I say* vibes, and since I'm a man who prefers not to argue with a woman when she's on a mission, I do as she says.

I spread my body over hers while also doing my best to tuck her dress under me. "It's a good thing you're not into meringue tidal wave dresses."

Her brows pull together. "What's a tidal wave dress?"

"Those wedding dresses that look like a small country's entire supply of fabric was required to make them."

She continues to frown. "Right, but a tidal wave? Where do you get that comparison?"

"I thought we didn't have time for questions." When she simply waits me out for my answer, I continue, "Got it. No time for *my* questions. A dress reminds me of a tidal wave when it overwhelms the bride with so much material and movement that it looks like sea foam crashing into her."

Her frown eases and she studies me thoughtfully. But only for a second because right after I give her my answer, George says, "Boss, the muscle is getting closer. They're three cars away."

It turns out my partner in crime likes getting intimate with new friends in more ways than one. At George's announcement, she grasps my neck tighter, and before I have a chance to object, she pulls my mouth to hers and kisses me.

It's not an all-in kiss. It certainly doesn't match the boldness with which she made her move. But hell if it doesn't silence the world and make me forget everything on my mind.

Her lips are the softest I've ever known, but that could be because it's been a long time since I've kissed a woman and my memory fails me. I'm only just getting acquainted with them when she drags her mouth from mine and blinks up at me with an apology.

"I'm sorry," she whispers.

"Don't be."

"No, really. I've barged my way into your life and now I'm making you shield me and kiss me."

"There are worse ways to spend a day."

"One car away now," George says.

The look of panic in the blonde's eyes lets me know what she needs from me. Within a second, I've got my mouth on hers again and this time we're not fucking around. This time, I claim the kiss I want.

My tongue slides over hers, and I deepen the kiss while taking hold of her face. My thumb trails slowly along her jawline as every nerve ending of mine awakens. The sensations of her curves molding perfectly against mine; her floral scent intoxicating me; her lips moving in synchrony with mine; and her fingers burning heat into my skin all unleash desire through me. It's been too long since I've lost myself in a woman and I could get so fucking lost in this one.

When she moans into my mouth, I'm helpless but to grind against her and growl my response.

Fuck.

It's her wedding day and my behavior is inappropriate.

I tear my mouth from hers. "That was out of line. I'm sorry."

She doesn't let my neck go. "I'm the one who demanded you kiss me."

"Right, but you didn't demand I force myself on you like that."

"It didn't feel like you forced yourself on me."

"Well, I certainly didn't act like a gentleman."

Her fingers loosen their hold on me. "Trust me when I tell you you're the only gentleman I've had contact with in years. You have absolutely nothing to apologize for. This is all on me."

In years?

My curiosity reaches new heights but now isn't the time for more questions because my complete focus is on separating my body from hers. "George, where are we at?" I ask my driver.

"The threat has passed and it looks like we're about to start moving again." I hear the silent laughter in his voice. After working together for five years and having built a friendship in that time, we can read each other in all the small ways. He's finding this situation highly amusing.

"They've gone?" the blonde asks, hope rising in her tone.

"Yes, ma'am," George says.

I smile down at her as the car begins inching forward again. "My job here appears to be done. Are you good if we refrain from kissing again? I did give you my sunglasses, after all. I think they'll do the job from here on out."

Her eyes twinkle. "You're probably right."

I move off her and when we've both gathered ourselves, I nod at her purse where I can hear her phone going berserk. "You think that's your groom?"

She shakes her head. "No. He's busy fucking another woman right now."

"Right." My mouth snaps shut as a thousand emotions course through me at what she just said. "Fuck." Infidelity isn't something I tolerate and any mention of it always stirs my dark side.

"Yeah, that covers it." She slides my sunglasses on and I take that as her indication she's still in a no-answering-questions kind of mood. I don't blame her. That would be my mood too if I were in her shoes.

"So, I'm heading to my brother's wedding. After George drops me there, you're welcome to have him take you anywhere."

She bites her lip. "I don't have anywhere to go." I can't see her eyes, but I can hear her tangled feelings and uncertainty.

"You don't live in New York? Or you don't want to go home?"

"I don't live here. And I don't want to go to a hotel. Or anywhere, really."

"If I asked you questions about that, would you answer them?"

"Let's just say that I don't want to be found today."

"Well, we better throw your phone out the window then."

Her eyebrows almost hit her hairline and she immediately removes her cell from her purse, drops it to the floor, and smashes it with her heel. She then presses the button to lower her window. Before I can stop her, she dumps the phone.

"Okay, now I really am wondering if it's the mafia we're running from." I was only joking about throwing the phone away. I certainly didn't expect her to do it.

"It's not the mafia." She takes a deep breath. "Can I ask you a huge favor?"

"I'm not sure that's a safe thing for me to agree to since I know you're willing to engage in wild antics."

She laughs and I like that I helped her do that. "Can I stay with you today? I mean, in your car while you attend your brother's wedding."

I process her question while also processing everything that's happened since she ran into traffic and caught my attention. This has to go down as the strangest way I've ever met a person.

When I don't answer her straight away, she says, "Sorry, just ignore that question. It's asking way too much of you." She appears embarrassed as she turns her gaze out the window.

I reach for her arm and gently curve my hand around her wrist. When I've got her eyes on me again, I say, "No, it's not. I wasn't taking my time answering because I thought that. I was thinking that I've never met anyone like you. And yes, my car is all yours for as long as you need it."

"I appreciate this. I just need a moment to catch my breath and figure out where to go from here." Her gratitude is woven through every word she utters.

"If you decide you want George to take you anywhere, just say the word. I don't need the car after I get to the wedding."

"This is very kind of you."

"No. Kind was me letting you faceplant in my lap." I grin for a moment. "*This* is just what humans should do for each other when they're having a bad day."

If I'm not mistaken, this means a lot to her. I get the impression she's close to tears. But she locks her emotions down fast and says softly, "Thank you."

We're in the middle of this when George slams on the brakes and curses.

"What is it?" I ask, not seeing any reason for him stopping when I glance out the window.

Before he can answer, the blonde whose name I still

don't know exclaims, "There's a puppy in the traffic! We need to help it."

"Honey," George says. "We don't have time to chase a dog. My life won't be worth living if I don't get Ethan to this church on time."

He's right. Olivia will have words for both of us if I'm any later than I already am. However, I'm not sure I have it in me to leave a puppy to flirt with harm in busy traffic.

I'm still working through these thoughts when my runaway bride takes matters into her own hands and opens the car door before George starts driving again.

"Fuck," George mutters as she makes her way into the traffic to save the dog. He looks at me in the rearview mirror. "This chick is a handful. I hope you know what you're getting yourself into."

I chuckle. "*Getting* myself into? I think I've already gotten myself into whatever this is." I look at her running after the puppy. "I'll be back in a minute."

"You hope," he says as I leave the car.

I jog to the blonde and together we save the dog while horns blare at us for the second time today.

"For a woman who was hellbent on not being seen, you're living dangerously now," I say as we walk back to the car, puppy safely in her arms.

She looks up at me. "We couldn't leave a puppy, Ethan."

Her use of my name reminds me I don't know hers. "What's your name?"

"Maddie."

"Okay, Maddie"—I open the car door for her—"let's make a deal." I follow her into the back seat. "If you stop running into traffic, you can have my car tomorrow too if you want."

Remorse fills her face. "No more stopping. I promise."

I catch George's look of disbelief and return a look that says to cut her some slack. I may not have decided to stop for the dog before she made the decision, but I know I would have gotten to that choice too.

As we continue the drive to the church, I watch as Maddie allows the puppy to lick her face and excitedly jump all over her. I get the impression from the joy that fills her entire body that she's a dog lover.

"Do you know what breed she is?" I ask as the dog jumps into my lap and proceeds to lick my face.

Maddie smiles as she watches the puppy show me love. "A Maltipoo." At my blank look, because I've never heard of this breed, she elaborates. "A cross between a Maltese and a poodle." She squeezes the dog. "She's so cute."

She's not wrong. The tiny puppy is a handful of cream fluff with eyes and a little face that I would challenge anyone not to get sucked in by.

We spend the rest of the drive to the church alternating between talking about the dogs Maddie grew up with and laughing at how enthusiastic and excited this puppy is.

The drive takes us close to twenty minutes, which is a ridiculous amount of time for this short drive. There must be something happening in Manhattan today that's caused more people and cars to be on the roads.

"So, I'll call the Health Department and find out how to reunite this pup with her owners," Maddie says when the car pulls into the church driveway.

I don't mention the fact that she's got a wedding mess to sort through. Every indication she's given me strongly hints at the fact that she wants to avoid that for as long as she can. The dog will provide her with a good distraction for a little while.

I open the car door as I think of something. "You don't have a phone. I'll call my assistant and ask him to help you. Do you need cash?"

"Ethan, no. I don't need cash or your assistant's help." She smiles. "But I appreciate the offer."

I watch her for a moment, trying to figure out if she really doesn't need anything. How the hell she intends on making a call without a phone is beyond me. In the end, it's the fact I'm now almost at the point in time where Callan will disown me that forces me to let this go.

"Okay." I get out of the car and take the suit bag that George has retrieved from the trunk. As I'm about to close the car door, the puppy begins barking. I duck my head back in to say goodbye and am greeted with the dog jumping into my arms. I fumble catching her due to the bag in my hand but manage not to drop her. She crawls up my torso and nuzzles her nose into my neck, curling up against me.

Maddie gets out of the car and joins us with a huge smile on her face. "She likes you."

"You know who won't like me if I don't get my ass inside this church in the next minute?" I attempt to pry the puppy from my neck.

"Your brother." She reaches for the dog who resists being taken from me.

I glance down at the tiny animal who seems to want to stay in my arms. "Sweetheart, I've got four brothers who are ready to kill me, so you're gonna have to let me go. Today is not my day to die."

When she doubles down in her efforts to stay with me, Maddie tries to help but the dog really doesn't want to be shifted.

"Here's what we're going to do." Maddie takes charge. "I don't want to be the reason you die today, so we'll all go inside. I need to use the bathroom and then I'll take the puppy." She removes my hat and sunglasses that she's wearing and places them in the car, and then is three steps ahead of me before I start moving. Turning back to me, she makes wide eyes. "Hurry up, Ethan. Today is not the day for you to die."

I grin.

What a weird fucking day this has turned into, but then, none of my family will be surprised that I've turned up to Callan's wedding with a stranger and a puppy in tow. Doing anything but what they expect is the story of my life after all.

3

MADELINE

GATECRASHING a wedding while wearing your own wedding dress isn't something I recommend. For more reasons than one, but mainly because it's rather awkward and not at all respectful.

Fourteen questioning sets of eyes are now on me after I followed Ethan into the room at the back of the church where it looks like the bride and bridesmaids have been getting ready. I'm unsure how this many people fit in this tiny room.

I blame the puppy for me even being here. I should have just taken the dog from Ethan outside but she appeared so anxious about letting him go that I wanted to give her a few more minutes with him.

I'm jolted back to the reality of my life when one of the bridesmaids spots me and exclaims to Ethan, "Holy fuck. Why is Madeline Montana standing in this room with you?"

I can't be here.

Ethan turns to me, his mouth curving into another

one of his gorgeous smiles. I've never met a man who smiles so much. It's refreshing. "That's your name?"

The bridesmaid's mouth falls open in shock. "How can you not know her name? Everyone knows her name."

This conversation is not one I want to be having. I'm saved from it when a very serious looking man with salt and pepper hair joins the group. He's older than the four guys who were already in here. My guess is they're Ethan's brothers and this man is his father. That hunch is proven correct when he looks at the groom and says, "Let's get you married, son."

It's chaos after that as everyone frantically finishes getting ready.

I take the puppy from Ethan. "I'm going to go." I glance at the dog who seems okay in my arms now.

Olivia, the bride, who is wearing the most stunning red wedding dress, interrupts us. She looks between Ethan and me with a kind smile. "You're welcome to stay. Anyone who is a friend of Ethan's is a friend of ours."

"Oh," I stutter, "We're not friends. We—"

Ethan cuts me off, humor in his eyes. "I don't know, Maddie. I only let friends put their face where you put yours today."

I blink up at him, feeling warmth flame its way up from my neck to my face and out to my ears.

Olivia laughs. "I'm not touching that." She places her hand on my forearm. "You're very welcome here."

I'm still in the middle of recovering from the shame over what Ethan's just reminded me of, so the only thing my brain can come up with is to blurt, "I'm wearing a wedding dress." Even if I wanted to stay, there is no way I'd attend a wedding in a wedding dress.

A mischievous look plays across Ethan's face. "Feel free to take it off."

Olivia rolls her eyes but I see the affection she has for him. "Seriously, do boys ever grow up?" Then, her features soften as she regards me with care. There's a knowing look in her eyes and I'm fairly certain she knows who I am and what today was supposed to be for me. "Are you okay?"

With that question and all the concern coming from her—a complete stranger—my throat suddenly clogs with feelings and emotions. I try to swallow them down as I nod. I also try to answer her but no words come. Instead, tears threaten and anxiety floods me. I'm in danger of breaking down in a room full of people I don't know and if I do that, I'm not sure I'll be able to get myself under control.

As I madly blink to stop my tears splashing down my cheeks, Ethan's hand comes to the small of my back and he steps into my space. Softly to Olivia, he asks, "Do you have any spare clothes here?"

God bless her, Olivia grasps the situation. "Blair practically brought her entire wardrobe and she's probably the same size as you." She gives my hand a quick squeeze. "Come and see what she has."

When I hesitate, Ethan presses his hand gently against my back and leans down to bring his mouth to my ear. "Let Olivia help. She loves helping people."

I appreciate Ethan more than he will ever know. It's been a long time since I've had anyone help me the way he has today.

After I shoot him a *thank you*, I follow Olivia to Blair who really may have brought her entire wardrobe with her. There are so many dresses to choose from. I quickly select one to change into because I really don't want to hold this wedding up even more than I already have.

Olivia doesn't appear concerned about that though. "Is there anything else we can do to help you?"

"No, please, go and get married. I feel awful that I kept Ethan from getting here sooner and that I'm now keeping you from your wedding. I'll just get changed and then I'll go." I look at Blair. "I'll leave your dress with Ethan. Thank you."

Blair regards me with interest. "How do you know Ethan?" she asks.

Before I get a chance to answer her, Olivia's mother interrupts us. "Darling," she says to her daughter with a look of concern. "If you don't go and get married now, you'll be waiting a long time until we can get this church again."

The other bridesmaid joins us. "And we'll then have to wait all that time before our karaoke battle, and honestly, Rhodes and I are ready to win tonight, so can we please hurry this along?"

Blair arches a brow. "There's no way you and Rhodes are taking this battle."

"Agreed," Olivia says quite decisively.

Now, Blair looks at her. "You and Callan aren't a shoo-in either."

"Of course we are."

Blair crosses her arms. "Tell me, when was the last time you heard Hayden sing?"

Olivia frowns but doesn't get the chance to reply because her mother gives her a look that says *this wedding needs to happen NOW.*

Everyone moves into action after that. A few minutes later, it's just me and the puppy left and the silence is heaven.

I take a minute, close my eyes, and inhale a deep breath.

God knows I need it.

Running from my hotel room without planning that move was not the best choice I've ever made. I only managed to slip past my two security guys because I told them Tucker had messaged to tell me there were crazy fans trying to get up to my floor. After they'd taken off to look into that, I ran for a different elevator and was lucky to escape without them knowing. I do feel for them, though. Tucker will be livid and likely fire them. I make a mental note to have my assistant ensure they're taken care of if that's the case.

Thank goodness for Ethan. It was everything to me when he stood in that traffic and asked if I needed help. I was lucky he didn't turn out to be a serial killer, but at that point I think I would have gotten into a car with just about anyone.

The puppy cuts into the silence with a bark that is surprisingly loud for such a small creature. I open my eyes and smile at her. "Okay, I'm going to get out of this dress and then we're going to leave. And I'll beg George to stop and buy you some food."

Removing my wedding dress might be the best moment of my day. Probably of my entire month. It's like the weight of all my commitments in life are also being removed.

I discard the dress, knowing I won't be taking it with me, and quickly put on the black dress Blair loaned me.

It's a super fitted sleeveless maxi dress with a low scooped neckline, thin shoulder straps, and skinny cross-back straps that reveal a lot of skin. Not a style of dress I've ever worn but I love trying something new. Something not chosen for me.

I'm on my way out of the church when I hear Bruno Mars's voice and the lyrics he sings about it being a beautiful night and that he thinks he wants to marry his baby. I come to a halt. This is the song Olivia chose to walk down the aisle to? "Marry You" by Bruno Mars? I'm so fascinated with this fun choice that I'm drawn into the chapel to see for myself.

Holding the puppy close to my chest, I quietly slide into the pew at the very back and watch while Olivia walks to her groom. His smile and look of adoration actually steal my breath a little. Tucker *never* looked at me like that.

I glance to his right and find Ethan watching Olivia in the way a brother would watch his sister getting married. I'm so touched by all the emotion I sense between the three of them. That's something else I've never experienced and that thought causes me to think about my mother.

A sharp pang of sadness engulfs me and for a moment, I struggle for breath. I've been thinking about her a lot this past week. About her final piece of advice before she died.

Find someone to love you, baby, and when I say love, I mean adore. They should admire you, respect you, and value you. Loving someone is easy; adoring them through miscommunications, disagreements, and turmoil is hard. When you find the person who can do that, who will do whatever it takes to have you never let go of them, you hold on just as tightly.

How did I ever think Tucker was the man I could spend the rest of my life with? He doesn't have a clue how to adore a woman. My mother would never have let me get all the way to today, dressed in my wedding gown, ready to give my heart to him. She would have had serious words for me the moment I announced my engagement. Hell, I wouldn't have even made it to *that* moment if she were still alive.

Tears pool in my eyes.

Why did you have to die, Mom?

It's a question I haven't asked in three years. Not since I met Tucker and numbed myself with a toxic relationship and fame.

God, I've been so dumb. Made stupid choices. And gotten myself into a mess that's going to be painful to get out of.

The sound of laughter erupting around me brings my attention back to the wedding and when I glance up, I find Olivia and Callan kissing. She's got a hand curled around his neck and I get the impression she's the one who instigated the kiss. When she pulls her mouth from his, he's grinning and whispering something in her ear that causes her to smile.

That's what I want.

A soulmate in silliness. An accomplice in mischief. A partner who would happily let me lead him astray.

A man who'd kiss me at the beginning of our wedding ceremony rather than at the end when we're supposed to kiss.

I sit through their vows, alternating between

swooning over the love they clearly have for each other and feeling a myriad of emotions over my own non-wedding. Emotions that may take me a very long time to even begin unpacking, let alone processing.

As the ceremony ends, I slip out of my seat and take the puppy outside. She has to go to the toilet and I need some fresh air.

Guilt hits me when I see Ethan's driver leaning against the car waiting for me. *Shit*. He's been waiting for me all this time.

I let the puppy do her business and then make my way to George, giving him an apologetic look. "I'm sorry for keeping you waiting."

He doesn't appear annoyed. "You wouldn't be the first of Ethan's women to do that."

It doesn't surprise me to learn that Ethan has had a lot of women. He's one of the best-looking men I've ever met, with his thick, dark, tousled hair; strong, angular facial lines; and a square jawline covered in scruff that screams masculinity to me. He's also got a whole lot of sex appeal going on. His presence alone is sexy, let alone his mannerisms, his voice, his self-assured magnetism.

And don't get me started on the way he kisses.

Embarrassment fills me again as I think about the fact I kissed him. On what was to be my wedding day. What kind of person does that? He must think the worst of me. It's a good thing we'll never see each other again.

I direct my attention back to his driver. "Can I convince you to take me to the store so I can buy some dog food?"

His lips quirk. "Let me guess, you're gonna need me to go into the store for you?"

I grin. "I like you, George. It's not often I meet a man who can read a woman's mind."

He gives me a shake of his head. "I imagine you don't have any trouble getting what you want."

If only he knew.

The wedding guests spill from the church as he opens the car door for me. I've just settled myself in the back and am deep in thought over just how much trouble I do have getting what I want when Ethan comes over to the car.

He opens the door, places one hand on the roof, and leans his face down into the car. "Hey." His eyes search mine like he's assessing me. "Are you okay?"

"Yeah." I try to give him a reassuring smile but fail. It's a wobbly smile at best.

His brows furrow at the same time the puppy jumps toward him, excited to see him again.

As he catches her, I murmur, "And right when I'd calmed her down you come and stir her up all over again."

His eyes flick to mine while he accepts licks from her. There's concern etched into his face. "You know, you don't have to be alone today if you don't want to be." At my confused expression, he continues, "Why don't you come to the reception with me? Unless that's harder for you, of course, but the offer's there if you think being with people might be easier."

My natural instinct is to decline. I hate putting people out. Dragging them into my troubles. But there's something about this man that pulls me to him. That makes me feel like I'm safe with him. That he might be able to help me forget, if even just for a few hours, the shambles my life is in.

However, we have a puppy to return to her parents. I reach out to pat her. "I need to get this pup back to her owners."

"George can do that."

"We can't expect him to do that."

Ethan grins. "Trust me, I've asked him to do worse things."

And just like that, for the second time today, I make a new plan and have no idea where I'll end up.

4

MADELINE

THE FUN VIBE of Ethan's brother's wedding continues into their reception and helps lift my mood. The champagne I drink helps too. I'm onto my third drink when Ethan stands to give the best man's speech.

Smiling as he casts a glance around the room, he says, "The year was 1999, the class was grade three. Callan was into video games, baseball, camping, and"—he grins—"pulling Jenny Johnson's pigtails. She was *not* into him pulling them, but as much as she kept rejecting him, he just kept on trying. That is, until the day our new neighbor marched up to him after school one day and announced that she wanted to learn how to ride a bike and that he should be the one to teach her." His gaze meets Olivia's. "He never did pull Jenny's pigtails again after that day. Instead, he taught our bossy neighbor how to ride a bike, how to play baseball, how to pitch a tent, how to catch a fish, and a whole lot of other things I'm sure none of us need to know about." He pauses while everyone laughs. "For those who don't know me, I'm

Ethan, Callan's younger brother and one of Olivia's oldest friends, and along with my three other brothers, I've had to sit through twenty-two years of watching these two figure themselves out and realize they were made for each other."

I relax a little more as I listen to Ethan share some stories about Callan and Olivia before reading out the congratulatory messages from friends and family who couldn't be here. I'm struck again by his easy manner and charismatic way of engaging with people.

After he reads the messages, he praises the bridesmaids and then turns to Olivia. "Liv, we've been through a lot together over the last couple of decades. Some down times, but more good times than bad. You've been the sister to me that I never had and while I know Callan is the luckiest and happiest man here tonight, I'm coming in a very close second. You've always been a member of our family but now there's no getting away from us and I am more than glad about that." He pauses for a moment, his affection for Olivia blazing from his eyes. "You look beautiful today, happier than I've ever seen you." He looks at his brother before looking back at her. "And you've made my brother happier than I've ever seen him." He reaches for his glass and raises it in a toast as he looks around the room. "Please join me in raising a glass to the happy couple. To a long life together, filled with the kind of memories that make a fulfilling and wonderful marriage." He gives them one last smile. "May you always be friends as well as lovers."

There are tears in Olivia's eyes as she mouths *thank you* to Ethan. Callan also appears emotional after his brother's toast. I also feel emotional even though I don't know these people. The speech was touching.

Callan and Olivia share their first dance to the song "At Last" by Etta James and my smile throughout is the most genuine smile I've experienced in months. I may have had a wedding day calamity today, and I may have just discovered that my fiancé has been cheating on me for years, but I will always be a romantic at heart. I write love songs for a living after all. I love getting lost in all the feels of love. Attending this wedding and reception has reminded me that there are beautiful love stories out there.

"That's a smile worth celebrating," Ethan says, leaning in close as the first dance comes to an end and the couple's parents join them on the dancefloor.

Thanks to being Ethan's guest, I'm sitting with him at the bridal table. I've enjoyed the conversation between everyone as they talked about Callan and Olivia's honeymoon plans and reminisced over years of shared memories. Mostly, though, I enjoyed feeling anonymous and not having the spotlight on me.

I look at Ethan who is close enough for his scent to invade my senses. It's spicy, dark, and musky, and I find it quite distracting. "Thank you for inviting me," I say softly. "I think being around people was exactly what I needed today."

"I'm glad. I was a little concerned it may have been hard being here."

I shake my head. "It wasn't hard to be here."

He studies me silently, questions no doubt filling his mind. He doesn't ask them, though. Probably because I wasn't in a question-answering mood earlier.

"I must seem like an awful person to you," I say.

"Why?"

"Because I walked out on my fiancé without telling him."

"You had your reasons."

"I did. But still, it's not a nice thing to do, leaving someone in that way. Especially when I've had my doubts over the wedding for six months."

"Did you know he was cheating on you all that time?"

"No. I only discovered that last night."

"Why'd you wait until today to leave him? I mean, six months is a long time to be having doubts."

"Rocking the boat isn't something I do. I tried to make it work rather than ending the engagement and upsetting a lot of people. But when I found out about his cheating, it didn't hurt in the right way and that was when I knew I couldn't go through with the wedding."

"What do you mean it didn't hurt in the right way?"

"It should have made me feel so much more than just having been taken advantage of." I stop talking, trying to untangle my thoughts so I can explain this to him. "I should have felt like my heart had been ripped out of my chest and I couldn't breathe. I should have wanted to scream at him and throw things at him. And I should have felt torn over leaving him. I felt none of those things."

His eyes search mine. "What did you feel?"

I struggle to answer him. To admit something I feel ashamed about. "Relief."

He gives me the space to sit with that before saying, "I can see you're wrestling with this and I get that, but I appreciate a person who invites chaos into their life. I don't think you're an awful person. Just a human who's trying to make sense of feelings you're yet to understand."

I frown. "Why do you like someone inviting chaos into their life?"

"If you want change, it's the only thing to do."

Ethan is unlike anyone I've ever met. "I've never thought of it like that."

"Do you want change?"

"God yes."

"Then carry on."

He's given me a lot to think about. For now, though, I'm thinking about Tucker. "I should probably call my fiancé." *Ex-fiancé.*

"Why?"

"Because it's the right thing to do."

"The asshole cheated on you, Maddie. In my book, you don't owe him a damn thing."

He may be right but I was raised a good girl who followed rules and always used my manners. And I'm still that girl, so doing the "right" thing is still important to me. However, today may be the day I begin altering my definition of certain things, beginning with what the right thing is.

I drink the rest of my champagne and follow Ethan's gaze to the dancefloor that's filling up.

When I spot his brother, Bradford, I say, "Your brother is a senator."

Ethan looks at me. "You caught that, huh?"

I did. I also noticed the handful of professional football and hockey players here. If there was ever a wedding to be crashed where privacy would be pretty much guaranteed, I found it. My fear of the paparazzi catching wind of my whereabouts was put to rest when I realized the company I was in.

"I did."

"So, it turns out that hellish traffic today was all your fault."

"You caught that, huh?" He's right. Thanks to a social media leak, people knew Tucker and I were marrying in New York today. We did everything we could to keep the venue a secret, but I know our fans were out in force trying to find us.

His lips twitch. "At the time, no, but Sasha has enlightened me." The bridesmaid who recognized me.

I exhale a breath. I've enjoyed not talking about myself today but I knew that couldn't last forever. "I told you it wasn't the mafia."

Now, he full on smiles. Then, he turns serious and pulls his cell phone from his pocket. "You should call your family and let them know you're okay."

I stare at the phone.

I don't have any family.

I don't even have a friend to call.

I meet his gaze again. "Thank you."

He watches me for another moment before pushing his chair back. "I'm going to find my brother."

After he leaves, I stare at his phone again while all my messy feelings twist and tangle some more. How did I get to this point in my life? I'm a twenty-seven-year-old woman with millions of fans around the world but not one person in my life who would be desperate to hear from me right now.

My heart sits heavy in my chest as I pick up the phone

and call Leigh, my assistant. She actually may be desperate to hear from me but not in the way I wish.

When she says, "Dear God, Madeline, do you have any idea of the mess you are in right now?" I sigh. It's time to get back to work.

5

ETHAN

MY BROTHER, Hayden, spins Olivia on the dancefloor while I walk to Callan who's standing a little away from the dancing, talking with a friend. Their conversation wraps up fast and as his friend walks away, my brother eyes me. "You came home."

This is the first chance we've had to talk alone since I arrived and it's safe to say it won't be the easiest conversation we've ever had. I left the States fifteen months ago after we had a fallout and we've spoken less than five times since then. Callan's not only my brother but also my best friend and I never imagined we'd ever go this long without seeing each other.

"You knew I would."

His expression tells me he had his doubts. "Liv knew you would. All I knew was that you've shut me out for over a year and I wouldn't have been surprised if you canceled on me." He doesn't sound bitter, just hurt.

"There's no way I'd miss your wedding day." I release a long breath. "I know I've let you down, and I know we've got a lot to work through, but can we let all that go for today so we can celebrate the fact you're a married man now?"

It's a weird fucking place to be when I can't read my brother's mind anymore. Callan and I were inseparable our entire lives up until our mid-twenties. We always knew what the other was doing and thinking. I was the idiot who let a woman come between us and I fucked everything up.

He takes a few moments contemplating what I said, and just when I wonder if he's not going to run with me here, he nods. "Yeah, I don't want to get into it tonight." He looks at his wife who's laughing with Hayden and Gage now. "You were right."

"I'm always right."

He arches a brow at me. "You're rarely fucking right."

I grin. "What was I right about this time?"

"I would have given highlining up for her if that's what she needed. Growing old without her isn't something I ever want to do."

He's referring to one of the only conversations we've had since I left. The one in which I told him to think about whether he'd be happy as an old man who'd had a lifetime of highlining but not a lifetime of Olivia. "You would have gotten to that decision without me."

"Maybe. Probably. But I don't ever want to be in that position again where I don't have you to talk to." He glances at Olivia once more, for a brief moment, before fixing his gaze back on me. "Don't ever cut me out again, Ethan."

Callan isn't the kind of guy who wears his heart on his sleeve. With Olivia, yes, but not with anyone else. He doesn't ask for help or admit he needs it. For him to be so raw with me right now is telling.

"I don't plan on it."

Olivia's laugh draws our attention and we find her coming our way. She slides her arm around Callan's waist when she reaches us and pulls his mouth to hers for a kiss before looking at me and asking, "Who did you pay to write that speech? It was a ten out of ten from me and I don't recall any of your essays in school ever being that good."

I chuckle. "Fiverr came through for me this one time."

She laughs. "It was beautiful. Thank you."

"I enjoyed going through our memories. It helped remind me of the things I'd left behind. Things I don't want to leave behind anymore."

Her eyes soften. "I'm glad. And please tell me this means you're not traipsing off to another country any time soon."

"I'm staying, Liv." I look at my brother. "I've got relationships to mend."

"Speaking of relationships that need mending," she says, looking past me. "I know your mom has been waiting patiently for today. She's missed you, Ethan."

I follow her gaze and find my mother watching me. Hesitation clings to her. It's just as familiar to me. Mom and I have never had a close relationship.

Looking back at Callan and Olivia, I say, "Go dance. And prepare to lose that karaoke battle. I think I'm going to win tonight."

Olivia rolls her eyes. "Seriously, I thought you'd know by now that you can't sing to save yourself."

I smirk. "It's not *my* talent that's going to win me this battle."

Olivia's eyes go wide. "Oh my god, no. That's cheating if you drag a professional singer up on that stage with you."

I shrug. "A man's gotta use every tool at his fingertips."

Callan laughs and pulls his wife close. "Come on, Ace. It's time to shake your ass for me."

I can't help but think how fucking perfect they are for each other as I watch them walk to the dancefloor. Olivia's talking his ear off and if I had to bet, I'd say she's going over her strategy for winning the karaoke competition tonight. She's always got a strategy when it comes to karaoke.

"Ethan." Mom interrupts my thoughts when she joins me.

I pull her in for a hug. "Mom."

She wraps her arms around me tightly and it feels like she doesn't want to let go, which is unusual because I've never felt this from her before.

"You look well," she says when she finally pulls away.

"I'm really well. How are you?"

"I'm good. Happy you're home. Are you planning on staying or will you be heading back to Europe after the wedding?"

We're as stilted as we always have been, our conversation shaping up to be another unremarkable exchange. Just one more in a long line of the same with her.

It's always the usual back and forth between us. *How are you? What have you been up to?* I've always craved so much more. I gave up on a deeper relationship with Mom a long time ago, though, so none of this is unexpected.

"I'll be staying. I've just sold my company, so it's time to figure out what's next."

Surprise fills her face. She's the first in the family to hear my news. "Are you happy about this? What are you thinking you might do?"

"Yeah, it's what I wanted, but I'm unsure of what's next. At the moment, I'm just happy to have time for photography again."

"I hope you take all the time figuring it out, Ethan." She touches my arm. "And I hope that whatever you choose to do keeps making you happy. You deserve that."

I don't get much of a chance to think about what she's said before my father joins us. He regards me with scrutiny like he always does. "Son. It's good to have you home."

Somehow, I manage not to call bullshit. The last thing my father said to me before I left New York was, "*I've never been so fucking disappointed in one of my sons. I gave you everything you needed to succeed and still you screwed it all up. I can't look at you like this, Ethan, and I don't want to. Not until you sort yourself out.*" He hasn't called me since I've been gone. A few texts, sure, but tapping out a message takes very little compared to making the time for an actual conversation. A phone call, in my opinion, means so much more.

"He's staying after the wedding," Mom informs him and fuck if an entire lifetime of Mom managing Dad and me doesn't flash before my eyes.

"I can speak for myself, Mom."

She flinches.

"Ethan." Dad's admonishment is sharp. The look in his eyes sharper.

"No." Mom gives a quick shake of her head to Dad. Then, to me, she says, "You're right. You can. I'm sorry."

"I heard that you were courting an offer for your company," Dad says. Nothing gets by the old man. He's got eyes and ears everywhere.

"I signed the contract just before I flew out of Paris."

"And what do you plan on doing with your time now?"

And there it is. His silent judgment. My father has always taken issue with my choices in life. Not even developing and managing a billion-dollar app was good enough for him.

"I have no plans yet."

Mom steps in again. "There's no hurry to figure it out."

Dad's expression would say otherwise but he doesn't get into it with me. Instead, he allows Mom to direct the conversation away from business talk. She wants to nail down our next family weekend away, so we chat about possible dates for that and where I'd like to go.

Blair ends up dragging Mom away to help her get everyone ready for the cake cutting. After she leaves, Dad eyes me. "Will you be seeing Samantha now that you're home?"

Fuck.

"We're long over, Dad."

"You forget I was the one who found you after she destroyed you. And that I saw how intent you were on chasing her even after what she did."

"That was nearly a year and a half ago. A lot's happened since then."

He nods at the table where Madeline is sitting. "She's what's happened?"

I clench my jaw at his patronizing tone. "Tell me, what's it going to take for you to stop treating me like I'm a fucking idiot?"

"You're not an idiot, Ethan, but you make questionable choices at times. My job as your father is to help you."

"No, Dad, your job as my father is to love me. That's it. I'm an adult and can ask for your help if I need it, and right now, I don't need it or want it."

"I'm not convinced. You skipped Bradford's wedding and now you've turned up to Callan's with a woman who skipped her own wedding to come to this one. For once, I'd like to see you with a woman who has some sense about her. And I'd like to know that *you* know where you're heading in life. I'll sleep a hell of a lot easier at night once you've got those things in order."

His mention of Bradford's wedding infuriates me. I step closer, getting in his space as all my anger and hurt over the shit he's pulled on our family throughout our lives pushes me closer to the edge of snapping. "I didn't come home for Bradford's wedding because I didn't want to ruin it for him. Because I fucking would have if I'd had to look at you then. You think I'm a fuck-up? At least I know how to be faithful to a woman and love her well. You're the fuck-up, Dad, and you screwed your entire family over with the choices *you* made. Don't ever talk to me about my choices again."

With that, I stalk away from him before I ruin Callan's wedding. I leave the room and head for the escalator to take me downstairs. I need some fresh air and a whole lot of distance from my father.

I spend fifteen minutes out on the sidewalk, people-watching. It's something I've always done. As a child, it allowed me to escape my own life and imagine someone else's. As an adult, I think about the angles I'd photograph people from to find their unguarded self. To find their candid, unglamorous truth. I'm always looking for human rawness in its purest form. And while photographing people was once my job, I'm almost certain it was therapy for me. Liberating another person of the mask they wear for the world helped me find the kind of connection I've always needed. It helped me know I'm not alone in a fucking lonely world.

Tonight, all I can manage is a brief escape and to shake some of my father off. If it wasn't for Callan and Liv, I'd leave so I didn't have to see Dad again.

I go back inside and weave my way to the table where Maddie's still sitting.

She finds my eyes as I take the seat next to her. "Something's happened. I'm not sure what, but Olivia seems worried."

My brows pull together as I search the room for my sister-in-law. "I'll be back," I say when I spot her at the corner of the dancefloor with Callan, Mom, and her parents.

It turns out Olivia *is* worried. Her father collapsed while dancing. He's conscious but complaining of chest pain.

"We've called the paramedics," Callan informs me, his face creased with concern. "And we're going to take Liv's mother to the hospital."

"Do you need me to do anything?"

"No. Hayden will make an announcement after we leave. He'll sort everything out."

"Fuck. I'm sorry, Cal."

He scrubs his hand down his face as his attention turns to his wife. "Yeah."

I let him go and watch as Olivia grips his arm when he reaches her. I'm glad she's got him to support her through this.

"The reception is over," I tell Maddie when I take the seat next to her again. I fill her in on what's happened and then ask, "Did you call your family?"

"I called my assistant."

Interesting choice to call your assistant rather than a family member or friend. It makes me wonder about her family. I don't touch that, though, because if there's something I understand, it's fractured relationships. "And?"

Her shoulders lift and then drop as she takes a deep breath. "And I've got a mess to clean up."

From the few facts I gleaned from Sasha earlier, that was a given. But not the information I'm after. "Do you have somewhere to go tonight?"

If I had to bottle and label Maddie's visible response to that question it would be named *Adrift*. Uncertainty and vulnerability blaze from her, but more than that, she seems lost. And after she gives a quick shake of her head and swallows hard, I offer her an anchor for the night.

"I have a spare bed if you want it." When her eyes widen a little and she doesn't respond, I add, "I'll stay at a hotel if you'd feel safer being there alone." She doesn't know me, and who knows what she's been through in life. Staying with a stranger wouldn't be the safest choice to make.

"No, I'm not worried about that. I'm just . . . I'm overwhelmed by your kindness. No one has ever been so generous with me." She pauses before saying softly, "Thank you."

"So that's a yes to staying at my place?"

"Yes. And I have another favor to ask?"

"I shudder to think what I'm about to agree to."

Her smile lights up her face. "You're fun, Ethan, but I promise not to make you go along with any more wild antics. I just want to ask if I can give your address to my assistant so she can have my things brought to me."

I give her my address to send to her assistant, along with my phone so she can send that text. I then say goodbye to my family and lead Maddie out to the sidewalk where George collects us.

After Maddie asks George how he went with returning the puppy to her owners (he had success), she and I settle into an easy conversation about Callan's wedding. We've just discussed the fun vibe of it when Maddie's expression turns serious and she says, "I saw you talking with your father. It didn't look like an easy conversation. And if you don't want to talk about this, I totally understand, but sometimes I think it's easier to talk to a stranger about hard things than to people we know."

That's been my experience in life too. After a quick glance out the window at the passing cars, I turn back to her. "Dad and I have always struggled. I'm not like my brothers. I've never wanted the things he's encouraged in all of us and this has caused problems between Dad and me."

"What kinds of things?"

"They've pursued wealth, power, success. I just want something simpler."

"You don't want any of those things? I mean, it looks to me like you already have wealth."

"Yeah, I sound like an entitled asshole. I get it. I have all those things. But I didn't go searching for them."

Her smile is gentle. "What did you go searching for?"

"People. Honesty. Conversation." I pause, taking in the way she's watching me closely. "I went searching for the threads that hold us together, which isn't something I could ever say to my father and have him understand."

Maddie is quiet for a long moment before finally saying, "I understand what you're saying. People think I write songs and sing them for the fame and fortune, but I don't. I write them because I'm trying to make sense of people and love. Of how we connect and disconnect. Of the pleasure and pain love brings."

I turn my body so I'm facing her. "Do your parents understand that?"

A bolt of sadness streaks across her face. "My parents aren't alive. But if they were, they'd understand." She smiles, her sadness ebbing away. "My father wrote songs. And my mother had the kind of depth I don't come across often."

"I wish I could say the same about my mother."

"You're not close with her?"

"No."

"Where did you get your depth from if not from your parents?"

I smile. "That's an unusual compliment." Not once in my life, has a woman expressed a similar sentiment.

"It's also a genuine question."

And not one I've ever been asked or had to contemplate the answer to. "If I had to guess, I'd say it comes from a longing to be known."

Maddie nods slowly like she's thinking about the fact every word I just uttered was pulled from my soul. From my *bones*. And I have no fucking clue how I know that's what she's thinking, but I'm surer of that than I've been of anything in a long while.

"You just want to be seen," she echoes softly.

I hold her stare while I think about the fucking mysterious ways of the universe. Of all the days and all the ways to meet someone. "Yeah. Isn't that what everyone wants?"

"Yes, but I don't know anyone who actually thinks about this, let alone talks about it. Everyone's so busy trying, trying, *trying*. To fit in. To reach for more. To be more. All the while not having a clue why. We never put words to our real why and so we just keep on striving for things we maybe don't even want."

Fuck, I wish we had more than one night for this conversation. Since we don't, and since we'll likely never see each other again, I cut straight to the question I'd love to know the answer to. "When you said you tried to make it work with your fiancé because you didn't want to upset people, who were you referring to if not your parents?"

"I was engaged to Tucker Brandt. Have you heard of him?"

"No."

"God, it cannot be stated enough just how much I like

that." She exhales a breath and I get the impression she's got a great deal of heaviness to discard over her ex. "Tucker is the biggest selling country singer in the world. Has been for years. I met him when I was sent to write a song with him, and the rest is history. The—"

"When you say, 'the rest', I'm gonna need you to fill those details in."

"Let's just say it was a whirlwind romance. I was living with him five weeks after we met." At my surprised expression, she makes wide eyes at me and says, "I know. Dumb."

"No, not dumb. That's not what I'm thinking." I shrug. "The heart wants what the heart wants, Maddie. Fuck anyone who tries to make you feel stupid for following it."

"Yeah, but even you just looked shocked at the fact I shacked up with him so fast."

"Not shocked. Surprised, yes, but only because it's a rare occasion I meet someone like me."

"What?" Now, *she's* surprised. "You've done something like that too?"

I laugh. "My entire life has been one long succession of following my heart and getting it banged the fuck up."

Maddie appears amazed at my admission. But there's also some disbelief mixed in there. "Right, but have you ever moved in with someone five weeks after meeting them and then practically signed your life over to them?"

My grin meets my ears. "If this is a competition, you're going to be sadly disappointed when I win."

Her grin matches mine. "Show me what you've got."

"I moved my second girlfriend out of her place that she shared with a guy who abused her and let her stay with me. We'd met the night before in a bar. No sex, nothing, just her crying on my shoulder about her boyfriend. She lived with me for just over a year, and in that time I gave her not only my heart but also my car, whatever cash she wanted, and one of my closest friends. My next girlfriend—"

"Wait." Maddie holds up her hand to stop me. "When you say you gave her a friend, do you mean she left you for them?"

"She cheated on me with him for most of our relationship."

Her face darkens. "Assholes."

"I thought so."

"Okay, your next girlfriend."

"Brianna. She moved herself in after our fourth date. Tried to convince me to get her pregnant. We were twenty-year-old kids and I was crazy blind in love. It's a wonder you're not looking at a father of an eight-year-old child."

A laugh bubbles out of her. "Maybe you will win."

My mood shifts from fun to something darker as I think about sharing something I've waged a war with myself over for the last year and a half. "My last girlfriend stole half a mil from me before leaving me. That was after two years of slowly coming between me and my brothers to the point that when Callan tried to talk sense into me, I chose her over him. The truly fucked-up thing is that I would have forgiven her and given her more if she'd asked for it. So, yeah, I've practically signed my life over to someone else. You and I have that in common."

Maddie is quiet for a moment. Then, she cracks her heart open and gives me her unglamourous truth. "I was going to marry Tucker today because I didn't want to rock the boat with my management or the people who took a risk on me when they gave me my career." Her voice turns to an almost-whisper when she adds, "I didn't want to upset them or my fans because I fear losing that career. And I don't know what kind of person that makes me, Ethan. To think I could marry someone to keep a career."

"It makes you human."

"It makes me someone I never imagined becoming and I'm not sure what to do with that."

I reach for her hand to get her full attention again because she's drifted from me a little, deep in her pain. "I know that feeling all too well, and the best advice I can give you is to take some time away so you can start to hear yourself again. Fuck knows the world will tell you how you should think about yourself if you let it." I pause. "Don't let it, Maddie. Go away. Be by yourself. And here's something to think about: that career you think those people and those fans gave you? I call bullshit. They gave you a chance. *You* gave yourself what you have now and no matter what happens, your heart and talent hasn't gone anywhere. Don't ever forget that."

Her fingers tighten around mine. "Thank you for saying that. I hope I can be brave enough to do something with your advice."

Her last truth she shares touches the chaos inside me. There's something about another human admitting their struggle that helps me get good with my own battles in life. And tonight, I really fucking needed this.

6

HOLY SHIT, girlfriend. @madelinemontana was a runaway bride yesterday! Say sike rn! Seriously, though, we just can't. And right when we were ready to stay in our cowgirl era forever. Did you all catch that photo of @tuckerbrandt last night about to board a jet plane to Sadsville? Our tears for him. I mean, not only has he lost his bride, but what about the world tour he and Maddie had planned together for next month? There is SO. MUCH. TEA. to sip here, bestie! There's been no word from Maddie, though. Gasp! And no sightings. I mean, are we sure our girl hasn't been kidnapped by a serial killer? Surely, no girl in her right mind would run away from Tucker. We're on strict #MaddieWatch and will report back the very minute we know more!

7

MADELINE

ETHAN BLACK MIGHT NOT HAVE GONE SEARCHING for wealth, but the man sure as heck found it. I mean, he *was* born into it, but based on his condo, I think he's done a good job of amassing his own money.

His condo is jaw dropping. And that's saying something because I've lived with Tucker and he loves to splash his cash all over the place. Ethan lives in a tower in Brooklyn Heights. His condo takes up the top two floors and has insane views of New York Harbor, Manhattan, and the East River. The attention to detail is amazing. He gave me a quick tour when we arrived here last night and while I prefer a white and airy style, I can appreciate the sleekness of the darker tones he's chosen. The black and gray throughout, along with the minimalism, fits in with the sense I've gotten of him. Ethan strikes me as a man who is very comfortable in his masculinity and not fussy in any area of his life. I think he's a guy who likes to get to the point and get there fast.

I slept better last night than I have all year and while I

could put that down to the most comfortable bed I've ever slept in, I know that's not the reason.

I feel free.

Sure, that freedom is actually a state of utter disorder, but still, I can breathe now and that's not something I've been able to say for a very long time.

After we arrived at the condo last night, Ethan gave me a tour and then Leigh arrived with my belongings. Ethan gave us space to talk and she relayed to me just how much shit I'm in.

Darren is on the warpath. Not surprising to me. Tucker too. Again, no surprise. What *was* a surprise is that Leigh knew Tucker was cheating on me, as did, according to her, most of the people we work with.

She strode into Ethan's condo last night with a plan for how we're going to tackle this. Leigh already disliked Tucker and hated Darren as much as I do, but I've never seen her as passionate as she was last night. I imagine she's probably like that with her friends and all I can think is that I wish I had a friend like Leigh. Perhaps I wouldn't be in this mess if I did.

She handed me a new phone, already programed with the numbers I need. Then came my suitcase, a list of properties for sale in Nashville that she thinks I should look at to find my new home, and a list of potential new managers. As I glanced at her lists, she told me I should also find a new lawyer. "Actually," she'd said with a whole lot of certainty that helped me feel okay about my actions, "you need a whole new team, Maddie. Tucker has really fucked you over by getting you to sign on with his people. I swear they've screwed you over with your percentages. And I'm not even a little bit sorry if I'm talking out of line here. I think you need someone in your life who will give you the hard facts."

She was right.

They have screwed me over.

And I've known that for a long time but I've been buried under my gratitude for being "rescued" by Tucker that I've done my best to ignore it all. Besides, I'd planned on being his wife and spending my life with him, so I didn't think it mattered in the scheme of things.

Oh, how dumb I've been.

I've undervalued myself for too long.

"I know," I'd admitted and smiled at her wide-eyed shock.

"Well, why the fuck were you still with them?" she'd demanded.

We'd talked for an hour or so after that and I told her I was done with being taken advantage of. I also admitted that I had no idea what my next move was. She left with everything hanging in the air. And while I know she felt apprehensive about not having a solid plan, because if there's one thing Leigh and I have always had it's a plan, I also know she has great trust in me and my ability.

"Everything's going to work out," I whisper to myself as I stare at the river through the window of the bedroom Ethan let me stay in. "I'm going to figure this out and everything's going to be okay."

I'm still pep talking myself as I go in search of coffee. Pep talks and me go way back. My entire life has been one long internal motivational speech and I don't see that changing anytime soon.

"Morning," Ethan says when I walk into the kitchen.

I glance up from my phone where I've been scrolling

the news posted about my wedding and come face to face with bare skin and muscles that render me brainless.

I come to an abrupt stop.

Ethan's shirtless and if I die today, I'll die knowing I've seen the kind of muscles every woman should have the pleasure of seeing up close at least once in her life.

It's because I'm suddenly without a brain that I allow my eyes to spend all the time in the world making their way down the chiseled ridges of his chest, his abs (seriously, how many abs can a person actually have?), and down to the hypnotizing V that—

Ethan's low rumble cuts into my thoughts. "We're gonna find ourselves in a world of trouble if you keep looking at me the way you are."

My eyes snap to his. "Sorry." Honestly, where *is* my brain? And how can a man just steal it away like that? And *also*, why has no man ever managed to do this to my brain?

Before I have time to circle the rabbit hole of why my fiancé never came close to causing this state of bewilderment, Ethan's mouth shifts into a lazy smile and he says, "Don't be sorry."

I truly am a bad person. This time yesterday, I was preparing to put a wedding dress on so I could marry Tucker. Today, I'm wondering what Ethan's abs would feel like.

I decide to ignore everything that's just happened, along with the fact a half-naked man is looking at me like he's also wondering what it would feel like for me to touch his abs. Instead, I say, "I'd kill for coffee."

Ethan continues smiling at me, and goodness if it isn't one of the sexiest smiles I've ever been treated to.

"Are you hungry too? I was just about to make an omelet."

"No, I don't want you to go to any trouble. I'll take a coffee and then I'll get out of your hair."

He studies me for a long moment. "Does this come from your ex or did someone else fuck you over before him?"

I frown. "This?"

He rests his hip against the countertop and I wish I was not aware of that because keeping my eyes off that hip and all the skin surrounding it is a real struggle right now. "Thinking that someone making you breakfast is putting them out."

I really have never met anyone like Ethan. "You just cut to the chase, don't you?"

His eyes now hold mine without effort. "Life's too short not to. It's also too short not to let people do things for you when they want to."

"This doesn't come from Tucker." At Ethan's silence that says he's waiting for further information, I elaborate. "It was just me and Mom for most of my life, looking after each other. For a little while, it was just me looking after the both of us. And then, it was me on my own before Tucker." I swallow down my rising emotions. "I guess I just got used to looking after myself."

"Even while you were with him?"

I nod.

"Fuck," he curses softly. Then, he lifts his chin at the stool on my side of the island and says, "Sit your ass down and let me make you breakfast."

I arch my brows. "Are you always this bossy?"

"Only when it's called for."

I've spent three years with a man who pretty much *was* the boss of me. Allowing a man to boss me into anything is something I've decided I won't ever do again. However, Ethan's style of bossy feels a whole lot different and I find myself pulling out the stool.

He moves into action, taking all those abs of his and that deep V of his to the fridge to gather ingredients for our omelets. It's at this point that I realize he's wearing the holy-mother-of-quads gym shorts of gym shorts. Before I can censor myself, I blurt, "Do you spend entire days in the gym?" Surely, he must, to have the body I'm staring at. "And do you often wear shorts like . . . like *that*?"

He looks at me with amusement. His gaze follows mine down to his shorts. "This is a problem for you?"

"This would be a problem for any woman who's into men."

Ethan chuckles. "It was leg day."

I blink rapidly because my eyes can't figure out where to look. It's as if they're having a seizure right alongside the dilemma of what to do. Seriously, his shorts sit halfway up his quads and stretch over him like a second skin. They're not a problem as such, but blatant ogling seems rude.

I stare at him. "You say that like it explains everything." I drop my gaze again. Yes, my descent into very loose morals is almost complete. "Those shorts are so fitted. And so . . . short."

As I continue to dig the hole I should consider burying myself in, Ethan turns serious, watching me like he's figuring something out. "I'll change."

Once I'm alone, I chastise myself. Only I could make a scene like the one I just made. And *this* is on Tucker.

I've spent the last three years suppressing my sexuality to be the perfect sweet country girl that he and Darren decided was right for our couple image. It started after the first time Tucker and I were photographed together in public. I was wearing a very demure dress that covered a great deal of skin. It wasn't on purpose, but Tucker's fans were intrigued because his image had always been very sexual and he'd never dated a woman who presented as sweet as that outfit made me look.

I've also spent the last three years watching everything I say and do with other men. Tucker had particular expectations of my behavior while I was in public. "For our brand, babe," he always said. He reminded me repeatedly that even a casual wink at another guy could cause us a scandal. Three years of those expectations has me all fucked up. *Don't smile too brightly. Don't speak too much. Don't flick my hair in a sexy way. And for the love of God, don't fucking wink.*

The thing about denying parts of yourself is that over time you either forget or get confused about who you are. I've forgotten what it's like to engage with a man. Or maybe I've forgotten *how* to engage with a man.

When Ethan returns, dressed in jeans and a black T-shirt, he doesn't mention what happened. He simply carries on with making breakfast, which I'm grateful for.

"So, what's the plan today?" he asks while chopping omelet ingredients like he's a highly skilled chef.

I glance at the knife he's good with. "Do you cook a lot?"

"Yeah. I find it distracting in a useful way."

"Maybe I should take it up."

"You don't cook much?"

"Never. At least not since I moved in with Tucker. Before that, yes."

"Well, it seems the timing might be right to get back in the kitchen." He meets my gaze and I read the question in those blue eyes of his. *The plan for today?*

"I'm going to see my mom."

Ethan's confused. "Your mom?" His confusion is warranted. I did tell him she was dead.

"She's buried in Sedona. I haven't been back to visit her in over three years. And since your advice was to go away and be by myself, that's what I'm going to do. I think a road trip sounds like a plan. I haven't driven in years and I miss it."

"I'm not sure a road trip by yourself is in your best interest. Not with all your fans out there."

He's not wrong about that. "I'm going to ask Leigh to come with me."

He doesn't appear convinced. "What about security? You should take some with you."

I release a breath and rest my elbows on the island. "I understand your point but I'm tired of always traveling with an entourage. I'm tired of schedules and checklists and rules. I just want to have some fun and live moment to moment for a little while."

He gives me a knowing look. "You want to run away for a bit."

"Yes."

"And you don't want to take your usual security guys?"

"I don't have access to my usual security."

"Why not?"

I sigh again. Mostly because I feel like an idiot. "Here's the truth of my life: I don't run very much of it. My manager does. I'd have to go through him to arrange security and he's the last person I want to talk to at the moment."

"You could outsource."

"I mean, I could, but I don't have the first clue how to do that." God, I really do feel dumb.

"I could help you."

"You could," I say slowly, trying to get a handle on what my gut's telling me. It's twisting and turning at the thought of going on a road trip with strangers.

"But you don't want to." His voice is threaded with understanding. "You need people you know around you," he adds softly.

"Yes."

"I get that," he says and everything about the way he says it, and the look on his face tells me he really does get it. "I could go with you."

I smile at the thought of Ethan trying to keep me safe. "You would attract far too much attention, especially if your entire wardrobe is made up of those hot-quad shorts. I really don't think you were put on this earth to be anyone's security."

He's amused at my shorts reference but doesn't touch it. "I'm being serious, Maddie."

"You don't even know me. Why would you give up your life to tag along on a road trip with me?"

"I love a good road trip and it would hardly be giving my life up. I can work from anywhere at the moment."

His lips quirk. "I promise to stay fully clothed at all times and to leave the hot-quad shorts at home."

I stare at him. "See, this is how you almost ended up the father of an eight-year-old child."

"I could swear I just heard you say you wanted to have some fun. I'm your guy for that. I'll make sure we break some rules along the way."

Before I know what I'm doing, and before I can stop myself, I'm agreeing to his impulsive offer and he's immediately making plans to come with me. In my entire life, I've never acted as spontaneously and recklessly as I have over the last twenty-four hours. Running from my fiancé was one thing, but running away with another man is a whole other thing.

It can't be denied, though: I think breaking some rules with Ethan Black is exactly what I need in my life.

8

ETHAN

IN THE HOUR and a half since we left my place, Maddie and I have talked about surface level shit that I'm fairly certain neither of us are that interested in. My car. My condo. My gym routine. Her gym routine. The places I spent time in Europe over the last year. The fucking weather. It's when we get into the weather that I glance at her and say, "We need a road trip playlist, and you need to choose our first song."

"Why?"

"We can't do a road trip without a playlist."

"No, why do I have to choose the first song?"

"Because I said so."

"I'm beginning to think you're actually very bossy."

When I just arch a brow, waiting for her to comply, she grins. Then, she admits, "I don't know my password to log in to make a playlist on the app I use."

I reach for my phone. "Use mine."

"Do you share your phone so easily with everyone? Or just with strangers?"

"Do you often go away with strangers?" I give her a pointed look. "We're not strangers anymore."

A smile settles across her face. "No, we're not." She taps my phone. "You really should put a password on here."

"I've never lost a phone. I think I'm safe."

She stares at me with disbelief. "Seriously? Is that how you do everything? No safeguards in place?"

"You'd get on well with my assistant. He emails me a list every week with suggested precautions I should consider putting in place."

"Let me guess, it's the same list every week because you never action any of it."

"See, not strangers. You already know shit about me."

"And wow, your music tastes are fascinating."

I glance over and find her scrolling through my playlists.

"I haven't heard of half these bands," she says as she taps the phone. The sound of John Mayer singing an acoustic version of "Free Fallin'" fills the car.

"You haven't heard of John Mayer?"

She looks at me. "LOL. Everyone's heard of John Mayer, Ethan."

"Jesus, you speak in acronyms. We may have just encountered our first bump in the road."

"I'm pretty sure everyone speaks in acronyms."

"I don't."

"How boring your life must be."

I can't help the lift of my lips at her banter. It's been far too long since I've done this with a woman. "Should I anticipate a fuckload of googling just so I can keep up with you?"

"I mean, how fast are those thumbs of yours, grandpa?"

I lift my chin at her. "How about you start adding some songs to our list?"

"In the time you've grumbled about not wanting to be dragged into the twenty-first century, I've already added five songs. Would you like to hear the second one?"

"John Mayer made it to first spot?"

"Well, I don't know about the first spot. We'll need to add all the songs and then rearrange them into order. And let me give you a heads up, Grandpa Ethan doesn't get the final say on our number one song. God knows, you'd probably choose some old-timer song no one's ever heard of."

"All I heard just then was that we'll be rearranging the list after we've compiled it and I agree with this method."

"Oh, so you're deaf as well as stuck in your ways?"

I grin at her. "Just play the damn song."

She laughs right before Tom Cochrane singing "Life Is A Highway" blares from the speakers.

Maddie's choice both surprises and impresses me. I'd expected country, but I should have known the unexpected was likely from her. And then, fuck me, she starts singing and every thought in my head is stripped away.

Maddie's voice is liquid gold. Rich and velvety with a hint of raw vulnerability that adds depth to every lyric. It holds me captive without effort.

When I don't join in on the singing, she stops and says, "Don't tell me you have a no-singing rule on road trips. That really would be boring."

"That's your singing voice?"

She half laughs, half frowns at me. "Huh?"

"Is that the voice you sing on stage with?"

Her frown deepens as she inspects me like I've grown a second head. "How many singing voices do *you* have?"

"Fuck, ignore me. I've just never heard a voice like yours."

Her face smooths into understanding. I imagine she must have this starstruck experience often. "Right, so singing is allowed then?"

"Sing as much as you want."

"Will we be duetting?"

"I'm not a man who has a road trip playlist that doesn't get belted out, so yes, we'll be duetting."

Her smile is pure beauty. "Thank god for that. Do you want to hear the third song?"

"Play them all for me and feel free to give me a running commentary as to why you choose each song."

"Okay, so while I support this suggestion, I also go by feel when it comes to music rather than too much thinking."

I look at her. "So tell me your feels for each song."

She turns silent, watching me with a look on her face that says she's thinking deeply about something. When she speaks again, I expect to hear about her feelings over either the next song or the last one, but again, she gives me something else. "I've lived for twenty-seven years without anyone but my mother asking me for my feels. I wish there were more people out there like you." Then, she gives me a cheeky smile and says, "Also, did you actually just speak in slang or did I mishear that?"

"Fuck, I did. I've spent too much time recently with a friend who speaks almost entirely in slang."

Still smiling, she settles back against her seat. "That's

great news. I no longer feel the need to alter my language so that you don't have to hurt your thumbs trying to google." She taps my phone. "Okay, so I've just added this next song for two reasons. First, I love it. And second, I want to hear your singing voice on it. And just in case you're a shy guy, we can duet this one so you don't feel under the spotlight."

I give her an amused look. "A shy guy?"

"It's a thing."

"I get that, but do I strike you as a shy guy?"

"Well, you might be when it comes to singing."

I shake my head at just how far off base she is. "Play the song."

With one last grin, she taps the phone and I immediately know the song before Jon Bon Jovi even begins singing. When the bass kicks in, Maddie turns the music up and starts nodding her head in time with the beat. By the time, Jon's voice sounds from the speakers, her entire body is in sync with the song.

We both sing the opening line of "Livin' On A Prayer" and Maddie's joy is written all over her face at this. We sing together, Maddie's eyes firmly on mine while I glance between her and the road. There's no way I can't look at her while we share this moment.

When we get to the chorus, Maddie closes her eyes, tips her head back, and belts it out. I match every lyric with her, wondering why I've never searched for a woman to do this with.

"Oh my god," she says as the song ends. "Can we spend all day doing this?" Her face is lit up so fucking beautifully and electrically that I wish I could press pause on life and figure out how to help someone keep a feeling forever. If I could give her anything right now, it would be that.

"How much of your time is actually spent singing?"

The light disappears from her eyes. And go me for achieving that. "It's not even about the amount of time I get to sing, it's the honesty in it that means more to me. This"—she gestures between the two of us—"was more honest than any singing I've done in a long while."

"That says a lot because I can't even sing."

"You were in every second of that song with me. That's everything to me."

"I think you might have to help me understand this. Surely, your fans are in every second with you when you're up on a stage with them?"

"They are. God, it's my favorite part of my work. Singing with them doesn't even feel like work. It's all the other bullshit I hate."

"The business of it all?" I get it if that's what she's referring to.

She nods. "Yeah, that, but mostly it's the manufactured brand that Tucker and Darren have created that I've struggled with. There's very little truth in it, and it kills me that our fans think it's all true."

"You don't have any say in it? Control over your own brand?"

She laughs and I feel the jaded mood of it. I sense her exhaustion. "The songs I write are at Tucker's and Darren's direction. There's not one song on any of my albums that's truly mine, that tells my fans something about me. I've had very little say in Madeline Montana from day one. I mean, Montana isn't even my real surname."

"Is Madeline your real name?"

"Yes. I got to keep that part of myself at least. Pretty much everything else is a performance designed to keep fans and find new ones. And even when I do something that wasn't planned, I've had it drummed into me to always remember people are watching and judging."

I'm not surprised about any of this. Not after watching my brother go through everything he has for his political career. And not after all the things I know about my friends who live in the public eye. The world puts the people they want to idolize through their paces, that's for damn sure.

"Okay," I say, "Play me a song that tells me something about you that no one knows."

Hesitation flickers in her eyes and it's in line with what I know of Maddie so far. I think her ex has taken her identity from her and I wonder if she'll be able to give me a song. I think she's confused as fuck about herself.

Just when it seems like she won't give me a song, she scrolls my phone and selects one. I don't know it and have no idea who the singer is but I'm immediately drawn to the lyrics.

It's essentially an anthem for women. The singer is telling herself and other women to embrace themselves. That all the confusion in a world full of comparison is natural but that they don't have to put up with this any longer. It's a song about the acceptance of imperfection.

"I've had "Girl" on repeat for months," she admits when the song ends.

"Who's the singer?"

"Maren Morris."

"Great lyrics." I meet her gaze. "Honest lyrics."

"I want to write lyrics like that."

"You don't already?"

"No. Well, yes . . . but I've kept them to myself. Actually, they're more like scribbled journaling than lyrics . . ." Her voice trails off and I get the impression there's a lot here for her to unpack about her work. But then, I think that's the lot of a creative person. There's a great deal of unpacking about our place in the world, what we actually have to say, what we *want* to say, and whether there will be acceptance of it.

Maddie finds my gaze again, more hesitation in her eyes. "This has been on repeat too," she says softly, and I know she's sharing a vulnerable piece of herself with me when another song comes on from the same singer. It's a cover of "Dancing With Myself" that Billy Idol originally sang. Maren Morris's version is slower, quieter. It feels more introspective. I think that for Maddie it speaks to not only her love life but also her career.

When it ends, we sit in silence for a long while before I turn to her. "You have over twenty million followers on Instagram. I wonder how many of them would kill to dance with the real Maddie? I bet it's more than you might think."

"You looked me up?" She's wide-eyed.

"No. Sasha was all about you yesterday during the wedding photos. And now I have no need to look you up. Sasha has ensured I have all your stats stored in my head."

A laugh busts out of her. "Oh, god. That's a lot."

"Based on my conversation with her, I'd say she's a superfan."

"Most of those twenty million come from Tucker. I

don't know how many of them are really there for me, you know?"

We're interrupted when a string of texts come through on her phone. I give her the space to check them and focus back on the highway. A few minutes later, I spot a gas station and pull in.

As I cut the engine of my Range Rover, Maddie finishes texting and places her phone back in the center console. "Sorry about that. Leigh's having issues with my manager." She looks pained when she adds, "He's threatened her career if she doesn't give him my new phone number."

"No need to apologize. You've gotta handle your business. Is Leigh okay?"

"Yes, she's not the kind of person to let threats get to her, but I hate that I've put her in this position. I've just texted Darren to take the pressure off her, so I imagine he'll start blowing up my phone any second now."

"You want me to take over the management of your phone?"

She laughs. "I can only guess what you'd say to him."

"Try me and see."

She inhales a long breath before releasing it. "I'm so glad you forced your way into this road trip. You're helping take my mind off everything."

"Forced is highly inaccurate."

She tilts her head questioningly. "Bossed?"

"Let's agree that I came along because I wanted to get to know you. I also didn't want you to end up in your very own version of *Misery*."

"What's that?"

"The movie where an author is held captive by a fan.

It's a Stephen King thriller. How have you never heard of it? How have you never watched it?"

"I don't do thrillers. Or horror movies."

"This is our second bump in the road."

"How many bumps before a friendship has to be declared impossible?" Her smile is infectious, or maybe it's just her presence that inspires so much enjoyment in me.

"I'm the guy who was almost the father of an eight-year-old, remember?"

"Right. You're also the guy who probably would have given up his entire fortune if asked. You don't let bumps deter you."

"The bumps make the ride interesting." As she thinks about that, I ask, "What's your real surname?"

"Miller."

"So much better than Montana."

She smiles and I think she likes that I asked for her real name. "It really is."

I reach for the door handle. "What snacks do you want?" We were nowhere near prepared for this road trip. It's time to load up.

To my great fucking delight, Maddie rattles off a list of junk food she'd like. I know far too many women with hang ups over their diet. It's refreshing to meet someone who'll eat what she wants.

I fill up with gas and food. Maddie starts eating a chocolate bar before we leave the gas station.

She eyes me as I start the car, holding up the Snickers bar I got myself. "How are you not already halfway through this?"

"Some of us have restraint."

She rolls her eyes. "Seriously. If you don't hurry up and eat it, I'll steal it."

"It's all yours, but I'm ready for some more duetting, so eat fast."

My phone buzzes with a text, then another, and another. When Maddie tries to pass it to me, I say, "Can you check it for me?" Another car has pulled in behind us, so I need to drive.

"Oh, you have a group chat with your brothers," Maddie says, reading my messages. "That's cute."

I steer the car back onto the highway. "It's practical."

She looks at me. "It's also cute. It's nice to see brothers getting along. I've just spent years with a guy who hated his brothers."

"We don't chat much through that group. It's usually just for making plans. What are they arranging?"

"Nothing. Gage texted first to ask where you're going. He says your father told him you were going on a road trip. Hayden and Bradford texted that they'd heard the same and are also wondering where you're going."

I messaged Mom and Dad earlier to let them know I was unable to come to the family dinner next week that they'd planned. Mom had texted back to have a good time. Dad hadn't been as kind. He texted his disappointment in me for canceling on my family. I should have expected that. I've been disappointing him my entire life.

"Ethan," Maddie prompts when I get lost in my thoughts.

I turn to her. "Can you text them back and let them know where we're going?"

"Sure." She taps out a text and then reads it out to me

to confirm it's okay. She appears highly concerned about getting the text exactly right.

"Whatever you send will be good."

"No, I want to make sure it's what you would send. Maybe just tell me word for word what to send."

I reach over and hit send on what she'd already typed. "It was good."

She blinks at me like she can't believe I just did that. "I'd started deleting what I'd typed." She glances down at the phone. "And your big finger added some extra random letters before you hit send. That message won't make any sense to your brothers."

"Good."

"Good?"

"Yeah, it'll give them something to pass their time with. Wondering what the hell I meant."

More blinking.

"Perfection is overrated, Maddie." At the sound of two new texts, I ask, "What did they come back with?"

She reads the texts, still giving off vibes of *I don't understand you right now*. Then, laughing, she says, "Oh, actually, this is fun. Maybe you're right. The text you sent ended up saying, 'I'm driving to Styiiiioop' and somehow you also managed to get a middle finger emoji in at the end of it. Gage texted back 'Is this a new game we're playing?' and Bradford replied 'This is Kristen and I like this game already. Tell us more, Ethan.' Oh, and Callan's just texted 'Olivia here and I'm thinking it's time this group chat had an upgrade. Kristen and I need to be added because you boys suck at games where you have to guess things. I'll add us in so we can help figure out where Styii-iioop is.'"

"Jesus," I say. "That group chat is never going to shut up now."

"Well, perhaps if you hadn't sent your text so hastily you wouldn't be in this predicament now."

"I'm detecting some passive aggressiveness there, Miller."

"And you would be right, Black."

I grin at her right as her phone starts ringing.

"Shit," she says checking it. "I have to take this call. It's my manager."

9

MADELINE

"DARREN," I answer the call, my voice tight. I don't think there's a single thing I could do to relax it or me right now.

"What the fuck kind of stunt was that yesterday?" He sounds murderous and I didn't expect anything less.

I inhale a breath, taking a moment to reply so that I can search for a little calm. "It wasn't a stunt, Darren. I didn't want to get married."

"That's bullshit. You've wanted your claws in Tucker from the first day you met him. Marrying him was always your goal."

"And this just shows how little you truly know me. I wanted Tucker because I thought I was in love with him. Marrying him hadn't ever crossed my mind until he started talking about it and then rushing me to the alter."

"Don't kid yourself, sweetheart. You ran around doing everything for the brand you were told to. Fuck, if we'd told you to get on your knees up on a stage you would have. You wanted everything that being with Tucker could give you and you went out of your way to get it."

Get loud, Maddie.

Get fucking loud.

The thing about never experiencing anger? When you do feel it, *finally* feel it, it feels like a magnitude 8 volcanic eruption. My skin is alive in a way it has never been. There's violence trapped inside it. Right under it. Explosive violence.

"Two things, Darren." I try to speak slowly, try to slow my eruption, but I can already feel that this isn't an explosion I can control. It's been building for too long. "Don't ever fucking call me sweetheart again." I suck in a breath, my body shaking. I want to harm this man like I've never wanted to harm another person. "And don't *ever* presume to know why I do anything. Yes, I did do everything for the brand that I was told to, but for very fucking different reasons than you think. If I really was the person you've just described, I would have stayed yesterday and signed my life away to Tucker and you."

"I'll call you whatever I want, Maddie. I own you." Venom spills all over his words. "Now, you need to get the fuck home so we can begin putting this shitshow back together. The tour depends on it."

Go home?

Put everything back together?

Go on tour?

"I'm unsure of what's not clear to you. I'm not marrying Tucker. There is nothing to put back together." And I'm certainly not going on tour with him.

"You *are* marrying Tucker. I don't care if it's before the tour or after, but it is happening."

"Go fuck yourself, Darren. The time when you get to order me around has passed. And if you think that tour's happening, you're deluding yourself." I think of one last thing. "And it was really nice to hear from Tucker himself, but I guess he's been too busy fucking Tee. Come to think of it, she might be who you're confusing me with. *She's* wanted her claws in Tucker since the day she met him." I stab at the phone to end the call, throw it into the center console of the car, and look out the window as I release a long breath. God, I hate that man. With a capital fucking 'h'.

Ethan doesn't say anything. He allows me the space I need to come down from that confrontation.

I'm in the middle of doing that when a text sounds from my phone. The text notification alone triggers more violence under my skin.

When I don't reach for the phone, Ethan says, "How you doing over there, Miller? Do you need me to take over?"

I smile as I stare out the window. My fury eases a little instantly. Ethan has a gift for cutting through the noise and quieting my inner turmoil. And the way he's started using my surname? I like it a lot.

I turn and find concern on his face. "I don't think I'm doing too well, to be honest. I think I've just ended my career."

"Your manager has that much control over the twenty million people following you?"

"I appreciate what you're trying to do but you don't know the industry like I do. Tucker is an asshole with far too much power. One word from him or Darren and I'll find it hard to get people to work with me. My career will be over before it's really even begun."

He's quiet for a moment. Thinking. Then he says,

"Sure, you may not be able to work with some people if your ex blacklists you, but there's a lot of talented people in this world waiting to be discovered. I imagine you could find your perfect collaborators if you really wanted to. And the fact you already have a large platform means the kind of opportunity that so many don't have." He pauses. "Point is, you aren't powerless, Maddie. Never forget that."

Another text comes through for me and this time, I reach for my phone. Ethan's right; I'm not powerless. And I have value. Tucker and Darren wouldn't still want me if I didn't.

> TUCKER
>
> You have a contract, Madeline.
>
> TUCKER
>
> And I highly fucking recommend you honor it. You won't like what happens if you don't.

And there's the asshole I was going to marry. I know he's referring to the tour contract, but the subtext is *get your ass home and marry me, or else.*

WE ARRIVE in Pittsburgh close to six p.m. That's after adding six more songs to our playlist in between having a long conversation about Ethan's work and the travel he's done as part of it. He's a photographer and has photographed people all over the world, although, he hasn't done much photography over the last couple of years after he developed an app that teaches photography. He's just sold the app and isn't sure what he'll do next, but I've got the impression he misses taking people's photos. It was that conversation that got me through the afternoon. If I didn't have Ethan to help with that, I would have spiraled into a black hole of worry over my career.

I tried to push Tucker and Darren to the back of my mind after Tucker's texts. I haven't replied to him yet and I'm still unsure of what I'll text back.

"Okay," Ethan says after he gets off a call with the hotel we've decided to try and book for the night. We're currently sitting in his Range Rover in the hotel parking garage. "There's some massive event on in Pittsburgh this weekend and hotel rooms are scarce. They can give us two rooms but they're on different floors."

I know what he's asking here. *Am I happy to be nowhere near him?* The answer to that is no. I feel panicky at being alone in that way. It's irrational, I know, but it's how I feel.

"Would you be okay if we shared a room?" I bite my lip. From the moment we met, I've been asking things of this man and I feel bad over that.

"I don't know. That's a big fucking ask of a guy." He grins.

Ten minutes later, he's booked us a room and we're in the elevator up to it. Thankfully, no one has recognized me.

The room we could get is a deluxe room with two queen beds that overlooks a park. Ethan lets me choose which bed I want and then asks if I want to order dinner in or go out for it. He suggests he could go out and get anything I'd like. It's at this point that I feel really awful for everything he's already had to do for me. It's also the moment where my anger at Tucker and Darren resurfaces because they're part of the reason Ethan and I are here in this hotel room together.

"Do you know what?" I say as I stride to my suitcase. "Leigh threw a wig in here for me, and I think I should put it on, and we should go out for dinner. It's not fair to you if I demand we stay hidden away for this entire road trip."

I've pulled the suitcase up onto the bed and am unzipping it when Ethan moves behind me and places his hand over mine.

"Maddie, stop." He's so close to me that his chest brushes against my back. "I knew what this road trip would be when I signed up for it. I'm happy to stay in for dinner and I'm more than happy to go out and get it for us. Please stop thinking that you're putting me out. You're not." His deep voice and closeness affect me, sparking flutters in my stomach.

I turn, ready to thank him for what he just said. However, every sense I have is overwhelmed by his close proximity and my good sense shuts down on me. There's a lot going on between this and the anger I'm feeling toward my ex, and this is the only reason I have for what I suggest next. "I think you should take me out and get me drunk."

His response is immediate. "I think that's the worst idea you've had since I met you."

"Worse than demanding you kiss me?"

"Far worse than that."

"Well, we could just get drunk here."

"Or we could just eat. I've worked out you really like

chocolate. I'll bring you enough to binge on so you don't feel the need for booze."

"It's a real wonder you aren't the father of an eight-year-old and a husband of that child's mother. How any woman ever let you go is beyond me."

That slows him down for a beat. He stares at me for the longest moment, like he's turning over what I just said in his head. "I have a running list of my faults as told to me by exes if you'd like it. It's a long list." There's no bitterness in his words, just candor, and I get the impression that Ethan is a very self-aware man.

"I don't care to read the list. I have my own."

"Fuck. Already?"

"It only has one item in the *Could Be A Problem* column."

"What is it?"

"Your quads."

His lips twitch. "That really is a problem because I can't do anything about them."

I cock my head. "I don't know about that. Surely, if one were to stop putting on hot-quad shorts to take part in leg day, the problem would eventually disappear."

He lets his smile out to play. "How boring would life be without hot quads though, Maddie?"

I return his smile and realize the tight feeling in my chest has disappeared. "I think you should go out and find us something to eat for dinner while I take a shower."

"What do you feel like eating?"

"Anything except spicy food. Surprise me."

He appears to like that suggestion and a few minutes

later, I'm alone in the hotel room. After I gather my thoughts, I grab my phone and send Tucker a text.

ME

I'm not marrying you, Tucker, and I'm not going on tour with you.

He comes straight back to me.

TUCKER

You're making a mistake here.

ME

You wanted to sleep with other women. Well, the world is wide open for you now.

TUCKER

The world never shut down for me, babe.

I stare at that last text for a long time and know deep in my soul that Tucker never loved me. He used me for his career. That's all I was to him.

Tears spill down my cheeks. Not because I'm broken up over our relationship ending. I'm not. I'm hurt that he used me in this way and I'm upset that it's taken me so long to see it.

I feel stupid.

I let two men run my life without question.

Well, never again.

I'd rather start fresh and see if any fans stick around. And if not, I'd rather have no career than no self-respect.

With more boldness than I'm actually feeling, I tap out a reply to Tucker.

ME

We're done.

His text comes back a minute later.

TUCKER

Good fucking luck to you then. Make sure your shit is out of my place tomorrow.

10

MFW I READ @tuckerbrandt's latest Insta post. Holy sheesh! The. Tea. rn. We are shook. It appears the magical love story between him and @madelinemontana wasn't so magical after all. He's come out with a statement about his runaway bride and it's not pretty, girlfriend. The marriage is OFF. He said he can't marry someone who doesn't love him like he loves her. Be still our broken hearts. He'll be going on tour without her. He's announced that @teebird will be his tour partner now. Which, I mean, she's cool, but she doesn't inspire my cowgirl era like our Maddie does. And speaking of our girl, where is she??? I'm not buying into any of this until I hear from her. I know all the Tucker stans have their pitchforks out for Maddie, but I've got TFW something just doesn't feel right. I'm going in search of more tea.

11

ETHAN

It's been a long time since I've shared space with a woman and I'm unsure how I've forgotten the mess they can make. When I returned from getting our dinner last night, Maddie had taken a shower and, in the process, spread all her shit from one end of the room to the other. My bed was the only area left free. The bathroom also had her beauty products strewn everywhere. When I stumble into the bathroom first thing Monday morning after very little sleep, I almost trip over her shoes. I curse loud enough to wake her.

"Sorry," she says when I come out from the bathroom. She's half sitting up in bed with the sexiest fucking bedhead hair and those beautiful blue eyes of hers looking at me with apology. "I'll be tidier from now on."

I try hard not to let my eyes wander down to her chest but it's an impossible task. One of the thin straps of the silky pajama top she's wearing has slipped off her shoulder and as I take it all in, I wish to Christ I'd tried harder to keep my eyes on her face.

I'm staring at a whole lot of skin and a nipple that's only just hidden by silk.

Tearing my gaze away, I head for my bag to find clothes. "I'm gonna go get coffee. Do you want anything?"

She pushes the bed covers off and gets out of bed and fuck me, those tiny pink silk pajama shorts may be the death of me.

"I would die for coffee. With creamer please. And if they have cinnamon caramel syrup, I'll have that too."

My eyes are in a mood for my demise today. They're glued to her long legs as she walks toward the bathroom. They're so fucking glued there I may need help removing them.

In the end, it's the bathroom door closing that breaks the spell. I can only hope Maddie plans on covering all her skin today. Otherwise, it's going to be a long day.

I find a coffee shop down the street and while I'm waiting for our order, a group chat text comes in.

HAYDEN

Have we figured out where Styiiiioop is yet?

OLIVIA

St. Louis?

GAGE

Why would Ethan be going to St. Louis?

KRISTEN

Does he know anyone there?

HAYDEN

I don't think so.

OLIVIA

I'm thinking of places that start with "St".

KRISTEN

Is sending texts that need deciphering normal for Ethan?

HAYDEN

No.

KRISTEN

Ooh, so this is new?

OLIVIA

The emoji is confusing. It doesn't feel very Ethan.

GAGE

Not confusing. If any emoji represents Ethan, it's the middle finger.

OLIVIA

Right, I get that, but it's not like he gives us the middle finger. It's odd.

BRADFORD

I called Troy. Ethan's on a road trip with the runaway bride. They're going to Sedona.

OLIVIA

God, I have no idea why I didn't think to call his assistant.

KRISTEN

You're kinda busy on your honeymoon.

HAYDEN

How's your father, Liv?

OLIVIA

He's doing well. He's recovering at home
after the stent surgery.

HAYDEN

Glad to hear it.

I'm distracted from the texts when I'm alerted that my
coffee order is ready. I grab the drinks and pastries I got
for Madeline in case she's hungry and head back to the
hotel.

When I walk through the door of our room, I'm
presented with Maddie bending over her bed,
rummaging in her suitcase while wearing only her
underwear. And those panties she's wearing? They put a
massive grin on my face.

"I see you're in your grandma era, Miller," I say as the
door shuts behind me.

She spins to face me and glances down at the big
granny panties she's wearing. Her smile matches mine. "I
don't think I'm ever going to leave my grandma era. Seriously, these are the most comfortable undies I've ever
owned."

I'm looking at the most oversized panties I've ever
come across. They're white with big red hearts all over
them and red frilly lace along the edges. There's nothing
sexy about them, but Maddie manages to look sexy in
them. Although, that could have more to do with the bra
she's wearing. No grandma bra to be found here unfortunately. It's lacy, and hot as hell. And if I thought her
pajamas killed me, I had no idea of the death still
awaiting me.

Helping a runaway bride was not on my bingo card

for this year and now I know why. Under any other circumstances, I'd ask Madeline on a date. Under these circumstances, that feels like a crass move and I'm in a constant state of pushing my interest down.

I give her the coffee and pastries I got her. "Do you often wear granny undies?" *And killer bras?*

She laughs. "No, not like this. These were a fun joke from Leigh that I just found in my suitcase. I doubt she's expecting the message I'll be sending her about finding more." She mercifully reaches for a black T-shirt from her suitcase and puts it on along with a pair of jeans.

I take a sip of my coffee. "Okay, I'm thinking if we leave around nine this morning, we'll make it to Louisville today. Probably around five p.m. based on the number of stops you insisted on yesterday."

Her brows lift as she drinks some of her coffee. "Me? I recall you wanted to stop to take photos."

"If we remove those stops from the equation, we're still looking at a fuckload of breaks for all kinds of odd things."

"Since when is having to use the bathroom an odd thing?"

"It's not the bathroom breaks that give me pause."

"Oh, hello, Grandpa Ethan. Who says 'give me pause' anymore?"

My lips threaten to curl up into a grin. "I can get behind stopping for snacks, for looking at historical markers, for collecting shit you see that gives you lyric inspiration, for looking at cute animals you see along the way, and for buying trip souvenirs, but stopping to gaze at cloud animals you see? That shit's weird, Miller."

I think she's also trying not to smile but she's doing a

bad job of it. "It's a good thing you enjoy bumps in the road of a friendship because I don't think I'll ever stop wanting to look at cloud animals. And honestly, I'm unsure why you don't like them."

"I've nothing against them, but they add time to our trip that we need to factor in."

"For a guy who seems to enjoy spontaneity, that is the most unspontaneous thing you've said since I met you."

"A guy can be both spontaneous and practical." I nod at the cup in her hand. "Drink your coffee. We've got half an hour till we need to leave but about five hours of packing ahead of us."

She can't contain her smile any longer. Sweeping her gaze around the messy room, she fakes offense. "I can't believe you just said that." She puts her hand to her heart. "I'm wounded."

"Can you save that for after we pack? You'll have at least six hours to feel all those feels in the car."

She walks my way and pats my chest. "Soon, you'll be talking in acronyms." With that, she moves past me and goes into the bathroom to begin packing. I'm helpless but to watch every step she takes.

12

MADELINE

I TRY to pack my belongings in half an hour. I really do. But when Leigh sends me a stack of texts outlining some things we need to do *immediately*, I fail.

Tucker made a statement about our relationship and the tour last night and it wasn't kind to me. Leigh is furious and so am I after I read it. I was already angry after the messages we exchanged yesterday, but this . . . *this* lights a fire inside me that I would never have imagined possible.

He can't marry me because I don't love him like he loves me?

That fucking asshole.

I need to make a statement of my own but Leigh has reminded me that not only do I need a new manager and lawyer, but I also need a new publicist. Every person on my team is also on Tucker's team, so I can't use any of them. I *won't* use any of them. Leigh has taken it upon herself to change all my social media passwords and compile a list of possible PR replacements. Until I hire someone, I need to decide what to do with my socials. And I have to decide whether I want to make a statement immediately or wait until I have someone to advise me of the best way to handle this.

Leigh, being the amazing assistant she is, texted me one she drafted as a starting point for me to tweak. I stop packing and sit on the bed to read it.

"You look like you're in physical pain," Ethan says, sitting on the bed across from me. It doesn't escape me that unlike all the men I've ever known, he doesn't appear annoyed that I'm slowing us down.

"I am."

"What's happened?"

I pass him my phone so he can read Leigh's draft. "I don't know what to do."

He reads the statement and then looks at me. "You have no gut instinct on this?"

"Oh, I do, but it's probably not the right instinct."

"What's it telling you?"

The violence that crawled under my skin yesterday blazes to life. "Well, first, I want to go clothes shopping and buy all the kinds of clothes *I* want that Tucker never let me wear. And then, I want to take a photo of myself wearing something from my shopping spree and post it on Instagram with the caption 'Fuck you, Tucker.'"

The look on his face says he'd be my collaborator on this. "Is there a middle finger involved in this photo?"

The violence under my skin says *fuck yes*, but I waver on this. "I don't know . . ."

He stands and lifts his chin at me. "Okay, let's go."

I blink. "No . . . god, no. That was just me being angry."

"No, that was your gut speaking. You're putting that wig on and I'm taking you shopping. We can leave the fuck-you-Tucker photo out of this, but let's see how you feel after shopping."

I stand, every inch of my skin desperate to follow his lead while my brain does everything in her power to put forth reasons why this is a very bad idea. "We don't have time for shopping, Ethan. Not if you want to get to Louisville by five."

"We can arrive at midnight for all I care. I was thinking about you when I planned for a five o'clock arrival."

"Huh? Why?"

"I wanted you to be there in time for dinner and an early bedtime. I think you probably need some kind of routine you can count on right now. Three square meals a day and decent sleep is a good start."

"You really are the most thoughtful guy I've ever met," I murmur.

"No, it's just what you do for people who are going through something."

I shake my head. "It's not. It's really not what most people do. Especially not for someone they just met. I hope you know how special you are."

Ethan doesn't reply to that, but I think he appreciates what I just said. I wonder if anyone has ever told him how special he is.

He starts issuing bossy orders like, "Move your ass, Miller, we've got shopping to do," and forty minutes later, I've got the brunette wig on that Leigh packed and we're walking into a shopping mall.

I'm not even feeling a little bit nervous about being

seen. Not anymore. Something shifted in me yesterday when Tucker wished me *good fucking luck*. I think I was hiding because I was filled with shame over running out on him the way I did. I no longer feel that way. Not when I was the only one who showed up honestly for most of our relationship. I'm not the one who should be feeling shame.

Let the world see me now. I have nothing to hide from.

I put the wig on though. For security purposes. I don't want to put Ethan or myself in a situation that could get out of control.

"Right," Ethan says while surveying the racks of clothing in front of us. "What are we looking for?"

I smile up at him. "Do you enjoy shopping?"

"Generally, not with women."

"But you're taking one for the team today."

"Yeah." He smiles down at me and doesn't look even the slightest bit like he wishes he was somewhere else.

I gaze out at all the clothes. "I don't really know what I'm looking for." I bite my lip. "I'm sorry, this probably wasn't the best idea when we're in the middle of a road trip."

"I don't know, this feels very much in alignment with this trip."

"What? Rash and impulsive?"

"I was thinking of liberation. Freedom. Empowerment."

It's funny how other people see us compared to how we see ourselves and I'm reminded that I used to think of myself in a whole different way before I met Tucker.

I was fiercely independent back then. I had to be after

my mother got sick when I was sixteen. She died the day before I graduated from high school and instead of drowning in my grief, I got on with life like she'd done when my father died.

I met Tucker seven years after that, and it was nice not to have to worry about where my next paycheck would come from because I finally had a steady one. It was nice to have a reprieve from the grief I'd been trying to ignore for years. And it was really nice to have some luxury and fun in my life.

I exchanged my independence for ease, and I now know that was a bad trade.

"You're right." I push my shoulders back. "Let's find some new clothes."

We spend two hours shopping. We search the mall high and low and if a piece of clothing draws my attention, I buy it. I push doubts and second-guesses from my mind and just go by feel. It's exhilarating.

Ethan helps by holding up possibilities as he finds them. It turns out he's a fast learner because he starts spotting things before I do once he knows my style. He wanders off to take a work call while I'm in the lingerie department and when he returns about ten minutes later, he's holding a pair of oversized black women's undies.

I contain my smile. "Are those for you?"

He's amused. "Smart-ass. They're for you." He holds them up and shows me the "Take No Shit" scrawled across the front in bright colors. Surrounding the words is a pattern of bright flowers and middle fingers. "They're so loud they assaulted me while I was walking through the racks, and I knew you had to have them."

"Oh my god." I laugh as I take them from him. "You're so right. I need these in my life."

"I looked for cloud patterns too since I know how much you love them. Sadly, there were none."

I roll my eyes at him but I'm still laughing.

We banter and laugh our way to the cashier. This entire shopping expedition has felt more domestic and natural than anything I've done in the last three years, and I've enjoyed every second of it. The fact it's stirring feelings for Ethan is something I try to ignore because I really doubt he's in the market for a woman as messed up as me. But what he's given me today is something I've craved forever with a man.

After we pay, I make him wait while I find a restroom to change my clothes. I put on the pair of tattered denim shorts I selected along with a grungy gray sleeveless top that has a phoenix with its wings spread wide as the focal point. The words "FREE BIRD" are written above the bird while underneath it says, "and this bird you cannot change."

The heated look Ethan gives me when I emerge from the restrooms unleashes butterflies in my stomach. "I thought hot-quad shorts were banned on this road trip," he says as we head for the car.

"These are hardly hot-quad shorts, Black."

He gives me a disbelieving arch of his brows before dropping his gaze to my shorts, and holy heck it's like my entire body decides to get behind those butterflies in my stomach. I almost lose the thread of our conversation while my body tries to run the show. "They fucking are," he says when his eyes find mine again.

Oh. Wow.

Ethan's as affected by my shorts as I was by his.

"Should I change?" I want to show him the same courtesy he showed me.

"Don't you dare."

By the time we arrive at his car, I'm all kinds of bothered. Mostly because of his reaction to my shorts but also because I've pulled up my memory of the kiss we shared the day we met. The one Ethan took charge of.

I didn't want that kiss to end. The way he'd taken hold of my face and grazed his thumb over my jaw had been so intimate. And the way he'd kissed me so thoroughly and then ground himself against me? I've lost count of the number of times I've thought about that. But the apology he'd given when he'd dragged his mouth from mine? *That* was everything even though it was so unnecessary.

I barely know this man, but I think he's shown me exactly who he is. And while good looks, smoldering eyes, and sexy magnetism are all turn-ons, I'm discovering just how much a man's heart turns me on more.

When Ethan opens my car door for me and takes all my shopping bags, I avoid eye contact and settle myself into my seat while he puts the bags in the trunk. I busy myself on my phone when he starts the car. I need a hot minute to shift my thoughts away from our kiss. Looking at him won't help me do that.

His deep voice cuts into my thoughts as we drive toward the exit. "Are we taking a photo?"

"No . . . maybe. I don't know." I madly keep my eyes on my phone, tapping, swiping, scrolling.

He stops the car in the middle of the parking lot exit. "Miller. What's going on in that pretty head of yours?"

I glance up and look in the rearview mirror. "You can't just stop here. There are cars behind us."

"I don't give a shit about those cars, Maddie. I give a shit about why you're being weird with me. What gives?"

I've only dated three guys in my life. I didn't have a boyfriend in high school and didn't lose my virginity until I was twenty. I've never had a one-night stand. I've never kissed a random stranger before I kissed Ethan. All up, I don't have a lot of experience with men or flirting. And I have no experience with the kinds of feelings I'm having right now.

I look at Ethan who is watching me like I'm the only other person in the world. He's giving me the kind of attention I've never known, and he's right; I am being weird with him. All I can give him is my truth. "I'm thinking about how much I liked shopping with you. No one's ever gone shopping with me and made it fun like you did." I pause before adding, "I really like hanging out with you."

Surprise is clear in his eyes. I don't think he expected that. "I really fucking like the way you share yourself so honestly."

A horn blares from behind us while my heart beats loudly in my chest.

"I was also thinking about our kiss the other day."

His piercing gaze smolders with an intensity that jolts electricity through my veins. "I haven't been able to get that kiss out of my mind."

My breathing feels very unsteady right now.

The horn blares again.

"We need to go," I say, even though leaving this moment behind is the last thing I want to do.

"Yeah." Ethan's voice is gravel, and it moves into my veins, too.

He doesn't stop looking at me.

The horn blares again, for much longer.

I smile. "You've got a photo to take of me, Black."

He's still not taking his eyes off me. "Will there be a middle finger involved?"

"I'm not sure yet. Let's see."

13

ETHAN

MADDIE'S BRAIN and body are in competition over allowing her to just be herself in front of my camera. She's the most beautiful woman I've had in front of my camera, and it's clear she's used to being photographed, but I'm looking for something more than just her beauty to show up in these photos. I want to see her essence and the only way we'll get that is if she discards her perfectly choreographed mannerisms and lets her soul do the talking.

We drove to the Pittsburgh Botanic Gardens to take these photos and the setting is gorgeous with the picturesque fall foliage as our backdrop. Maddie removed her wig, so we found a secluded space amongst trees that offered privacy, and we've spent the past fifteen minutes trying to get some good shots, but I haven't been happy with any of them.

"Is that one better?" she asks as I inspect the photo I just took.

It's a perfectly fine photo that a lot of photographers

would be happy with. However, it doesn't even begin to capture the Maddie I'm getting to know.

"We can do better."

She frowns. "Really? I thought that one would have been good." She walks my way. "Show me." After I let her look, she says, "Seriously, Ethan, what's wrong with it?"

"Everything."

More frowning. "Well, that's cleared things up for me."

"I want to see *you* in the photo, Maddie. I'm not seeing that."

"I'm seeing me in that photo."

"No, you're not. You're seeing Madeline Montana in that photo. Show me Madeline Miller. Show me what you're feeling right now, today. Show me your confusion and hurt. Show me your worries. Show me your hope. Hell, show me your anger and your middle finger. If you want to connect with the people who will look at this photo"—I move into her space and touch where her heart is—"*that's* what will make them look a little longer and think a little harder about who you really are."

Her breathing slows all the way down as she stares up at me. "How?" she whispers. "How do I show all that?"

"Do you have any of your notebooks with you that you write lyrics in? The lyrics you told me about that you haven't shared with anyone."

"Yes, I have one in my purse." She sounds anything but confident about where this is going.

"Okay, take it and go sit on that bench." I point to where I want her to go. "I want you to read what you've written. Connect with it. And I want you to think about everything you've given up to be Madeline Montana. Write more if lyrics come to you."

She nods but I see the hesitation in her eyes, which is good. Exactly what I was hoping for. I need her to feel vulnerable so we can peel back some layers and I wondered if sitting with her inner thoughts in public might get her there.

I snap photos while she sits on the bench with her notebook. I stand a good distance away, letting her immerse herself without my presence. She takes about ten minutes to start writing in her notebook and then it's another twenty minutes until I sense she's losing herself in her thoughts.

Moving closer, slowly, I take more photos until I reach her. When I sit at the other end of the bench, she continues writing for another minute before lifting her head and staring out at something in front of her. Then, she slightly angles her face down and toward me. It's a side profile and it's fucking perfect with the way her eyes are closed. I take the photo right before she opens her eyes and looks at me.

"I don't know who I am anymore, Ethan," she confides so softly I almost can't hear her.

I snap the photo.

"Did you write something new?"

She nods and I take the photo.

"Tell me."

She swallows whatever she's feeling and I get that one too.

Glancing down at her notebook, she reads the lyric out to me. "Lost in the shadows, trying to make myself whole."

I get every one of these photos.

She continues reading. "I've discovered the truth, I'm

not erased." Tears slide down her cheeks and she brushes them away as she closes her notebook and looks at me. "That's what I've been feeling for so long. Erased. But I'm not."

"No, you're not."

"I'm not going down without a fight."

I fucking love the determination in her voice.

"Good."

"I know the photo I want you to take." She stands. "I need some things from the car."

Five minutes later, she's retrieved a cowgirl hat and a long sleeve denim jacket that looks very western with the long fringes on it from her suitcase. We walk back to the area near the trees and she turns away from me before taking her shirt and bra off and putting the jacket on. It's long enough that it ends almost exactly where her shorts end. When she turns back to me, the jacket is undone and she's holding it closed. She's standing in front of me wearing her cowgirl hat, cowgirl jacket, frayed shorts, and fuck me, her mask is gone.

"I don't want to share a fuck-you-Tucker photo." She opens the jacket, letting it fall so that it covers most of her breasts but not all of them. "I want to share one that says, 'I'm broken and bruised, but I'm still here.'"

When she drops her hands to her sides and tilts her head ever so slightly, I take the photo and I know without having to check that it's the one.

Madeline Miller is standing in front of me.

She's ripped her heart out and offered it to me.

Her essence is bleeding from her.

And when I look at the photo, I'm struck by the way

the shadows cover most of her face, making her eyes hard to see. It's so fucking perfect in its imperfection.

This photo captures how exposed and naked she feels.

I hold out my camera and show her. "As far as I'm concerned, this is the one, but if you want me to keep going, I will."

She stares at the image for the longest time before finally lifting her face to mine. "That's it."

Yeah, it is.

That's the photo that shows Maddie's unglamorous truth.

14

MADELINE

WE ARRIVE in Louisville just after eight p.m. I made Ethan stop for cloud animals again, as well as souvenir collecting, snack gathering, and multiple bathroom breaks. Not to mention the shopping trip and photoshoot.

He didn't complain once.

We talked about fun stuff: our favorite movies (I had to admit I haven't watched a movie in three years; he was horrified and vowed to rectify this sometime this week); our hobbies (again, Ethan was horrified to learn I don't have any hobbies, while I enjoyed learning of his love for highlining, which I'd never heard of, motocross, tennis, golf, and beach volleyball); and our favorite music, which, of course, I had a lot to say about. I vowed to introduce Ethan to more country music this week and had to agree to watch *Misery* with him in exchange for him listening to country music. We added eight more songs to our road trip playlist, which has mostly songs from the eighties and nineties on it so far. Ethan also talked about a friend he has in Louisville, a guy who owns a bar there, and we decided to drop in and visit him after dinner.

We find a hotel and get one room again. We didn't even ask if there were two rooms next to each other available. I like that Ethan seems able to read me and that he's picked up that I don't want to be alone.

There's a new tension between us since we discussed our kiss. And since he photographed me. That photoshoot was unlike any I've ever been a part of. Having Ethan take my photo was an experience. He knows how to peel a person's layers away. It was like having a conversation about myself that had no words. One in which he got to see the vulnerable parts I try to hide.

"What are you thinking you might want for dinner?" he asks once we're in our room. "I know some great restaurants. It just depends what you like to eat." He tells me about some restaurants he's enjoyed here that I might like to try.

"I love a good steak, so maybe the steakhouse." A text comes in for me as I say this and I check it because I've been going back and forth with Leigh all day trying to make a decision about the new PR team I'll hire and I'm waiting on some information from her.

> LEIGH
>
> Okay, so you may want to sit down for this.

I'm instantly on high alert.

> ME
>
> What is it?

LEIGH

Are you sitting?

ME

Leigh, just tell me already.

She forwards me an Instagram link that I immediately click.

@THETEA_GASP

GIRLFRIEND, the news that broke today about our girl @madelinemontana and her ex @tuckerbrandt was so unexpected. And to be honest, we're not sure we wanna be a part of circulating it some more, but we know you're always looking to us for the tea updates so here we are. Just know, we won't tolerate any drama on this post and will delete anything nasty. Maddie had an abortion two years ago. This has been confirmed by Tucker in a post he just made in response to the gossip, and we quote him here: "It's true that Madeline had an abortion before our last tour. What you don't know are the circumstances under which she made that choice, so please respect her privacy and right to choose, and leave her in peace." You can read his entire statement on his Insta, but for real, we're torn over his post. Sure, he's come out in support of her, but was she okay with him posting this before she's had a chance to make her own statement? We're concerned the Tucker stans are gonna come after her even more now. And how about this thought: Maddie's been thrown to the wolves and we're wondering why Tucker isn't being clear about his part in all this. I mean, this is the guy who has talked a lot about the era of equality for the sexes, about men standing beside their women rather than in front of them. Where was the bit in his statement asking his fans to respect HIS right to choose? We've got TFW something just doesn't add up.

I SIT on my bed and stare at my phone for what feels like forever. My heart beats so fast and all the way up in my throat that I'm unsure how oxygen is even entering my lungs. I don't think it is. I think Tucker has just thrown me under all the buses in the world and I'm almost dead.

> LEIGH
>
> Maddie? Are you there?

I try to suck air in but it's a fight.
This is bad.
Really, really bad.
Because the sad fact about the music industry is it's filled with misogyny and even in this day and age, my abortion won't go down well. Tucker lied every time he said this is the era of equality. I was never the woman standing next to him; I was the woman standing about ten men back from him.

> ME
>
> Yes.

My fingers shake as I tap out my text, and not just from fear, but also from my rising anger over what Tucker's done.

LEIGH

What do you want to do? Should I draft a statement for you to check over?

ME

I don't know. I need to think.

LEIGH

Okay. Let me know.

LEIGH

And Maddie? I'm so fucking sorry this has happened.

My attention is drawn from my phone when my bed dips under Ethan's weight as he sits next to me. I glance up to find him studying me with concern.

"What is it?" he asks and despite the turmoil raging inside me, I'm acutely aware of everything about him—the nearness of his body, the way his gaze feels like a touch on my skin, the solid wall of his chest that feels like a comfort. *His genuine desire to know what's upset me.*

I take a deep breath, willing my voice to steady when it wants to shake, and hand him a piece of my soul. "I had an abortion two years ago," I whisper, the words sounding like ash. "No one knew. But it's on social media now. Tucker has commented . . . he made it sound like it was my choice."

His eyes search mine. "But it wasn't your choice."

I like that he didn't phrase that as a question. "He made it clear I had to get rid of the baby. And not just if I wanted a career. And he left me to do that on my own." I squeeze my eyes closed as all the memories of that time in my life flood my mind. Ethan remains silent, giving me the space I need to think. When I finally open my eyes

again there are tears in them. "I made the choice ulti-
mately. I own that choice. It was what I thought I wanted,
but damn, the choices women have to make at
times . . . We're damned if we do and damned if we don't."
I gulp down some oxygen. "My choice haunts me."

"Why?"

"Call me romantic, idealistic, but I want what my
parents had. I want a deep love that would say 'fuck it all'
to outside forces when stuff like this happens." I wipe my
tears from my cheeks. "And yes, I know that's unrealistic,
because hard stuff happens in life all the time that we
can't say that to, but it's what I wish everyone could have.
And if that's what I'd had with Tucker, maybe we would
have chosen differently."

Ethan's gaze is unwavering. "I don't think it's unreasonable to want a man to stand by your side and choose
you over everything else even when hard stuff's
happening all around you." His jaw clenches. "And it's
sure as shit not unreasonable to expect the man who says
he loves you to accept joint responsibility for making a
baby with you."

If I could stay in this moment for the rest of this night,
I would. There's something about Ethan that makes me
feel protected, and right now I just want to feel sheltered
from the world. But that's not possible, and I have to
figure out how to handle this.

Ethan's phone rings while I'm thinking about this,
and he grimaces when he sees the caller ID. He doesn't
answer the call though.

"You should call them back," I say after the phone
goes quiet.

"I don't want to leave you like this."

"I'm okay. And besides, I have to call Leigh and put together a plan to mitigate this." When he doesn't appear convinced, I add, "Honestly, I'll be okay while you make your call." I smile. "I promise to let you worry over me for the rest of the night."

He looks torn over this, but when his phone rings again, he curses softly, stands, and answers the call while exiting the room.

I exhale a shaky breath once I'm alone. The silence and four walls are suffocating. Or maybe that's my anger that feels like it's crushing my insides.

How fucking dare Tucker do this to me?

And now *I* have to be the one to explain myself to the world?

I push up off the bed, my movements jerky, my fury increasing. I could scream and throw things. I *want* to scream and throw things. But all the years of pushing myself down, of containing myself, of swallowing my thoughts, feelings, desires, *my everything*, make it so I'm unable to do either of those things. Instead, I switch into business mode and send Leigh a text.

ME

Can you please draft me that statement?

LEIGH

I've already drafted it.

She sends through a statement. It confirms the abortion and asks for privacy in the same manner that Tucker's post did. The only truth it reveals is the fact I ended a pregnancy. It shows none of my heart or real truth, and after I read it a few times, I contemplate whether I want to share it. Whether I want to continue the façade I've been a part of for years.

This is a crossroads I never expected to reach, and I'm again presented with a choice that feels like *damned if I do, damned if I don't*. That thought drives me in search of the minibar and what it may offer. I don't tend to resort to alcohol to cope with life, but tonight it feels like a great option.

I down the vodka first. Then, the gin. They burn all the way down. I'm in the middle of the gin burn when Leigh texts again.

> LEIGH
>
> Holy fuck, Madeline, if I end up in prison tonight for hurting someone because they hurt you, you must bail me out. Social media has lost its mind.

> ME
>
> I promise to bail you out, but don't tell me why. There's only so much booze in this hotel room and I suspect it won't be enough if you do.

She calls and I put her on speakerphone. "You're drinking?"

I eye the whiskey in the fridge as my veins begin to warm from the vodka and gin. "I am."

"Oh, god. Tell me Hottie McHottie is with you to stop you from drinking too much."

I reach for the tiny whiskey bottle while silently agreeing with her description. He really is a Hottie McHottie. "Why do they make these bottles so small?"

"Have you ever binged alcohol in a hotel room while mad and sad?"

"Never."

"Send me your exact location. Right now."

I laugh. "Why have we never talked like this? I like it."

"Ah, because you were my boss."

"I'm still your boss."

"Yeah, well, things are different now. There isn't time to fuck around with niceties when I'm worried you're about to wipe yourself out, destination unknown, and potentially no Hottie McHottie in sight to save your ass. Where is he?"

I down the whiskey, scrunching my face up at the way it burns. Way worse than the other two. "Whoa. Whiskey is nasty."

"Oh, Jesus. Please tell me the name of the hotel."

I rattle the name off and discard the whiskey bottle. "Hottie McHottie is outside taking a call. He'll be back soon. You can stop fretting."

"Are we posting that statement I drafted?"

"Yes. No. I don't think so." I spin at the sound of the door and watch Ethan walk back in.

"That's a decidedly unclear direction. Do you care to clarify?"

It really is. And I really can't clarify it right now. Not when I can't untangle the thoughts and feelings twisting up my insides, turning my anger into something sharp and cold and dangerous. Part of me wants to stay silent, let Tucker's lie stand because that's what I've always done —played the good girl. But the other part, the part that's fueled by cheap booze and years of burying everything I feel wants to burn it all down.

"Madeline?" Leigh presses.

I don't know what to do.

My life is a wreck, and *I don't know what to do.*

I bring my hand to my temple and rub it. "Hottie McHottie is back, so I have to go now. I'm hoping he'll take me out for a drink, at which point I will clarify for you."

Ethan watches me like he's assessing me.

"Right," Leigh says. "I'm taking that as a no for now. Please tell Hottie McHottie that you need to be cut off after two drinks."

Ethan listens in thanks to the speakerphone, his eyes very firmly glued to mine. "I'll cut her off," he says to Leigh. "You can rest assured."

"Thank God one of you can be trusted tonight," Leigh says. "I'm ending this call now. Please don't forget to text me your final decision about this statement."

With that, she's gone, and I'm left alone with the man who really should change his name to Mr. McHottie.

His gaze shifts to the empty alcohol bottles. "You got started without me, Miller."

"I had to. I need the booze to help me figure out what I want to say about Tucker's statement."

"Is it helping yet?"

"No, but it's making me feel good on the inside and that's a damn good start."

"And you still wanna go out?"

I know what he's really asking. *Do I want to go out in public after what's happened*? "Yes. And I might not even wear my wig."

The beginning of a smile settles across his face. "You're feeling frisky, huh?"

"I don't know what I'm feeling. Except mad. Really fucking mad."

"What's your gut telling you to do about that?"

"I never know what my gut's telling me."

"Yeah, you do. What's the first thing that came to mind when I asked you about it?"

I cock my head. "Is the first thing that comes to mind really my gut talking because I'm pretty sure if I did the first thing, I'd have no career tomorrow."

He takes a moment to answer, figuring out his reply, and I really like that he doesn't ever just offer easy answers or platitudes. That he respects me enough to sit with the complexity of a problem and help me find my way through. "Trust me, I get self-doubt. I've dedicated enough of my life to entertaining it. And at times, I've let it run the show." He pauses, his gaze intensifying, telling me that what he's about to say next is important. "None of those times ended well."

His words hang in the air, heavy with unspoken consequences. And while I wonder all the ways it didn't end well for him, I know he's right because I'm in the mess I'm in because I've given into my doubt over the years.

He taps his head. "It'll keep you stuck here rather than here," he shifts his hand to his heart. "And *here* is where you want to lead from. Your head can play catch up and figure it all out later."

When I don't say anything, he encourages me. "Say it, Maddie. You don't have to do it, but just say the words out loud and see how they feel."

My throat squeezes and my heart pounds even just thinking these thoughts. "I want to tell the world who Tucker really is. No, scratch that. I just want to tell the world who I am. Who I really am. But sharing that truth involves him and that feels scary."

"Invite the chaos in, Miller. Nothing changes without it."

"I don't know if I'm ready for everything to change," I whisper, struggling to push the words past the lump in my throat.

"There's no rush. You can take your time with this."

He has no idea about my world. "I don't have that kind of freedom, Ethan. I need to make a statement, and soon."

"Who made that rule?"

"The world. My fans won't still be there if I don't get on top of this. I've given myself three days off, and now it really is time to get back to work."

"I think you're letting fear make the rules." His phone rings again and he gives me a regretful look. "Sorry, this is time sensitive."

While he's on the phone, I find a dress to wear to dinner and go into the bathroom to change. I spend ten minutes fixing my hair and makeup while thinking about everything Ethan said.

I want to share my truth. I really do. But I don't know if I'm strong enough to do that and face the consequences. I'm in the middle of those thoughts when a memory from my childhood comes to me. A memory of my mother making a hard decision a year after my father died.

We were dirt poor, living in a tiny trailer, and she was struggling to put food on the table after using hers and Dad's life savings to get us through that first year without him. She was offered a job that paid well. Too well. She seemed conflicted over that. I'd overheard a phone call she'd had with the man offering her the job and she'd told him there was no way she'd ever do what he'd asked her to do. Not even for the kind of money he was trying to throw at her. She'd told him she had more integrity than that.

I don't know what the job was. All I know is that my mother then went on to work two jobs to feed us. Times were often hard, and she was exhausted, but she kept a roof over our heads, clothes on our backs, and food on our table, all without compromising her values or betraying herself. She refused to let go of who she was, even when it would have been easier to do so.

Somewhere along the way, I've forgotten that I always wanted to be like my mother. Ethan's right: I've let fear rule my choices.

I may not be ready for everything in my life to change, but I can't go on not being true to myself. I reach for my phone and open Instagram, and with shaky hands I invite chaos in by posting the photo Ethan took of me today and speaking from my heart.

@MADELINEMONTANA

WHEN YOU DISCOVER that the man you were going to marry has been cheating on you for the entirety of your relationship, you bet your ass you leave that relationship. And then, after he fails to stand up like a real man and own half the responsibility for making a baby and choosing not to have it, you bet your ass you get loud and start telling your truth. And to all the women out there who have stayed silent for too long, who have had to make damned-if-you-do-damned-if-you-don't choices, who have let someone push them down, I invite you to join me #getfuckingloud

I TAP the words out faster than I've ever written any post and hit share. I don't second-guess myself and I don't hesitate. I'm fucking angry and I'm done with being controlled and manipulated.

15

ETHAN

MADDIE and I skipped the steakhouse and headed straight to my friend's bar. I suggested that because I was concerned the restaurant might not offer as much privacy as a quiet, dark corner in the bar would, and I figured tonight she might appreciate that. We arrived forty minutes ago and ordered tacos for dinner, which we've just finished eating. My buddy, Dan, has tried to get away from serving drinks but so far hasn't managed to, so Maddie and I have spent the time talking about photography. She's guided the conversation and I've gotten the impression she's doing her best to avoid talking about herself.

There was something different about her after she got ready for dinner. She walked out of the bathroom while I was wrapping up my phone call and the way her shoulders were pushed back, along with the look of determination on her face, was vastly different to the way she'd looked when she walked into the bathroom.

I didn't ask for her thoughts because I figured we'd

already talked and she'd bring it up again if she wanted to continue the conversation. She's got a lot to think about and she doesn't need another man telling her what to do. I already felt I'd overstepped when I suggested she invite chaos in. I don't have a fucking clue about her work and the challenges she faces in it, so I need to start keeping my thoughts to myself when it comes to her career.

"So," she says settling back against the booth in the corner of the bar where we're sitting. "How long have you known Dan? And how long has he owned this bar? And" —she grins—"how are you friends with someone who loves bluegrass as much as Dan obviously does when you hate country music?" She's referencing the fact the music selection in the bar tonight has been nothing but bluegrass.

I chuckle. "I don't hate country."

She arches a brow. "That doesn't seem like a statement filled with truth."

Before I can reply to that, Dan slides into the booth next to Maddie, places a glass of bourbon on the table in front of him, and says, "What's that about truth?"

The smile Maddie gives him is lit like a Christmas tree. She gives him all of her attention, turning her body to face him. "Your boy here is telling lies about loving country music. I'm just calling him out on it."

Dan eyes me with amusement before looking back at Maddie. "I like you already, and I don't usually like any woman Ethan dates."

Maddie reaches for the bourbon I selected for her. She asked me to choose because the menu had too many options for her to wade through. "Mr. McHottie and I aren't dating,"

Dan laughs. "Mr. McHottie?"

She sips some bourbon. "That's what my assistant calls him." Then, giving me a flirty look, she adds, "It fits."

Fuck.

I feel every bit of that look she's throwing my way deep in my gut.

Dan eyes me over the rim of his glass as he sips his drink. I know him almost as well as I know my brothers, so I know what he's saying without uttering a word. *Get your act together, dickhead, and fix the non-dating situation.*

I ignore that and answer Madeline's earlier questions. "I've known Dan since we were kids. He grew up in New York."

"You went to school together?"

Dan nods. "Yeah. I moved here two years ago after inheriting this bar from my father."

"And," I say, "he's always loved bluegrass. Fuck knows why."

Maddie grins triumphantly, pointing at me. "I knew it! You do hate country."

"No, I'm not a fan of bluegrass, but your kind of country is okay."

That slows her down and she stares at me for a long moment. "You know my music?"

"Not before I met you, but I've listened to some since then."

"Wait," Dan interrupts. "You're a singer?"

"Yes."

"You sing country?"

Maddie's smile is huge, as is the way she relaxes right

in front of me. Over the last few days, I've picked up that she's not comfortable with her fame and I think she loves the fact Dan hasn't recognized her. "You're my new favorite person, Dan. And yes, country is my first love."

He's fully engrossed in this conversation now. Dan's the biggest music nerd I know. "Would I know your music?"

I laugh. "You'll know it." He likely hasn't recognized her because he's only about the music not the star.

"Why are you two being so fucking evasive?" he asks.

"We're not trying to be," Maddie says with a hint of disappointment. "I was just enjoying the anonymity for a bit."

I tap my phone, pull up my music app and Maddie's profile before sliding the phone to Dan.

After looking at it, Dan peers at Maddie and says, "Fuck me. I love your music. I'm sorry I didn't know who you are but I don't know what most singers look like." Then, he shifts his gaze between us before resting it on me. "How the fuck did I not know that you know her?"

Maddie answers before I can. "We met three days ago. He let me use him for a kiss that saved me from having to get married."

"Kiss*es*," I correct as my mind goes straight to those kisses.

Maddie's eyes meet mine, holding as much heat as I feel after thinking about her body underneath mine and my lips on hers. "Kisses," she agrees with the kind of sexy look any man would kill for. It's pretty clear she's remembering our meeting in the same way I am, but then that's no surprise. Not after the conversation we had this morning while some asshole sounded his horn at us.

Dan breaks the moment between us when he says, "And after that, you guys just decided to become friends and drive to Louisville to see me?"

Maddie laughs. "Yes, that's exactly what happened."

"Jesus, Ethan, this might be your most outrageous relationship yet."

"Fun, though, right?" Maddie says.

He looks at her. "Fun is Ethan's middle fucking name. I hope you're buckled in tight because this guy will lead you astray in a million different ways if you let him." He narrows his eyes at her. "How long are you planning on staying friends with him?"

Maddie turns her attention back to me, her eyes demanding mine without even needing to. There's no one else on my radar. "I think forever."

The way her "forever" lands with me is unlike any response I've ever felt. I would have hated to hear anything else. And fuck me, we're in dangerous territory now. I want something that I can't have right now. Not when Madeline's in the thick of a breakup.

"Right." Dan stands, grabbing our empty glasses. "While you two eye-fuck each other, I'm getting another round of drinks that Ethan's paying for. And when I come back, we're gonna talk music. I have many questions."

"No more drinks for us," I say, ignoring the eye-fucking comment that was right on the money. "We've got a long day of driving tomorrow." And I promised Leigh I'd keep Maddie out of trouble tonight.

"Well, I'm not driving tomorrow, so I'm having more," Dan says. "And you're paying my tab. You still owe me for our last drinking session that I funded."

I study Maddie while she watches Dan walk away.

That brunette wig she's wearing is fucking awful but even it can't hide her beauty. I could stare all night long.

"We could have had one more drink," she says when she finally turns back to me.

"You're at your limit, Miller."

She rolls her eyes. "I think you really enjoy bossing me around."

"Wait till you see what me bossing you around really looks like."

Her eyes flare with more heat and I remind myself to avoid any kind of comment that could be taken in a sexual way. I may want something more with her, but it can't happen while she's all fucked up over her ex. If anything were to ever happen between us, it'd have to be after she's worked her way through that and really knows what she wants. I'm not in the market for a relationship that's doomed from the start because my partner is unclear in her feelings and intentions.

Maddie doesn't make this easy for me, though, when she says, "Maybe you should try it and show me what I'm missing out on."

Fuck.

I'm hard now, thinking about the ways I'd like to boss her around. Mercifully, her assistant takes this moment to text her.

"Sorry," she apologizes as she checks the message.

She goes back and forth with Leigh for a couple of minutes, and I search her face for a hint as to her frame of mind. If I'd had my personal shit vomited all over social media like she has during the last three days, I wouldn't be as calm as she appears. It's confusing as hell to me, but that could be because my way of coping when someone hurts or angers me is to voice my feelings. And since the women I've dated have all been fiery and quick to temper, all I've known are showdowns. Maddie was angry earlier, but it was a quiet fury that she mostly kept on the inside, and she hasn't shown any sign of it during dinner.

"What?" she says after she finishes with Leigh and places her phone down. "You're looking at me like you're trying to figure me out."

"I'm trying to figure out if you're okay."

"I did promise to let you worry about me, didn't I?"

"You did."

She releases a long breath. "I'm okay."

"I don't understand that."

Her brows furrow. "What don't you understand?"

I try like hell to keep my mouth shut, to let her figure this out in her own way, but I've never been good at keeping my thoughts to myself. "How can you be okay after everything that's happened today?" I lean forward. "I don't understand how you can be so calm about it."

"You think I should be lashing out? Calling Tucker and unleashing my anger on him? Not enjoying myself with you?"

"Yeah, something like that. After you told me what happened and I had to go take that call, I expected to walk back into a trashed hotel room or to screaming and yelling. I've never met anyone who locks their anger up so tight."

"I'm pissed off, Ethan. Don't doubt that. In fact, I've never been so pissed off. I feel it *violently* in here." She jabs her finger at her chest with enough force that I finally see a speck of her anger. "I feel like I could explode. And like I can't breathe when I think about it. But, as much as I wish I could yell and scream to get it all out, I've never really let my feelings out in that way."

"You wanna try?"

She stares at me like this idea terrifies her. "No.... Maybe. I don't know."

I jerk my chin at her while standing. Reaching for her hand, I say, "Come on, let's go and do some screaming."

She doesn't take my hand. "You're joking, right?"

"Nope. Serious as fuck."

"Ethan." Her tone is all kinds of *what the fuck*. "This is a crazy idea."

I take charge of the situation and grab her hand so I can pull her up. "Have you forgotten we're trying to break some rules on this trip? This is a great fucking idea."

She allows me to lead her out of the bar. I let Dan know we're leaving, and he makes it clear I still owe him for drinks and that I also owe him a longer catch-up soon. A minute later, we're heading outside in search of somewhere I can encourage Maddie to let her anger out into the world.

Maddie's hand grips mine like she's relying on me to get her through this. Like she's as far out of her depth as she could be. I feel her apprehension in that grip, which makes me even more determined to help her.

There's a crowd outside Dan's bar, lining up for entry. It doesn't surprise me. His establishment is popular with its eclectic vibe and unpretentious charm. The crowd is rowdy tonight, thanks to a large group who appear to be here to celebrate something. Some of the guys in that group spill across the sidewalk, blocking our path, and one of them slams into Madeline after his friend pushes him.

"Shit, sorry," he slurs as he tries to get his bearings, grabbing her arms in the process. I hear how drunk he is, but that's also obvious from the way he's stumbling around.

My instincts kick in and within seconds, I've got my arm around Madeline's waist to steady her and to pull her in close, away from these guys.

"It's okay," she says to the guy while turning into me, letting me protect her.

"Oh my god," one of the girls in the line screams, her eyes going wide as she points at Maddie. "That's Madeline Montana!"

More screams of excitement erupt, and phones are pulled out, and before I know what's happening, the crowd is all over us. It's fucking chaos and Madeline appears bewildered.

"Get the fuck back," I growl to everyone while holding Maddie tightly against me.

One of the assholes shoves his phone in Madeline's face and I see fucking red. Moving Maddie behind me, I grab his phone from his hands. Then, I grasp his shirt and yank him to me, ignoring his outcry over the removal of his phone. "You need to get the fuck out of my face, and when you do that, you need to take all your asshole friends with you. And if I find any of these videos online, I will make it so whoever posted them really fucking regrets that decision."

He sneers. "Sure, you will. Fucking dickhead."

I clench his shirt harder, bringing his face right to mine and snarling, "Try me. You wanna violate Madeline's privacy by sharing an unauthorized video of her, you better believe I'll be sending my lawyer after you. And trust me, I have enough cash to waste on a million lawsuits if it comes to that. I also have people who know how to dig into a person's life and find the shit they'd rather stay secret. So yeah, fucking try me, asshole."

I shove him away as Dan's head of security joins us, bringing three other men from his team with him. He shoots me a look that says, "Fuck me, Ethan," before moving the group along. Some of the guys are hard to force away from me. It seems they're ready for a fight, but Jason isn't head of security for nothing.

Once he's got them all inside, he looks at me with a shake of his head. "I thought you were done causing me grief."

"It turns out I wasn't," I grunt, the words ripped from my chest. I pull Madeline in close again, a hard urgency to protect her driving me. My body is wired, my jaw is tight, and I have to force myself to loosen my grip a little so that I'm not crushing her.

"Do me a favor and get out of here. I'm not in the mood for trouble tonight."

I do him that favor. For Madeline. Keeping my arm around her, I steer her away from the bar toward the river a few blocks away.

"Thank you," Maddie says as I let her go once we're away from the bar.

I force a breath, trying to loosen the knot of tension in my chest. "I'm not sure I helped you back there." Fuck knows how videos of us surfacing on social media will pan out for her. Videos of me threatening people.

She shakes her head. "We don't deal in doubt, Black.

And at this point, I don't think it matters what else is posted about me online. People are gonna think what they want, right?"

Fuck me. She's made a 180 since we talked earlier and certainty looks fucking good on her.

"I take it you and the security guy go back," she continues.

"A few years, yeah."

"And you and trouble are besties?" Her eyes twinkle with fun.

"Let's just say that some of those grays you saw in his hair were caused by me."

"How bad are we talking here?"

"You wanna know if I'm a bad boy, Miller?"

"Oh, I already know you are. I just need to know what to expect going forward."

"My bad boy days are behind me. You don't need to worry."

"I don't know if I believe that. Not from what I just saw."

"That wasn't me being a bad boy. That was me making sure those assholes wouldn't hurt you. And if something like that happens again, I won't hesitate to protect you again. That's what you can expect going forward."

She turns silent while looking up at me with eyes that hold a universe of thoughts and feelings. But while she doesn't respond to what I've just said, the way she moves closer to me while we walk tells me everything. She's grateful.

From the little I know about her, I'm not sure Maddie has ever had someone in her corner like I am now, and that pisses me the hell off. This woman deserves so much more than she's ever been given.

"Okay," I say as the river comes into view. "Are you ready to give your lungs a workout?"

She glances around, taking in the people we can see. "I don't know, Ethan. Screaming in a public area doesn't seem like the best idea."

"There's hardly anyone around." There are only five people in sight. "Besides, it's dark and I know a place tucked away from view. And if anyone comes running to see why you're screaming, I'll deal with them."

She scans the area again before taking a deep breath. "Okay, but let the record show, I think it's a bad idea."

I take her hand. "The record knows exactly where you stand on this and it thinks you might enjoy this, even if just a little bit."

When we make it to the sheltered area that's hidden from everyone, I let her hand go and turn her to face the river while I move next to her. Then, I start a conversation that I hope will help her access her anger. "How did you find out Tucker was cheating on you?"

She stands perfectly still, not answering my question. It's dark, so I can't see every line of her face to get a read on her, but her stillness and the way her breathing turns shallow give me the information I'm after. Finally, she looks at me and I see her torment. She still doesn't answer my question, though.

"Well?" I prod.

She releases a breath and turns back to the river. "Things had been off between us for a while and then he came home the night before our wedding smelling of another woman's perfume, so after he passed out, I checked his phone. It wasn't hard to guess his password. I found messages that went back years, from women he'd had one-night stands with and women he'd carried on affairs with." Her chest rises and falls as she closes her eyes briefly. When she speaks again, pain bleeds into her words. "His actions were so blatant that night. Coming home smelling of her . . . he didn't even care if I knew." She finds my gaze again, her face a mess of hurt. "And that's what hurt. He didn't care about me. He never cared about me."

The fucking asshole.

"And?"

Her pain twists across her face. "And what?"

"How did you feel that night? Did you really think you could go through with your wedding the next day?"

"We've talked about this, Ethan. I don't really want to go over it again."

I move into her space, in front of her. "I know. I know you just want to force this into that box you have inside you for the hurtful things in your life, but that's not going to help you move on. You need to get this shit out of your body. Unless, of course, you just want to sit in your mess and pretend it never happened."

Her eyes widen, and I don't blame her. My tone was intentionally sharp. I want to help her get to her anger and if I have to make her angry at me first to do that, so be it.

"Do I look like I'm happily sitting in my mess?" she demands, and I sense the first stirrings of what I'm looking for.

"No, but what are you doing about it? Because from

where I'm sitting, it looks like you're scrambling to find all the ways to go on without letting it out of that box."

Now, her eyes are blazing with outrage. "And to think that I thought you didn't have any asshole in you."

"Everyone has some asshole in them, Maddie." I dip my face down to get even more in hers. "Tell me how it made you feel to know Tucker was out there fucking other women, for *years*, while he forced you to perform perfectly for the world, wearing what he told you to wear, writing what he told you to write, saying what he told you to say, and—"

"I hated him!" She smacks her hands to my chest, pushing me away. "I hated that he made me feel like a fool! I despised him and Darren for making me give myself up. But mostly, I hated myself for being so fucking naïve and stupid."

I want to tell her she's not stupid, but I don't think my opinion will count for much. Not when she's got years of wiring to untangle so she can believe it herself.

"Say it louder, Miller. Scream that shit out."

Her eyes, wild now, search mine madly. "I want him to hurt as much I am."

I make a hand movement to indicate I want her to turn this shit up. "Louder."

"I want Darren to hurt too." *Still too fucking quiet.*

I move back into her space and yell in her face, "Louder!" I jab her chest. "Here! Scream it from here!"

She snaps and it's so fucking beautiful to watch someone let it all out when you know they never have. She throws her head back, opens her mouth, and screams so fucking loudly that I'm sure I'll have to fend people off who will think she needs rescuing.

When she stops and brings her gaze back to mine, she's breathless and her eyes shine with freedom and abandon. Then, she lifts her face to the sky and screams again. This time, she extends her arms out and shakes them while her entire body vibrates with the release, her feet pounding the ground.

"Fuck!" she exclaims after finishing, still shaking out her hands and bouncing on the spot. "Maybe you're not really an asshole. That felt pretty good."

I chuckle. "I'll take the asshole tag. Plenty of people would agree with you."

Still breathless, she says, "I don't remember ever saying I hate someone."

"You feel bad about saying it?"

She thinks about that for a moment and just when I wonder if she'll say yes, she shakes her head. "No. I do hate them and I'm okay with feeling that." Lifting her face to the sky, she exhales a loud breath and flings her arms out, releasing more of the wild energy that I think has been trapped for a long time. "I kinda hate having to tell someone they were right." She turns her face to mine and smiles. "But you were right. Screaming was what I needed."

I have no idea what I did to earn this woman stumbling into my life and bringing a refreshing amount of realness with her. She's a breath of fresh air for me.

"You wanna scream some more or can we get out of here before the cops show up ready to arrest me?"

Her smile turns to a grin. "*Now* you're worried about the police? What happened to being a rule breaker, Black?"

"I'm not worried about myself. I'm thinking of you. I

don't wanna give social media something else to slam you with tomorrow."

Her grin fades, and her eyes—fixed on mine—hold a heat that makes my gut tighten. There's gratitude there, maybe, but there's also a simmering intensity that feels a hell of a lot like desire. "I'm done screaming." She steps closer to me, bringing with her that floral scent I like far too much, and says softly, "Thank you."

She may have uttered only two words with absolutely no context, but I don't need that or a whole speech of what she's really saying. I know what she's thanking me for.

I nod. "You got it. Anytime." My voice is rougher than I intended because that's what she's doing to me. Stealing my ability to get a handle on myself.

I lift my chin at her. "Come on, let's get you back to the hotel." *And out of this moment*, because if she continues looking at me the way she is, fuck knows what I'll do with it.

16

MADELINE

ETHAN HAS BEEN AVOIDING me since we arrived back at our hotel room. First, he said he had to go down to his car to get something. When he returned, with nothing in his hands, he said he had to step out to make a call. Which let's be real; it's late, so I don't believe that was true. Five minutes after coming back from that, he was hungry and went in search of something to eat.

I mean, it's after midnight. We ate just a few hours ago. No one's hungry, Black.

I think he's avoiding whatever it is that's happening between us. Because something *is* happening.

I'm confused by his actions. He's been flirty with me over the last couple days. I've been flirty with him tonight. We have a hotel room together. What's a little sex between consenting adults? Why is he doing everything in his power not to go there with me?

It's while he's out trying to find food (that I don't think he really wants) when I ask myself that last question and my thoughts come to a thudding stop. *Oh god*, maybe I've misinterpreted his actions. Maybe he wasn't flirting, but rather just being his usual fun self. Maybe this is all in my mind.

Despite the fact he said he couldn't get our kiss out of his mind, and despite the fact he sometimes looks at me with heat, maybe I'm not the kind of woman he'd ever be interested in. He did rescue me after I ran away from my own wedding, a hot mess, after all. And he's spent most of the time since then propping me up, seeing all the ways I'm not put together. He told me about some of the dysfunctional relationships he's had. Maybe these days, he's looking for women who have their shit together.

Feeling like a fool, I gather my pajamas and lock myself away in the bathroom. I'll take a shower and do my best to forget what I thought could happen tonight. It's probably for the best, anyway. I've got enough to deal with at the moment. I don't need to add another man into the mix.

I hear Ethan out in the room while I'm putting my pajama shorts on after my shower, and suddenly, I'm feeling awkward and weird about going back out there. It's like my teen years all over again when I had no clue about guys and put way too much thought into every-thing I said and did when I was around them.

Ugh.

I'm being ridiculous.

I'm a grown woman. Not a teenager. This doesn't have to be weird. Ethan can't read my thoughts. He doesn't know I've been imagining his naked ass and wondering what it would feel like to touch him. To have him touch me.

I yank the bathroom door open a little more enthusiastically than I mean to, and in doing so gain all of Ethan's attention. And hot damn, he's shirtless.

Shit.

Don't look at his chest, Maddie.

Or his abs.

Don't do it.

Don't—

"Why are you avoiding me?" The words fly out of my mouth before I can stop them and shit, shit, shit. I hold my hand up. "No, just ignore that." I really don't want to get into a conversation about why he's not interested in me.

I remove my eyes from him and hurry out of the bathroom to my suitcase, intent on putting my dirty clothes there before crawling into bed and hiding under the covers so I can forget this moment ever happened.

"I'm avoiding you because if I don't, I'll be putting my hands on you and asking for something I shouldn't be."

Just the thought of Ethan's hands on me causes need to pool low in my stomach, let alone the gravel in his voice.

I twist to face him, sucking in a breath at the raw desire in his eyes. "Why shouldn't you be asking for it?"

He appears torn over this. "I'd be taking advantage of a hell of a lot, Maddie."

"Of what?"

"Fuck, of everything. You're not sharing a hotel room with me because you want to have sex. I'm trying to remember that."

I close the distance between us, loving the way *he* sucks in a breath now. "You think I wanted to share this room with you tonight because I didn't want to be alone?"

He looks down at me and I think it's taking everything in him to get through this conversation. "You're telling me that's not the reason?"

"It's some of the reason." I glance at his chest, all hard planes and shadowed hollows that I'm desperate to explore. "But it's not the full reason."

"Fuck," he curses, his voice raw. "Don't look at me like that."

I was dumb to think he wasn't flirting, wasn't interested.

Ethan wants this as much as I do.

I ignore what he says and keep looking at him like that. "You wouldn't be taking advantage of anything if you fucked me tonight."

The look in his eyes says he's *this close* to giving into what he wants. "You always have a filthy mouth when it comes to sex?"

I move into him and place my hand on his chest. Touching him sends lust racing through every vein in my body and I have to stop myself from just taking what *I* want. "No, but I might embrace it going forward." I slowly trace the contours of his chest and enjoy the way his muscles tighten beneath my fingers. "I haven't had an orgasm in a long time, and I want you to be the one to change that."

He grasps my hand, stopping me. "I'm concerned you'll regret this in the morning." With every gruff word he utters, I want him even more.

"Have you ever regretted sex?"

"Yes."

I'm not expecting that answer, and it slows my thoughts down.

"You've had a hell of a day, Maddie. Maybe you should sleep on this."

"You think I want sex to forget my day?" He's way off base. "I'm so into you, Ethan, and I want to have sex with you. And I really want you to stop being a gentleman and just give me what we both want already."

"Fuck," he growls, and before I know it, he's curved his hand around the nape of my neck and has his mouth on mine, and *holy fuck*, I might just die and go to heaven tonight.

His kiss is hungry, desperate, possessive. He holds me in place, his grip on my neck firm, his other arm wrapping around my waist and pulling me against him as if to say there's no escape now.

I reach for his neck, clawing his skin as we collide, moaning when his tongue slides over mine.

Ethan groans in response and I feel that sound *everywhere*. He deepens our kiss while moving his hand down from my waist to my ass and pressing me into his erection. Then, dragging his mouth from mine, he rasps, "Is this really what you want? Because if we keep going, I'm gonna find it really fucking hard to stop."

I'm already drunk on his kiss and his touch. The way he's looking at me like he can't get enough of me only intensifies everything. "Don't you dare stop now, Black."

He hesitates for one more moment before finally—*finally*—reaching down and taking hold of my ass to lift me into his arms so he can carry me to his bed.

Dropping me on it, he runs his eyes down my body, drinking in every inch of me, and I decide there's nothing better in this world than having Ethan Black look at me like he is now. I feel his gaze like it's actually caressing me.

He puts one knee to the bed, then the other, and brings his attention to my shorts while moving in between my legs. "These are hell on a man, Miller." His eyes find mine. "In case you weren't aware."

I smile, pulling my bottom lip between my teeth. "Good to know."

He places his hands on either side of my body on the bed and bends his face. Dropping a kiss to my shorts, right above my clit, he says, "I think it's only fair if I return the favor."

I'm barely breathing while I watch him hook his fingers under the fabric of my shorts and slide them down. I don't know what he means about returning the favor, but I don't care what he does so long as he doesn't stop touching me.

He gives me a sexy smile as he removes my shorts. "No granny undies tonight?"

I grin. He even makes sex fun. "I would have left them on for you if I'd known you *were* interested in me."

He stops what he's doing, a fleeting look of confusion passing over his face. Then, he moves over me and brings his face closer to mine. "How the hell did you do the math on that and come up with me not being interested? I told you I couldn't get our kiss out of my mind. That's not something a guy says when he's disinterested."

I put my hands to his chest, my heart practically galloping now he's so close and saying things I like. "I don't know. I overthink everything and come to bad conclusions."

"Well, since you told me you're into me, you should know I'm just as into you."

His eyes spend the longest moment searching mine and it might be one of the most intimate moments of my life. It's like he's searching my soul, connecting with me in a way no man has ever taken the time to. And then when he dips his mouth to mine and kisses me *oh so slowly*, deepening it with every swipe of our tongues, it feels like he's joining us, soul to soul. Even if just for the night, he's giving himself to me.

I thread my fingers into his hair and wrap one of my legs around his body while we lose ourselves in the pleasure. Ethan settles his weight over me, slides his hands along my jaw and into my hair, and kisses me like it's the only thing he's ever wanted to do.

We spend so long kissing. Just kissing. It's unlike any sex I've ever had. It's actual making out and I am here for it.

When Ethan finally lets my mouth go and lifts his face, he says, "Fuck, I could do that with you for hours."

He unleashes a million butterflies in my stomach with that declaration.

The corners of my mouth curve into a smile and I glide my fingers from his hair down to his shoulders. "Me too."

He traces his gaze over my face, taking his time, and I get the impression Ethan isn't a man who gets in, takes what he wants, and gets out fast. I think I've found a man who dedicates himself to pleasure.

He kisses my jaw. "So, we're done with your doubt now?"

I grasp his face and pull his mouth back to mine and

we go back to making out. This time, my hands are all over Ethan's chest and his abs. *His muscles*. I've never touched muscles like his.

I end our kiss, breathless and needy. "The only doubt I have is about why your hands aren't on me?"

His mouth kicks up, sexy. His eyes heat some more. "Why are we in such a rush, Miller?"

"Because I'm way past ready for my first orgasm."

He arches a brow and he even makes that look hot. "Your first? You're making some pretty big assumptions there. I might not have more than one in me."

I roll my eyes. "Seriously, I'm pretty sure you're not the kind of guy who doesn't hand out orgasms like they're going out of fashion."

More of that sexy grin. And then another kiss that curls my toes and steals my breath. "How many are we talking here?"

I grind myself against his hard length, my impatience for him reaching new heights. "Is this a ploy to make me so desperate for your dick that I'll beg you for it?"

The look in his eyes says this is exactly that, but he doesn't answer me. Instead, he kisses his way down my neck to my throat, then down to my chest. He pushes my silk cami up so it bunches at my throat and starts kissing one of my breasts, and is almost to my nipple when he glances up at me. "Is this hell yet?"

I recall what he said earlier and put it all together. "This is you returning the favor?"

He sucks my nipple into his mouth. But only for enough of a moment that the pleasure hits my veins and then gets interrupted. "It's only fair," he murmurs, and I hear the distraction in his voice. I hear just how much it's taking for him to slow this down.

I bury my fingers in his hair and tighten my leg around him. "You are hell on a woman, Black," I breathe. "In case you weren't aware."

"Fuck," he rasps before teasing my nipple with a lick and then a hint of a bite. And then, *then,* he finally stops teasing and gives me what I want.

He spends an exorbitant amount of time with my body. He uses his hands, mouth, tongue, teeth. It turns out that when Ethan Black dedicates himself to something, he goes all in. Nothing can sway him from what he's doing, not even me.

He edges me closer and closer to my first orgasm, all without touching me where I really want him to, and when I try to shift his attention to my pussy, he takes hold of my wrists and pins them to the bed, not stopping what he's doing with his mouth for even a second.

"Ethan," I whimper. "I need your mouth on my pussy."

His grip on my wrists tightens as he looks up at me. "Soon."

When he goes back to my breasts, I take matters into my own hands. I've never been this bold during sex, but Ethan makes me feel more confident than I've ever felt.

I force my hands free and push his chest, and then we're sitting up and I'm in his lap with my arms around his neck. The approval in his eyes spurs me on. "Soon is too far away."

He presses a kiss to my neck before looking at me with a mixture of amusement and lust. "I wouldn't have picked you as needy."

"And I wouldn't have picked you as being so slow, grandpa."

He chuckles but the sound dies quickly on his lips as heat fills his eyes again. "I want to take my time with you, Maddie."

And just like that, I melt.

I squeeze myself against him, even needier now, but for something else. "Say that again."

Everything about this moment shifts as Ethan wraps his arms around me, tightly, possessively, and looks at me like I'm the only woman in the world. "I want to take my time with you." His lips brush over mine, grazing me so lightly that I should hardly be affected, but I think this man could affect me from the other side of the world without so much as a touch. "I want to taste every inch of you." The brush of his lips turns into a whisper of a kiss. "I want my hands all over you." His kiss deepens. His hands come to my face to hold it. "I want to get to know every hollow of you." He stares into my eyes. "I can't speed this up, Miller, because I would be missing out on so much if I did that."

Our mouths collide, thanks to me. I no longer want him to take things faster, but I desperately need his mouth on mine, and I need that *now*. I kiss him like a starved woman, and he gives all of that back to me, just as starved.

When we come up for air, he keeps me close, not letting me move an inch. "You're going to lie down now and you're going to let me take my time."

My arms stay tightly around him too. "Is this you being bossy?"

"This is nowhere near me being bossy."

My core betrays me, loving what he just said even though I've sworn off bossy men.

I stay in his arms for a moment longer and then I unwrap myself from him and do as I've been told. Ethan hangs on my every move, his gaze intense, and once I'm lying down, he says, "Take your top off."

Holy god.

One order from him and I can't comply fast enough.

A second later, I have his eyes on my breasts, and I've never enjoyed a man's eyes on me as much.

"You are so fucking beautiful," he says, moving over me, saying words I believe simply because he said them.

He kisses me again and I let him take all the time he wants. And I love every second of it.

Ethan's a man who likes to explore. A man who likes to appreciate. His kisses show me how much he enjoys time with me. His erotic touch says he's turned on by every second he has with my body. And his whispered words let me know he likes what he's discovering.

When he finally gets to my panties, he peels them off, and with his eyes on mine, he circles my clit with his tongue. The pleasure I feel is indescribable. Unlike any pleasure I've experienced.

It's in my veins, my core, my mind. It's in my *soul*.

My back arches up off the bed as he uses his tongue over and over before sucking my clit into his mouth.

"Oh god!" I cry out and when he grasps my ass to lift me higher against his mouth, I curve a leg around his neck.

His stubble grazes my skin as he eats me, his hands hold me firmly, and his tongue, *oh his tongue*, does filthy, beautiful things to me. And I'm undone.

Ethan lets me go so he can finger fuck me while his tongue goes back to my clit. Every touch, every stroke sends me further into this exquisite oblivion. I come with my eyes closed and my hands tightly gripping the sheet. My orgasm rushes through me, the sensations making it so I forget everything but how good it feels.

All I know is this is bliss.

Pure, amazing, delicious bliss.

I'm boneless by the time Ethan kisses the inside of my thigh and says, "Orgasms look good on you, Miller."

I crack one eye open. "Do I have to talk right now?"

"No." He trails more kisses along my thigh. "Are we anticipating another orgasm still or are we thinking you're about to pass out?"

A smile pushes its way across my face. This man.

I open both eyes and take him in. His dark hair, perfectly messed up from my fingers. His face, his strong jaw, so fucking beautiful. His blazing masculinity that also holds just enough softness that says he'll do whatever I want while ignoring how turned on he is right now.

I sit up and crawl into his lap, looping my arms around his neck, and kiss him. It's a deep kiss that I don't rush, exactly how he prefers, and when I'm finished, I say, "We're chasing another orgasm, Black. Don't think you're getting out of it."

I reach a hand down between us, and with my eyes still on his, I slip into his sweatpants and find his cock, eliciting a groan from him as I wrap my hand around him and stroke.

He's got one arm around me and brings the other one up to caress my breast, tweaking my nipple. His eyes are so hooded, his breathing hot and fast as we watch each other while I pump him.

There's something so wanton about this. Hot in an indecent way. Maybe it's because I don't really know Ethan. Or it could be that most of the sex I've had hasn't been like this. I'm used to missionary and quick, mostly unsatisfactory encounters. I've never straddled a man like this and jerked him off while we watched each other. The record needs to show that I want a whole lot more sex like this.

"Fuck, that feels good," he groans, breaking eye contact to kiss my throat and bite my neck. His breathing grows heavier as he kisses his way back up to my mouth. "We need a condom." When I moan at the roughness in his voice, the need I hear, he growls, "You make that noise again and I'm gonna come before I get inside you."

"I don't have a condom. Do you?"

"Maybe."

I like his answer. A lot. I like that he's not the kind of guy who's always prepared.

I stop stroking him. "You should go find out."

His lips demand another quick kiss before he moves off the bed in search of his wallet. I'm so wildly turned on and ready to be fucked that I think I'd offer everything I own to the gods to be assured of him finding a condom.

It turns out the gods are on my side tonight. Ethan finds a condom.

He strips out of his clothes and rolls it on and then we're a tangled mess of limbs and lips and hands, and he's lifting one of my legs over his shoulder before pushing his dick inside me.

I grip his biceps as he sinks into me. "Oh god," I pant, finding it hard to breathe at the way he fills me.

His eyes are glued to mine as he pulls out and thrusts in again. "Fuck, Maddie," he says, his voice strained, his breathing growing ragged.

I rock with him, and we find our rhythm. It's neither fast nor slow but it's intense and *fuck me,* Ethan goes deep and discovers the right angle I need.

My hands move to his shoulders when his thrusts become faster and harder. And as my orgasm edges closer, I close my eyes and let the pleasure consume me.

I completely lose myself with my fingers digging into his skin; the world shrinking down to the feel of him, the scent of him, the taste of him, until there's nothing but him.

Ethan grips my leg harder and pushes it tighter against me as he drives his dick into me after I orgasm. Then, with one last thrust, he comes.

"*Fuck*," he rasps afterward, collapsing onto the bed next to me. His chest heaves as he tries to catch his breath, the rapid rise and fall gradually slowing.

I smile and turn my face to him, still a little breathless myself. "That covers it."

He looks at me, his eyes still dark with the remnants of desire. A lazy, satisfied smile tugs at the corners of his mouth. "That was fucking good," he murmurs, his voice low and husky as he reaches out to trail his fingers along my arm.

My smile grows and I find the energy to roll toward him. Snaking my arm across his chest, I tease, "Good is such an underwhelming word to describe something, don't you think?"

Amusement covers his face. "If you're looking for something more flowery, I'm not your guy." His hand curls around my forearm over his chest. "I'm a simple man, Miller, but you should know that in my mind, there's not much better than 'fucking good.'"

I press myself into him some more, enjoying the feel of his skin against mine. "Okay, I agree then, that *was* fucking good."

With a smile, he bends his mouth to mine and steals a kiss before leaving the bed to dispose of the condom. When he returns, my attention is drawn to one of the three tattoos I vaguely noticed while we had sex. This one is on his left bicep and is an intricate pattern of black lines that are spiraled and looped to resemble butterfly wings.

"What's the story behind this?" I ask, lightly brushing my finger over the tattoo as he settles himself on the bed again, pulling me in close. I have no doubt it means something to Ethan. I can't imagine he'd permanently ink himself with something that's meaningless to him.

He glances down. "It's the Lorenz attractor, a symbol of chaos theory."

Invite the chaos in.

"What is chaos theory?"

"It's the science of surprises and teaches us to expect the unexpected. It deals with the nonlinear and unpredictable like weather, our brain states, the stock market, and so on. Have you heard of the butterfly effect?"

"I've heard of it, but I don't know anything about it."

"It's the concept that says even the smallest action can lead to unexpected and profound changes. So, for instance, a single flap of a butterfly's wings can create a storm halfway across the world. It may take a long time, but the connection is real."

"So, you're not just a pretty face. You're a sexy science nerd too." I could listen to him recite facts for hours.

He gives me a smoldering look as he reaches down to bring my leg over his body. "I'll take sexy."

"What about the nerd bit?"

He rests his hand on my thigh. "Yeah, that too. I read a lot of shit."

"What do your other tattoos mean?"

He raises his arm that's around my shoulder and shows me his inner forearm where four simple symbols are inked in a line. "This represents the idea of letting chaos in if you want change."

"And the one on your chest?"

"That one wasn't my best decision in life."

Color me intrigued. I push up onto my side and look down at him, noting the grimace on his face. "Okay, so now you definitely have to tell me about it."

Still looking slightly pained, he says, "I was barely nineteen when I got that one. I was trying to impress a girl, which in hindsight was a waste of my effort because she was the one who cheated on me."

"What does it mean?" It's a beautiful tattoo but he's giving me the impression he's not a fan of it.

"It's the Sanskrit symbol for breathe."

"You say that like you don't like it."

"It's not something I would choose to get, but I was young and dumb. Lyra wanted matching tattoos and I couldn't have jumped any higher or faster to do what she wanted."

I study the tattoo again. "I think it's lovely."

"It's a reminder for me now."

"To breathe?" I try not to smirk.

"Smart-ass." He grins. "No, it reminds me not to jump so fucking fast all the time."

I lightly run my finger along his jaw. "I don't know, Ethan, you do seem to like inviting chaos in. If you weren't as spontaneous as you are, I wonder if you'd be bored in life. I, for one, am glad you are because otherwise, I would have missed out on our conversations, which are helping me make changes in my life." I push up to sit cross-legged on the bed and add softly, "Before we left for dinner tonight, I posted that photo you took of me, along with a post about my relationship and abortion."

I've got all his attention now. "How are you feeling about that?"

"It's a little scary, but I went with my gut and stopped letting fear make the rules. I'm not sitting in my mess anymore, and that feels good."

"Fuck, Maddie," he curses with a look of regret, sitting up with me. "I was just trying to force your anger out when I said that to you. I—"

I place my finger to his lips, silencing him. "No, you were right. I was scared to deal with all of this, but if I just keep piling more lies and half-truths on top of what's already out there, nothing changes. And I desperately want things to change."

His studies me silently and I see his mind working. "That's a brave fucking thing to do."

"It might also have been a dumb thing to do, but I can't take it back now." I smile, remembering what he said to me earlier. "My head can play catch up and figure it all out later, though, right?"

"It absolutely can," he says before reaching his arm around my waist and pulling me onto his lap. "You're capable of anything, Miller. Don't ever forget that."

My breath hitches at the way Ethan's looking at me, like he's captivated by me. And at what he says. No one has ever said anything like that to me.

He slides his hand along my jaw and into my hair. "You believe that, right?"

"Yes, but I've never felt like anyone else believed it."

He scowls at my admission. "You're spending time with the wrong people then."

"Yeah, I have been." I bring my arms up and loop them around his neck. "But now I'm spending time with the right person and I'm hoping he might be up for another orgasm."

He gives me a knowing look. "We're not sleeping tonight, are we?"

I laugh, loving how easily he can go from fun, to sexy, to serious, and back again. "I don't think so, Black."

With that, he pulls my mouth to his and gives me what I'm after.

17

ETHAN

I WAKE with blonde hair strewn across my face. And the sexiest woman I've ever known claiming almost every inch of the bed for herself. It's beyond me how someone so tiny manages to spread herself across a bed like Maddie has.

She stirs when I reach for my phone on the nightstand, uttering words that are completely indecipherable and repositioning herself so her body is now strewn across me.

I stare at her with a shake of my head. If she wasn't so damn cute, I'd push her off, but the truth of the matter is I fucking like her there.

My phone tells me it's just after eight a.m. It also alerts me to the fact my father has sent a text.

> DAD
>
> When will you be home? I have a proposal for you to consider.

"Fuck," I mutter as I scrub a hand down my face. Dad's proposals always involve me joining the family business. The last thing I'm interested in doing.

Maddie lifts her face when I swear. "Is everything okay?" She's groggy with sleep, disoriented.

I cup the back of her head. "Yeah. Sorry I woke you."

As she blinks herself awake, she puts her hands to my chest and rolls off me. I miss her warmth instantly. "God, sorry! Did I sleep on you all night?"

"No, but you *are* a bed hog, Miller."

Her eyes go wide. "Take that back."

I chuckle. "I never take back the truth."

"Ugh. You suck." She flings the bed covers off and leaves to go into the bathroom and I'm helpless but to stare at her naked ass until I can't see it anymore.

Sex with Maddie was the best sex of my life. And goddamn, I wish it wasn't because now I want a whole lot more of it, and I swore to myself that nothing would happen until she'd worked through her feelings over her breakup.

My phone vibrates with a text, interrupting my thoughts over Maddie, her ass, and the sex we had.

CALLAN

I just caught you on the news, Ethan.
Looks like a rowdy road trip.

GAGE

Fair warning, Dad's already called asking if I've heard anything from you about it.

BRADFORD

He called me too. You okay, Ethan?

OLIVIA

> Please let me know if you guys need any
> PR advice. I'm sure Madeline is all across
> this, but just in case, I'm here for you.

I'm guessing those assholes from last night posted their videos of Maddie and me outside Dan's bar.

"You're looking at your phone like you want to murder it," Maddie says, coming back into the room, distracting the hell out of me thanks to the fact she's naked.

My eyes linger on her breasts, and I think about fucking her again while also fighting with myself over not deepening whatever this is with her yet.

"Don't look at me like that," she says in that sultry voice of hers that comes out when she's turned on. That voice could convince me to do almost anything.

"It's fucking hard not to," I rasp, moving to the other side of the bed so I can sit on the edge of it and pull her onto my lap.

She slides onto me with an easy smile and then moans when I cup her breast and pinch her nipple. All my good intentions not to start something with her fly out the window when her pussy rubs against my hard dick. Before I can stop myself, I'm pulling her in for a kiss.

"Ethan." She attempts to push me away. When I place a hand to her back to keep her close, she presses against my chest and says, "My morning breath is so bad. I'm not kissing you."

I don't ease my grip on her. "I don't give a fuck about morning breath."

She doesn't remove her hands from my chest, and I

figure pretty quickly that we're gonna need to brush our teeth before she'll let me do what I want to her.

Letting her go, I jerk my chin at her. "Let's move this to the bathroom. We'll brush our teeth and then we'll get in the shower."

Heat fills her eyes. "So bossy."

I move in close like I'm going to kiss her. "Now, or else I'm taking what I want here in this bed."

Her phone rings and she glances at it briefly before shifting off me and ignoring the call.

She's halfway toward the bathroom when it starts up again.

"You gonna get that?" I ask, following her.

With a shake of her head, she says, "No, I want to brush my teeth so I can have your dick."

"You've got a filthy mouth, Miller." I hook my arm around her waist so I can pull her in close and growl against her ear, "I want it around my dick."

"What will I get out of that?"

"I seem to recall you've already received some orgasms. How about we call it even once you've blown me?"

She turns and loops her arms around my neck as her phone starts ringing again. Her eyes hold a sexy promise I want her to make good on. "So, just to get this straight, I owe you for those orgasms?"

My lips quirk. "You're the one who asked what you'd get out of a blowjob, so it seems I'm the one being asked for payment here."

Her body presses to mine, and I swear she almost kisses me. I fucking wish she would. "I like waking up with you," she murmurs.

I like many things about Madeline, but it might be her pure honesty that I like the most. Simple truths like the one she just gave mean a lot to me. The women I've dated never shared this kind of honesty so easily. I've always had to play a lot of games and jump through many hoops, and I'm damn tired of that shit.

"I like waking up to you sleeping on me."

Her smile is broad. And then, I receive a roll of her eyes. "Smart-ass."

I let her think I'm teasing and when her phone rings for the fourth time, I remember the texts I received about hitting the news with her. "I think you should take that call. We made the news overnight. It might be about that."

Her easy smile disappears but she doesn't let me go. "I wanted to stay in our bubble for a bit longer." She sighs and then removes her arms from around my neck before reaching for her phone.

"Hey, Leigh," she says, not an ounce of enthusiasm in her voice.

I let her take the call in peace and head into the bathroom to take a shower. Something tells me there's no blowjob in my future.

When I emerge from the bathroom with a towel around my waist, Maddie's wearing her pajamas and is sitting on her bed reading something on her phone.

"How bad is it?" I ask, coming to stand in front of her.

She looks up at me and where I assume to see distress of some kind, I see only exhaustion. And not the kind from little sleep. Standing, she passes me her phone. "Take a read."

.   .   .

BESTIE, great news: @madelinemontana was not kidnapped by a serial killer! She showed up on socials last night and let's just say, girl made a statement of her own and we were here for every word. After we fell off our chair reading it, we gathered ourselves up and mentally prepared for the next shot to be fired in this saga. We seriously thought it would be from @tucker-brandt but it came from OOMF who spotted our girl out in the wild. And bestie, we are shook! How did we not know that our girl Maddie is friends with @ethanblack #gasp They got themselves into a little altercation at a bar last night, and it has to be said that Ethan BMS when he went all OTT protective over our girl. We stan a protector king. And we're so ready for a new love story to follow. Tucker Who?

"BMS? OOMF? OTT?" I place her phone in her hand. "What the hell do all those letters mean and why the fuck can't people just use plain English?"

Amusement forces its way past her exhaustion. "Oh, grandpa, we need to get you educated so you can keep up with this century."

A series of text messages hit her phone, ending her moment of reprieve. The way her shoulders slump sparks regret in me.

"I'm sorry I caused this for you."

She shakes her head. "This isn't on you. And I have zero regrets about last night, so please don't think I do."

"But?" Because there is a but here. I'm just not seeing it yet.

She sighs. "It's time to face the music. Darren's been blowing up my phone this morning, making all kinds of threats on behalf of Tucker, and my label has requested a meeting."

"You're going home."

"Yes. Unfortunately."

The disappointment I feel over that is far greater than it should be after only knowing this woman for three days, but then I've never believed that the length of time knowing someone can predict the depth of feelings you have for them. Emotional connection is not a fucking scientific equation, as much as some people in my life would have me believe.

"I'll drive you."

"No, you've already done so much for me. I can't keep taking from you."

"It's a three-hour drive, Miller. That's hardly taking anything from me."

She moves into me, smiling gently. Putting her hands to my chest, she says, "You're such a giver, Ethan. I've never met anyone as generous and supportive as you." She brings one hand to my jaw. "And so selfless." Her lips brush over mine, lingering for nowhere near long enough. "I don't ever want to take advantage of you. Leigh has a car waiting downstairs for me."

I'm still processing the speed of all this as she showers, dresses, and packs her suitcase. I didn't fly home on Saturday intending on spending this week road-tripping with a woman I just met, but here I am, and now I have to rearrange my thoughts over what I imagined might happen.

"Okay, I think I have everything," she says, surveying the room, hand on her suitcase that sits next to her ready to go.

"If I find anything you forgot, I'll send it to you." Or drive it, her desire for me not to do that be damned.

Her gaze settles on me, calm in the storm of emotions I think she's probably feeling. "Thank you."

We turn silent for a beat, just watching the other. I wonder if her thoughts are as deafening as mine right now. We started something here and the abruptness of the ending is fucking with me.

The silence is broken when Maddie's phone rings. If I could throw that phone out the window, I would. Her expression says the same.

Pulling a face, she apologizes before answering the call. It's her assistant and I get the gist they've got a busy day of work to get through once Maddie arrives back in Nashville.

After ending the call, she releases a breath. "I have to go." She says this like it's the last thing she wants to do.

Not wanting to keep her from her work, I move into action, taking hold of her suitcase and bag. "I'll walk you down."

"You don't need to do that, Ethan."

My eyes bore into hers. "Let me do this one last thing for you, Miller. Besides, there could be fans downstairs now that they all know you're in Louisville."

She doesn't argue with me, and we ride the elevator down to the hotel lobby, silent, both lost in our thoughts.

Thankfully, there are no fans or paparazzi to harass her, and we make our way out to her waiting car without any problems.

Once I've got her bags in the trunk, I meet her gaze. "Let me know when you're home safely."

Her eyes smile just as much as her mouth does and she moves into me, gripping my shirt. "I'm so glad you were stuck in that traffic on Saturday."

I try like hell not to put my hands on her but fail. I've got one hand in her hair and the other around her waist before I can stop myself. And as much as I try to keep things light, I fail at that too. "Last night was nowhere near enough for me, Maddie. I fucking hate one-night stands. I know you have to go and handle your business, but you need to know I'm not happy about it."

The smile in her eyes shifts into something more. Something intense and searing. She lets go of my shirt to bring her hands to my neck. Then, gripping me tightly, possessively, she pulls my mouth down to hers and shows me that she feels the same way.

She keeps hold of me after she drags her mouth from mine. "I've never had a one-night stand and I don't want to start now, Black."

"Thank fuck." The way I feel that in my gut is something new to me.

With one last kiss, I open her door and make sure she's settled in safely before saying goodbye. I then watch her drive away, wondering what the fuck we're getting ourselves into here. Maddie lives an entirely different life to mine. In Nashville. And she's in the middle of a shit-storm that will demand all her attention. But hell if I can even begin to bring myself around to not pursuing her. I've never wanted something more than this. I want to see what Maddie and I could have.

18

MADELINE

THE TRIP HOME, which should have taken around three hours, ended up taking almost five, thanks to a tractor-trailer wreck we encountered near Elizabethtown. I should have just flown, but I wasn't in the mood for that.

I spent most of the time working. I decided on the new PR team I'll hire and had a call with them. Leigh and I narrowed down my choices for a new manager and she arranged a meeting for tomorrow with the guy I'm interested in working with. We also discussed the fact I need to find a new lawyer because terminating my contract with Darren is likely to be hell and I need legal advice on this as soon as possible. I looked through the properties Leigh has found as possible new homes for me, not really loving any of them. And . . . I dedicated a great deal of time to thinking about Ethan.

I hated leaving him like I did this morning. It felt too fast and furious for me, and I think he felt the same. I could not have loved it more when he told me he hates one-night stands and that he wasn't happy about me leaving. I've no idea where we'll go from here, or how, but I'm enjoying this bit of happiness in amongst all the turmoil.

Leigh's waiting for me at the hotel where I'll be staying until I figure out my living situation. She gets straight down to business when I walk into my suite.

"Judy's on her way over." My new publicist. "She'll spend the afternoon working with you on a plan for damage control, social media strategy and management, media relations, and campaign planning. She'll drive to and from the record label meeting with us so we can maximize the afternoon." She consults her phone before continuing. "I've got the name of five lawyers for you to consider. If we can choose one now, I'll push for an appointment late this afternoon or tonight."

I collapse onto the sofa, needing a minute to catch my breath.

Leigh gives me two seconds only. "Tucker has hit back, Maddie. We don't have time to waste on this."

"What was his response?"

"He said you're lying about everything and that he's devastated you've done this to him after he loved you so well."

I stare at her with disbelief. "You're joking, right?"

Her lips press together as she shakes her head. "No."

"I fucking hate that asshole." I put my fingers to my temple as a headache makes threats I really don't want it to follow through on.

"You and me both, but sitting here ranting about him won't fix the situation." Leigh is nothing if not efficient and businesslike. I've always valued those traits in her, but today, I could do with a little less of being managed. I'm tired after not much sleep last night, and it's affecting my ability to process everything as fast as she would like me to.

"Okay, give me a minute to freshen up and then we can go over the list of lawyers."

She approves of this, and I leave her to go into the bathroom, where I shut the door and slide down it to sit on the tiled floor. The coolness of the tiles is what I'm searching for, along with the quiet hum of the bathroom.

I close my eyes and do some box breathing to help calm my overloaded system. While I do this, I try to shut off my thoughts, focusing on the sound of the ventilation system in the bathroom. The continuous whir always helps me in times like this but today I'm unable to rely on it. There's too much noise in my head. Too much uncertainty to be able to switch it all off.

"Shit," I whisper as I open my eyes and exhale a breath. Leigh's right: sitting around ranting about my problems isn't going to fix them. I started this when I ran out on Tucker, and now I have to finish it.

I push up off the ground and splash cold water on my face while staring at myself in the mirror. I look tired and stressed, and I refuse to let my record label see me like this, so I get to work fixing my face and finding something to wear that screams *I've got this under control*.

Fifteen minutes later, I emerge from the bedroom ready to tackle the rest of this day. I find my new publicist sitting with Leigh on the sofa, deep in conversation. They stop talking when they hear me. Judy smiles and stands. Leigh narrows her eyes at me like she's trying to decide my state of my mind.

"Hi." I extend a hand to Judy. "Thanks for making time on such short notice."

Judy's grip is firm, and she exudes an air of confidence and control, which I find highly reassuring. "I'm glad to meet you, Madeline. I've been a fan for a while and that statement you made last night reminded me why."

I did not expect that, and it stuns me into silence for a moment before I find my voice again. "Thank you. I appreciate you saying that."

She smiles knowingly. "I imagine it's been a rough few days."

"You could say that. All my own doing, though."

Her brows furrow. "That's inaccurate. You may have chosen to end a very public relationship, but you didn't choose the social media nonsense that's occurred. If I could get my clients to believe one thing, it'd be that while they chose their line of work, they didn't agree to the bullshit that goes with it."

I've never thought of it like that, and I appreciate her saying that, too.

She indicates to the table in the corner of the suite. "Let's start by getting to know each other a little and then I'll take you through my ideas for managing this crisis and redirecting your brand. And let me just say before we begin that the response you've had to your post last night shows that we're starting from a solid foundation." She pauses and eyes me like she wants to ensure I'm listening. "Tucker might be out there calling you a liar, but your get-loud hashtag is trending on all platforms. You've struck a chord, and I don't think your fans are going anywhere."

I've avoided my post all day, not sure I was ready for any nastiness I might read in the comments. The relief I feel at this news is immense and helps get me in the right mindset for our conversation.

We spend half an hour talking about how she plans to help me shift my brand away from Tucker's and manage the negative publicity I'm currently facing. I'm impressed with everything she suggests, and I can tell that Leigh is too. By the time we leave for the meeting with my label, I'm feeling a lot more confident about everything and hopeful about my future in this industry.

"Never have I ever been so appalled by the misogyny of this fucking industry," Leigh rages as we push our way through the door of my record label's building and walk out into the sunshine that feels a lot warmer than I do after the meeting I've just had.

I think I'm in shock. Not that I know what that feels like. But if it involves clammy skin, nausea, a racing heart, and a faint feeling, then I'm definitely in shock.

"Surely, they can't do that," Leigh continues her tirade.

I'm going to vomit.

That's all I'm sure of right now.

"Right?" Leigh stops and inspects me. "Shit, are you okay?"

I claw at the top buttons of my blouse that aren't letting me breathe.

"Fuck," Leigh curses as the sun blinds me and I stumble. Her hand cradles my elbow, and she guides me to the park bench on the grass near us. Once I'm sitting, she shoves a bottle of water in my face. "Drink this. You are not puking on my watch."

I push the bottle away and lurch in the opposite direction of her just in time, hurling over the grass instead of her lap.

She thrusts a tissue at me, and I wipe my mouth while my stomach settles. When I'm sure I'm not going to vomit again, I turn back to her. "I think they can do whatever they want, and they just did."

"But you have a contract that I imagine is ironclad and states they can't terminate you based on that bullshit they just spewed at you."

"It clearly isn't that ironclad. They wouldn't terminate me if it was." And *god*, why do I not know this information? Past Madeline has a lot to answer for.

The record label execs cited a variety of reasons for terminating my contract but mostly they relied on a morality clause, saying that my recent behavior is unacceptable and damaging to the label's reputation. Read: Tucker, their number one artist, demanded they fire me.

I am so fucking angry at him. I thought he might do something like this, and truth be told, it's probably why I took six months to leave him and ruin all the business plans he and Darren built around our relationship. Fear of him trying to cancel me by throwing his power around in this way kept me engaged to him.

Having to listen to those men today tell me that women need to tread carefully in this business so as not to ruin all the hard work their team put into cultivating their brand has pissed me the hell off. Why should women have to tread carefully? Why does Tucker get to go out there and do whatever he wants, but I don't get to do the same?

Aaaargh!!!

Unable to hold in the fury grinding in my chest for a second longer, I throw my head back, open my mouth, and scream.

It's long.

It's loud.

And damn it feels good to get it all out.

Fuck those people who want to keep me down.

Fuck. Them.

I'm a Miller and we don't stay down. We stand the hell up and handle our business, and we don't ever give up.

Ethan was right when he told me I'm not powerless. Tucker can screw with my career as much as he wants but I have so many resources I can tap into.

The only person who can stop me is me.

"Wow." Leigh stares at me when I finish screaming, eyes wide, mouth open. "That was . . . unexpected."

I shake out my arms, every inch of my skin buzzing. "You should probably expect more of that."

She blinks. "Right. Good to know, but I'd like to suggest we maybe keep that kind of outburst to private spaces only." She motions at all the people staring at us. "God knows who just filmed that."

"Let them film. I'm holding my head high now. The only things I've done wrong in all of this have been not listening to myself, allowing people to make decisions for me, and not paying attention to the details. Lesson fucking learned." I take a deep breath. "I'm not burying my head in the sand anymore, Leigh. I'm taking charge and we're not fucking going down."

With that, I stride toward the car, my shoulders pushed back. If Tucker wants a fight, I'll damn well give him one.

19

ETHAN

"HAVE YOU SPOKEN WITH DAD YET?" Hayden asks me quietly during our family dinner on Wednesday while everyone else is engaged in a lively conversation with Luna, Gage's five-year-old daughter, about her new teacher, who she adores.

"Yeah, we had a quick chat this afternoon." I spent two days driving home from Louisville and then went straight into a meeting this afternoon with the company that acquired mine so we could iron out some details regarding my continuing presence as an advisor. I called Dad after I stepped out from the meeting.

"And? Did you say yes?"

"Fuck no." I look at him like he's lost his mind. He knows I have zero intention of ever accepting a job at Dad's company. "What have you been smoking today? He wants to turn me into a venture fucking capitalist and you know that's never gonna happen."

He lifts his glass of whiskey to his mouth. "I'm just checking to see that all the time you spent in Europe didn't turn you into someone I don't know. Glad to know it didn't."

I grin and at the same time, Luna comes around the dining table to crawl up onto my lap. I welcome her with open arms and help her settle in, at which point she grips my shirt and says, "Uncle Ethan, Daddy said you're coming to my birthday party. Will you take photos of me?"

Fuck, I love this kid and have missed her. "Of course." I squint my eyes questioningly at her. "What are you dressing up as this year? I'll need to bring the right props." This is something Gage started with her first birthday. He went overboard and dressed her up as a princess, and since then the two of them have made a tradition out of selecting her outfit and dressing her up each year.

Her eyes sparkle with joy. "Daddy bought me a unicorn tutu dress! It's so pretty."

"Excellent. I will find the exact right props for your birthday photos."

"And Sarah is coming too! She has to be in the photos with me."

"Who's Sarah?"

"My best friend, silly."

I chuckle. "Right. Got it. She'll be in all the photos too."

"No." She shakes her head madly. "Not *all* the photos. Mommy and Daddy will be in some. And Michael."

"Remind me again who Michael is." I'm sure I've never heard of this guy, but my memory may be failing me.

Eyes still alight with joy, she says, "He's going to be my new daddy when Mommy marries him."

Her new daddy? I glance across the table at Gage and catch his darkened gaze. He doesn't correct his daughter, though. Gage is the best father I know and not once since his divorce from Luna's mother has he succumbed to the kind of nasty behavior I often see exes engaging in over their children. Shayla, his ex, has, but not Gage. Luna's wellbeing is his priority, and I can't imagine he would ever want to take away her excitement over having another family member in her life.

I smile at Luna. "Okay, so there will be lots of photos with all the people you want in them. Will you send me an invitation so I know where and when your party is?"

Her forehead crinkles with a frown. "Daddy already sent you one." She looks at her father for confirmation.

Gage nods to verify he sent the invite. "Uncle Ethan has been away, so he probably hasn't had a chance to read the invitation yet."

"I'll look for it tonight," I promise her.

Once she's satisfied that I'll be at her party, she slides off my lap and runs to her grandfather who lifts her up with a smile. The two of them then talk quietly and I'm struck by the easy way Dad immerses himself with her and the obvious affection they have for each other. It's so unlike the way he raised his sons. Sure, he spent time camping and fishing with us, and taught us stuff, but there were always strict expectations and not the kind of affection I'm observing now.

Gage arches his brows at me. "I heard you're moving to Nashville."

"Smart-ass," I mutter, but it's no lie that my mind goes immediately to Madeline at the mention of Nashville. She texted me yesterday to let me know she arrived home safely but we haven't texted or spoken since. My thoughts have been returning to her obsessively, thinking about the time we spent together. Remembering her kisses, her touch. The sex. *Fuck*, the sex. And in amongst all those thoughts, I'm hoping she's okay with all the shit she's dealing with.

"So?" Gage nudges. "Will you see the runaway bride again?"

"Yeah." *Fuck yes.*

"Did you take that photo of her that she posted the other day? It looked like one of yours." Bradford says.

I look at him. "Since when do you go on social media?"

"Since my wife takes it upon herself to shove her phone in my face to help me keep up to date with my brothers' lives."

I grin, my gaze meeting his wife's who is sitting next to him. So far, I've only spent time with Kristen at Callan's wedding, but that was enough to know I like her. I also like the way she's softened Bradford's edges. "Promise me you won't ever stop shoving your phone in his face."

Her smirk matches mine as she looks up at Bradford before glancing back at me. "I promise. How would he ever know what's going on in the world otherwise?"

I laugh and take in the way my family watch Kristen with fondness while Bradford looks at her like she hung the moon, the stars, the entire galaxy. Then, I answer Bradford's question. "Yeah, I took that photo of Madeline."

"It's a beautiful photo," Kristen says. "Do you think you'll ever go back to photography?"

I nod slowly. "Maybe. It's certainly on my mind."

"You were always happiest when you were traveling the world taking photos," Mom murmurs with a smile. We haven't spoken much since I arrived for dinner but I've gotten the impression she wants to pull me aside for a conversation.

Dad looks up from Luna, the easygoing expression on his face now gone, replaced with a stern one. "He's twenty-eight, Ingrid. Roaming around the world taking photos is hardly work that will sustain him for the rest of his life."

A hush falls over the table as I stare at Dad and fight the urge to tell him what I think of that. "I don't know, Dad," I say as lightly as I can, "I roamed around for years taking photos that sustained me. I think I could make a go of it again."

"Not to mention the fact he could live off the sale of his company for the rest of his life," Gage drawls.

Dad's gaze stays firmly on mine. "I'm not talking about money, son. I'm talking about settling down and being a responsible adult."

"Dad," Bradford says quietly, cautioning our father in the way he sometimes does when Dad tries to pull me into line.

"No." I shake my head at my brother. "Let him say what he wants. He's obviously got some thoughts on the matter." Then, turning to Dad, I ask, "Is it the photography that's the problem or is it the fact that I'm just not doing what you want me to do? That my idea of a dream job doesn't look like yours? Or,"—I cock my head—"is it that you just wish I'd find a woman you approve of, marry her, and live a respectable life like yours?"

"You're putting words in my mouth, son, but is it

wrong for a father to want his children to find happiness and live a good life?"

"No, but when the happiness and good life have to look a certain way, that's wrong." I push my chair out and stand. "I don't want to keep going over this with you. As far as I'm concerned, I'm a responsible adult, I'm happy, and my life is good."

I stalk out of the room, needing to put distance between us before I really get into it with him.

Mom follows me into their grand salon, calling out, "Ethan. Wait."

I slow my stride and stop even though I'm not ready to get into a conversation about this with her. Turning, I find her looking at me with compassion. "I don't have an argument in me, Mom."

"I'm not going to argue with you. I just want to make sure you're okay. Your father . . . well, we both know he can be difficult at times."

"At *times*?"

"You're right. He's always difficult with you, and I'm sorry about that."

"You don't need to apologize for him. That's not on you."

"It is on me." She stops talking and a thoughtful expression fills her face, like she's trying to figure out exactly what she wants to say. "Well, no, that's not quite right. What I mean is it's on both of us, the way your father is with you I mean."

I frown. "What do you mean?"

She releases a breath. "Our marriage is complex, which you know." I know she's referring to the fact their marriage was one of convenience so they could join their families for political power. I also know she's referring to the fact Dad cheated on her in between Callan's and my birth. "After you were born, I had postnatal depression, which I know you're aware of, but it isn't something I've ever talked about with you boys.

"Your father and I were distant with each other while I worked through my devastation over his cheating. And I was distant to you boys. Especially to you, Ethan. And the depression didn't help." Her entire face is filled with regret. "I made sure you had all the physical things you needed but I didn't give you love in the way you needed, and for that I am sorry."

Fuck me.

This is the conversation I never imagined us having. Never imagined her opening up about.

"I'm still not following as to how this all fits into the way Dad treats me."

"He changed after he cheated on me. You have to understand that up until that point, our marriage wasn't based on love. We were two kids told to marry by our families. So, we did, and we tried to do what married people do. We had kids, we vacationed, we entertained, we tried to fall in love. But starting a marriage without a strong foundation of love and then having five children in seven years was a recipe for disaster.

"After your father cheated on me, we had to work through that. We had years of therapy and ended up falling in love. And I know that might not be something you can understand—that I was able to forgive him and fall in love with him, but it's what happened. Unfortunately," she continues with sadness, "you boys suffered throughout all of that turmoil, especially you. I was so lost after your birth and I just didn't have the emotional capacity to bond with you like I did with your brothers. As a result, I know you struggled to find yourself and your place in our family. You were lost and your father was extra hard on you because he worried so much for you. And he's still hard on you, but only because he worries, Ethan. He loves you more than you know."

I stare at her, lost for words. Lost for so fucking much. This is the kind of conversation I've wanted with my mother for my entire life and it fucking kills me that she's taken twenty-eight years to broach it with me.

"You're right that I don't understand how you can forgive him for what he did," I finally say because, fuck, I don't understand that and I'm not sure I ever will.

She gives me a small smile. "The thing about marriages is that the only people who can fully understand them are the two people in them. I don't expect you to wrap your head around our relationship, but I do hope you can separate the husband from the father and think about what a good dad Edmund is."

"When he says the stuff to me that he does, Mom, I'm not sure I can get to that point in my thinking. He treats me like I'm still a kid who needs to be told what to do next in life because I can't figure it out for myself. That doesn't make me feel good, you know?"

"I know, darling, and I'm going to talk with him about this."

I clench my jaw. "You shouldn't have to manage him or his relationship with me."

"Sometimes, that's the job of a parent. None of us are perfect, and sometimes we need our partner to help us see a different perspective." Her smile shifts into a soft loving one. "That's what love and marriage is for. Finding a partner to support us, counsel us, and love us as we grow into new understandings of ourselves and the world around us. I don't think of it as managing your father. I think of it as one way I can love him."

She reaches for my hand and squeezes it. "Please think about what I've said, and if you want to talk some more with me about it, I'm always here for you. I know things have been strained between us for a long time, but I hope we can change that."

I'm left staring after her when she walks back into the dining room, my thoughts all over the place. I stand rooted to the spot for a long while, thinking about everything she said. In the end, it's a text from Madeline that drags me from my thoughts.

MILLER

I'm thinking about buying these. Bad idea?

She sends through a photo of a pair of pink granny undies and the grin that spreads across my face is instant and so fucking welcome.

ME

Can you get a pair in every color? They're hot as hell.

MILLER

What's your favorite color?

ME

That depends. It's blue, but on you, it's red.

MILLER

Have you even seen me wear red?

ME

Not in person, but Google has been my friend.

MILLER

You stalked me?

ME

Damn right I stalked you. I need to know what I'm getting myself into here.

MILLER

I may have stalked you too.

Fuck, I feel that in my gut.

ME

Did you find anything interesting?

MILLER

I found your Insta and saw all the photos you've taken over the years. Ethan, they're stunning. You should become a photographer.

I laugh.

ME

You think?

MILLER

shrugs I mean, if you've got nothing better to do with your time.

ME

This asterisking of words is another bump in the road, Miller.

MILLER

grins Good to know, grandpa.

ME

How's your day been?

MILLER

Ugh. Next question.

I call her and she answers with, "I miss you. And I know that must sound ridiculous since I've known you less than a week, but it's true. And if that scares you away, so be it. I'm done with not telling the truth in my life."

Fuck.

"Did you just do one of those asterisk shrugs when you said, 'so be it?'"

Her laugh is the best thing I've heard all day. "Are you gonna leave a girl hanging, Black?"

"I miss you too. Now, tell me about your day."

"I need a new lawyer and I can't find one I like. And until I find one, I can't fire Darren as my manager because I need a lawyer to advise me on that. And Tucker's being a real dick. Like, the dickiest dick of all dicks and I would unalive him if I thought I could get away with it."

"Wow, the dickiest dick of all dicks. I see why you're a songwriter with your ability to string words together. And unalive? What the fuck is that?"

She laughs again. "I threw that in just for you. Kill, Ethan. I want to kill him, and if the FBI are listening in on this phone call and show up to arrest me, I'm gonna need you to come and save me from them, 'k?"

I chuckle. "Fuck, where do you get this shit from? The FBI listening in on your phone calls?"

"It's a thing! And since you're related to a senator, they probably really are listening in on your phone calls. This may be a bump in our friendship."

"I hope not. I wanna see your new granny undies on you."

"Oh god, we're gonna need burner phones if we start sexting. I barely manage one phone, so this may be another bump. I may need to reconsider hooking up with a senator's brother."

"You aren't reconsidering anything," I growl. I hate the thought of her on another man's arm, and that thought comes out of nowhere, smacking me in the face with the intensity of it.

Maddie is silent for a moment and when she speaks again, I hear how much I've affected her by her breathy tone. "I like that you've got feelings about that."

Hayden and Gage wander into the grand salon, deep in conversation over something.

"I have to go, but I may have a lawyer you'll like."

"Who?"

I eye Hayden. "My brother. I'll mention it to him if you'd like."

"Yes, please. I would love that."

"Okay, he's here with me now. I'll get back to you soon."

"Thank you," she says so fucking softly that it hits deep in my gut and I know I'd do anything to make her use that voice with me again.

"Go buy those undies, Miller. And when they arrive, I'm gonna need to see them."

"On me?"

"Fuck yes, on you." I don't even try to hide how much I want to see that.

We end the call with the sound of her laughing and I know I'm going to dream of those granny undies.

"Was that the runaway bride?" Gage asks.

"Can we stop referring to her as the runaway bride?" I scowl. "Her name is Madeline."

Gage's lips quirk, the asshole. "My apologies. Was that *Madeline*?"

His apologies, my ass. Gage is always across everyone's feelings. He can read people in a way no one I've ever met can. He just loves to fuck with people, especially his brothers. "Yeah. She needs a lawyer to look over some contracts." I eye Hayden. "Can you give her some advice?"

He grimaces. "I'm pretty busy this week while Liv's on her honeymoon."

"Surely, you can fit a contract in."

The look on his face tells me I'm pushing my luck, but he nods. "Give her my number."

I text his number to Maddie before he changes his mind.

She replies straight away.

MILLER

{This is a secret message the feds can't read: You are the best and the next time I see you I'm going to wrap my filthy mouth around your dick and pay you back for those orgasms you gave me}

Fuck. Me.

20

MADELINE

"So, what can we expect from you next, Madeline?" the radio host I'm currently talking with asks me early Thursday morning during my first interview of the day. Just like yesterday, I've got a full day of interviews thanks to the schedule Judy has put together for me.

I smile at the host. I've appeared on her show many times and I like her. "I'm writing new stuff that I'm really excited about. And I've decided to post more often on socials and share my process as I go." This is something I've always wanted to do, but Tucker and Darren never let me.

The host's eyes light up. "Oh, that would be amazing! I'm always fascinated to know how songs come together and I imagine your fans would love that too."

"I hope it'll be something fun for everyone."

She wraps the interview up and ten minutes later, I'm on my way out to my waiting car with Leigh and Judy. Leigh hands me a bottle of water while Judy rattles off information I'll need for the next interview, which is for a magazine cover story.

Judy hasn't found it hard to line up interviews. Everyone wants to know what happened with my wedding and what's in my future now that the news has broken about me being dumped by my record label. Darren has demanded I don't speak about my relationship with Tucker, but I haven't paid attention to any of his demands. Instead, Judy has helped me figure out how to talk about my hurt over being cheated on and the way my abortion was discussed publicly without talking too much about Tucker directly. We're keeping the focus on me and my plans for the future.

My phone rings as I'm settling myself in the back seat of the car and when I see Ethan's brother's name on my screen, I answer it immediately.

"Hayden. Thank you for calling me back."

"No worries. I'm in between appointments, though, so I'll need to be quick. Ethan told me you need a contract looked at. Can you give me some context?"

I fill him in on my contract with Darren and why I need it looked over. I don't hold anything back, sharing honestly with him that Darren and Tucker screwed me over with my percentages because I knew no better back then, and that I answered to them like I was an employee more than an artist in my own right. I hate having to admit my stupidity to Ethan's brother.

Hayden's reply, though, is what makes me decide he may just be the lawyer for me. "Send the contract through so I can take a look. It pisses me off when people screw others over because they know they can get away with it. You were young and new to the industry, Madeline, and they should have done better by you. Especially Tucker. I'll do everything in my power to help you get what you're owed, and we'll make sure this never happens again."

"Please call me Maddie. And I really appreciate this, Hayden, especially since I know how busy you already are." I did my research on Hayden and learned he's one of the most in-demand lawyers in New York.

After we end the call, Leigh looks at me. "Was that Hottie McHottie's lawyer brother?"

"Yes. Can you please email him my contract with Darren?"

"I'm on it."

Judy glances up from her phone. "A video of you has gone viral."

My new publicist has perfected her poker face, so I can't get a read on what she's thinking. "Good or bad?"

"It's not ideal." She hands me her phone with the video ready for me to watch.

I stare at myself wearing very little, talking dirty to the camera. It's a video Tucker took of me last year but he's nowhere in sight because he filmed it. The caption makes out that it's a recent video taken by Ethan, who social media hasn't stopped talking about since the video of us was posted two days ago. Speculation is rife that I left Tucker for Ethan and the comments on this video are nasty in their condemnation of me.

I pass Judy's phone back to her while my chest tightens with anger. *More anger.* It seems like every day brings a fresh round of it. "This is Tucker's doing. He made that video last year."

She nods. "I figured this is part of his campaign to make himself look like the injured party."

"God! How can someone be such an asshole?"

"The world is full of them, Maddie," she says casually and I get the impression she's used to this kind of stuff.

"So, what, do we just sit back and let him get away with this? Or do we, I don't know . . . is there *anything* we can do?"

"My advice is we go high. Ignore it and carry on as we are. No good will come from us playing tit for tat."

Leigh scowls. "I hate this. It's so unfair."

"I agree," Judy says, "But it's the nature of this business. People will forget and life goes on. We just have to give them a better story to be interested in, which we are." She looks at me. "People are interested in your story, Maddie. A woman finding herself, coming into her power. I think we should stick with our plan."

I force the heavy weight from my chest, trying to rid my body of the anger consuming me. My thoughts are the same as Leigh's, that this is unfair, but I've seen enough over the last three years to know Judy's right. "Okay, we stick with the plan. And maybe I surrender my phone to you guys so I don't accidentally make a post about what an asshole Tucker is."

Leigh holds her hands up. "Don't surrender it to me. None of us will have a job after I'm done posting exactly what I think of Tucker."

"Right," Judy says, taking charge, "I'll change your password if need be. Now, let's get back to focusing on what we need to get through today." With that, she brings us back to the task at hand, my next interview, and I leave thoughts of stabbing Tucker behind.

It's a long day and I don't return to my hotel suite until seven p.m. I'm hungry, but mostly I just want to collapse into a bath, close my eyes, and forget all the things I have to do tomorrow.

Hayden called a few hours ago to let me know he'll fly in tomorrow morning for a meeting with Darren and his lawyer. He's gone over the contract and advised that terminating my contract is possible. He also asked me to forward him all the contracts I've ever signed for work so he can start going over those too.

I need tonight to psyche myself up for this meeting. Not that I'll be in attendance, but I have no doubt Tucker will retaliate in some way. Leigh told me she's more than happy to take one for the team and personally deal with Tucker if he does. After joking about that, she'd given me a stern look and said, "Tonight is not the night to raid the minibar. Do I need to stay over to ensure you wake without a hangover tomorrow?" I'd had to spend a good five minutes assuring her I had no intention of binge drinking.

Walking into the sanctuary of my hotel suite is my favorite part of the day. The silence is everything I've craved for hours. I kick off my shoes and strip out of my clothes as I walk through the living room into the bedroom and then the bathroom. I run a warm bath and release a calming breath as I slide into the tub.

Usually, when I have a bath, I listen to music or a podcast, but not tonight. I just can't take any more noise today. Instead, I rest my head and close my eyes, enjoying the peace and quiet.

I'm about ten minutes into that peace and quiet when my phone sounds with a text. Chastising myself for not switching it to silent, I begrudgingly check the message. When I see Ethan's name, I can't read it fast enough.

> ETHAN
>
> This is a secret message that the feds can't read: it's time for you to wrap that filthy mouth around me.

I blink at the text, my heart speeding up at what I think he means.

> ME
>
> It's not a secret message without brackets, Black. They can read that. Abort.

> ETHAN
>
> {Get your ass to your door, Miller. I've come to collect my payment for your orgasms.}

> ME
>
> You're here?

I'm already out of the bath, scrambling to wrap a towel around myself so I can run to the door.

> ETHAN
>
> Yes.

I pull the door open just after his text hits my phone and *holy hell*, this man is sexy. He's standing in front of me wearing jeans that hug his quads and a casual black T-shirt that I'm all kinds of desperate to peel from his body. But it's the smile on his face and those blues of his that steal my ability to think straight. The way he's looking at me . . . like he sees everything he's ever wanted to see . . . I think I would do anything to have him look at me like this every day.

"Hi," I breathe, my first real smile of the day spreading across my face.

His arm is around my waist before I know it and he's pulling my mouth to his so he can kiss me. And god, he's everything I need right now. *Everything.*

He kisses me how he prefers, long and deep, before letting me go and rasping, "Jesus, I needed that."

My arms are around his neck as I stare up at him, the butterflies in my stomach going crazy. "You should do it again."

His eyes cover every inch of my face like he's taking the moment to learn all the contours of it, all my tiny details, before trailing down my body. Then, his arm tightens around my waist and he pulls my mouth back to his, and the rough groan he makes as he kisses me curls desire all the way through me.

This kiss starts slow but quickly ignites into burning passion. His lips are white heat against mine, his tongue exploring, possessing, *claiming*. I cling to him, my fingers threading through his hair, pulling him closer, needing to feel every inch of him against me.

Walking us into the suite, he backs me up against the wall, his body trapping me deliciously as he reaches down to remove the towel I'm wearing. "Fuck, Maddie," he growls after dragging his mouth from mine so he can look at me. "I've barely stopped thinking about you the last two days."

My head spins, overwhelmed by the sheer intensity of

the need blazing from him. I grip his neck so I can demand another kiss. When our lips collide again, I arch into him, a moan escaping as he presses his hips into mine, letting me feel the hard evidence of his desire.

I'm lost to the intoxicating scent of him, the heat of his body, the drugging sensation of his lips while he makes out with me like he did the first time we had sex.

When we finally break apart, we're both breathless. Ethan rests his forehead against mine, his eyes closed as he tries to regain control. My heart pounds wildly, its rhythm synced with my feelings for this man.

I curve my hands around his body. "I'm so glad you're here."

He lifts his head. "I would have been here yesterday if I thought that wouldn't freak you out."

My heart thuds and I whisper, "You feel this too?" *This connection.*

Ethan's gaze doesn't waver. Not even for a second. "Yes." He takes my face in his hands. "I'm in this with you, Miller." Then, he's lifting me to carry me into the bedroom.

"I see that I'm late for the strip show," he says as he notes the trail of clothes I left on my way to the bath earlier.

I nuzzle his neck, kissing it. "Such a shame. You would have enjoyed it."

His eyes blaze with heat. "You can get dressed after our first orgasm and give me my own show."

"You think I have more than one orgasm in me?"

He smirks as I repeat his words back to him from the last time we were together. Then, dropping me on the bed, he runs his eyes lazily over my naked curves. "I think we should aim higher tonight." He crawls on top of me and kisses his way up my stomach to my breasts, lingering there for a moment, sending my core into a frenzy of need, before continuing up to my throat, my neck, my lips. "Let's beat our record."

I reach for the hem of his shirt and pull it up over his head, discarding it on the floor. "You don't want me to be able to walk tomorrow?"

The look in his eyes at that question is pure hunger. Dipping his mouth to the side of my neck, he kisses me, his teeth lightly nipping. "I'd fucking love for you to not be able to walk tomorrow," he growls. "I'd keep you right here and demand more of that filthy mouth of yours."

His growly voice tips me over the edge. Not that I knew I was close to it, but now I'm falling so hard and all I can think about is how much I want him inside me.

My hands make quick work of his belt, the button on his jeans, his zipper. Then, I'm pushing his jeans down, his boxers down, and reaching for his dick.

"Fuck," he groans as I stroke his cock and reach for his balls. He thrusts into my hand and groans again before crashing his mouth down onto mine.

When he ends the kiss, he looks at me, his eyes hooded. "Less than a week, Miller." He kisses me again, roughly, his lips telling me how desired I am, and *god*, I want him to kiss me and touch me like this forever. He bites my bottom lip before saying, "That's how long it took for me to lose my mind over you."

I stare up at him, falling, falling, *falling*. Letting go of his dick, I bring my hands to his chest so I can push him up and force him onto his back. I'm fast, desperate, and he allows me to take charge, the heat in his eyes intensifying with my every move.

Straddling him, I put a hand to his neck, gripping him possessively. I want this man in ways I've never wanted a man. "How?" I breathe while my body floods with so many sensations and feelings.

He takes hold of my hip with one hand, a breast with the other, and I feel his raw need in the rough way he handles me. "How did I lose my mind so fast?"

I bend my face closer to his while rubbing my pussy against his cock. "No, how did we *both* do that?"

"Fuck," he growls as I grind on him. "I think it was those granny undies that did it."

"What?" I laugh and I love that he can make me do that during sex.

He gives me a sexy smirk. "Trust me, you look hot as fuck in them. But now that I think of it, it could have been the moment when you faceplanted in my crotch that did it for me." His smirk now looks like pure filth across his face.

I kiss that smirk right off his face before saying, "Your mind is a dirty place to live, isn't it?"

He grabs my neck, all rough manhandling in a way I think I may start living for. "It's nowhere near as dirty as your mouth, baby."

And just like that, with a term of endearment I've never really liked, but now am all about because it feels like a claim, I'm drowning in him.

I let him pull my face to his so he can kiss me.

I let him take all the time with that kiss.

I let him touch me everywhere.

But then, *then,* when I'm desperate to be in charge

again, desperate for him to look at me with raw hunger, I drag my mouth from his and make my way down his body. I kiss every inch of his skin, tasting him as I go, loving the way his muscles react to my touch. And when I reach his cock, I settle myself between his legs and meet his gaze while sucking him into my mouth.

The guttural sound he makes scorches its way to my core. It's a sound I know I'd do anything to hear every day.

His hand comes to my head, his fingers threading into my hair. "Fuck, you feel good," he rasps.

My eyes hold his as I take him out of my mouth and lick the length of him. Swirling my tongue over his crown, I say, "I want you to fuck me hard and fast the first time."

His eyes flash with fire and he thrusts his hips up, pushing his dick against my lips. "And the second time?" he demands. "How do you want it then?"

I open my mouth to let him in, taking him deep, and massaging his balls while sucking and licking my tongue along the length of him in a way I know he likes. "I want to ride you cowgirl style." I suck him back in for another round of the same. "I want to be in control while I grind on you." I take him back into my mouth, but this time, I lick his tip after, circling it over and over, oh so slowly, loving the way he's losing himself to the pleasure. "I want you to stare at my tits while I fuck you."

"Fuck," he surges up, "You've got a mouth on you that I really fucking love." He grips under my arms and pulls me up so he can reposition me on the bed under him. Then, he bends over the edge of the bed so he can locate his jeans, his wallet, a condom. Once he's got it on, he looks down between us, lines his cock up with my pussy, and thrusts inside me, and *fuck*, he's so fucking big that I forget how to breathe for a moment.

"I'm giving you what you want, Maddie." He pulls out and slams back in, hitting me right where I need him to. "This is going to be fast."

I grip his shoulders and wrap my legs around him. "Good." I barely manage to speak with the way he's fucking me, and all I can do is hold on tight and take every thrust.

Ethan makes good on his promise. He pounds into me, and since I'm so turned on and desperate for him, it doesn't take long for me to come. He orgasms right after me, his thrusts becoming erratic as he chases his release. His hips jerk, once, twice, three times. My nails dig into his back. And my inner muscles clench around him as I take all he has to give.

He collapses on top of me, his weight everything I want, his breath hot against my neck. For a moment, we just lie there, our bodies still joined, our hearts racing in tandem.

Slowly, he lifts his head, his eyes hazy with satisfaction. "It's gonna be a long night." His voice is a rough, sexy rumble that would be my absolute downfall if he always spoke like that.

I put my hands to his abs. "I need to eat something first."

"You haven't eaten yet?" His sexy rumble has disappeared. In its place is a serious tone that says he's moved onto thinking about feeding me.

"No."

"Okay, let's get you some food." He disposes of the

condom in the bathroom before coming back and putting his jeans on. "What do you feel like?"

"A hot chicken sandwich with fries." I leave the bed and move into him so I can have another kiss. "And if you wanna judge me for eating all that grease, I don't want to hear it." God knows, I never heard the end of it from Tucker whenever I devoured fried chicken.

He rests his hand on my ass. "I'll never judge you for anything you eat, Miller." He glides his hand over my butt, feeling every curve, and asks, "Where do you want me to go to get it?"

"Nowhere. The hotel makes a good one." I press myself into him, enjoying the sound of approval he makes as I rub against him. "I'm not letting you out of my sight, Black, so that means you have to choose your dinner from the hotel menu too, and I'm not even a little bit sorry if they don't have anything you like."

He grins as he squeezes my ass in the very best way. "It's a good thing I've already eaten since you seem more than happy to let me starve."

I reach for his neck and pull his mouth down to mine for a kiss before saying, "I'd never let you starve. You can eat me anytime you want."

"Jesus," he growls. "You're fucking filthy." Then, with a smack to my ass, he lets me go. "Put your clothes back on while I order your dinner. After you've eaten, I'm going to sit on that sofa in the living room and enjoy the hell out of you taking them all off for me."

21

ETHAN

FRIDAY MORNING ARRIVES FAR TOO QUICKLY, and with it, brings a new side to Madeline that I've not seen yet. She's wired over the meeting that's taking place today between Hayden and her manager. Not in an anxious way, but rather there's a hum of anticipation about her. There's also a bold glint in her eyes that I fucking love. Last night, she told me she's not looking forward to today because she's concerned about the repercussions. However, I can see that while she's uncertain about what will happen, she's ready for it. She's ready to have the freedom to move on.

Her alarm woke us at seven a.m. after only five hours sleep, and once I had my taste of her pussy, we fucked in the shower. Afterward, we ate a quick breakfast in her suite and then I came downstairs to the hotel lobby to find a quiet spot to do some work. Hayden wants to talk with Maddie here at the hotel before he leaves for his meeting and I wanted to give her some time alone to mentally prepare for his arrival.

Troy, my assistant, has sent me a list of admin tasks he needs my input on, and I'm knee deep in them when my brother interrupts my focus.

He sits across from me, placing his briefcase on the ground. "I didn't expect to see you here today."

I glance up and find him studying me. Of all my brothers, Hayden's the one who manages us, ensuring no harm comes to anyone. He's the one who pays attention to all the details and sees things others don't. It's why he's one of the top lawyers in New York; nothing gets past him. "You're trying to figure out what Madeline means to me."

"No. I've already figured that out."

I sit back. "What is it then?"

"I'm thinking about how relaxed you seem. Compared to before you left for Europe."

"I was a mess when I left. Anything would seem relaxed compared."

"Well, you could have come home in the same mess." He wears no smile and his voice is tight.

"You're pissed off. Why?"

"I'm not pissed off. I'm just working through my frustration with you." He leans forward, resting his elbows on the table, his gaze intense with emotion. "I was worried about you, Ethan. Dad found you in a state, coked-up and fucked up over Samantha, and you took off before we had a chance to get you through that. I understood why you needed to go away, but you shut us out. You didn't let us help you." His voice is thick with the same emotion that blazes in his eyes, which is highly unusual for Hayden. Out of all my brothers, he's the one who keeps his feelings locked up tight. "I swear, if you ever pull that shit again, I'll hunt you down myself and drag you home, kicking and fucking screaming if I have to."

He has every right to say all of this to me. I did shut my family out when Samantha betrayed me. I did lose myself in drugs and booze for a while. And I did refuse all the help they offered. I was an asshole and there's nothing I regret more in my life than the way I treated them over the last fifteen months.

"I'm sorry," I say and I've never meant it more. "You're right. I shouldn't have shut you out."

He watches me for another few moments before settling back against his seat, satisfied with that part of our conversation. "So, Madeline. Her ex is a piece of work. And her manager is even worse. How is she?"

"She's holding up."

"But?"

I release a breath, angry now that I'm thinking about those assholes. "No but. She's stronger than I think she realizes."

He nods slowly, thinking. "Good. She's going to need that strength today. It's going to get nasty with her manager."

There's something in his tone. "What doesn't she know here?"

He picks his briefcase up and stands. "Let's go up to her. I think she should be the first to hear what I have to say."

Ten minutes later, after he meets Maddie and they chat for a bit, he turns serious and, after we all sit, says, "The contract you signed with Darren is a shitshow. And that's being generous. But my job is to get the best outcome for you here and that's what I'm going to do."

It's unlike Hayden to speak so plainly with anyone but his family and friends.

Maddie takes a deep breath and holds her composure. "Okay."

Hayden details the appallingly high percentage Madeline's lawyer allowed her to agree to when she signed the contract with Darren, as well as the termination clauses that aren't in her interest, including a hefty penalty for early termination. He then goes on to tell her all the ways Tucker and Darren have screwed her over with poor royalties for the songs she collaborated on with Tucker, in particular the sync royalties for a song of theirs that was used in a movie. Rather than the same royalty split, Tucker took seventy percent, and since the movie was one of the highest grossing movies of the last decade, the income she's missing out on is significant.

Maddie doesn't crumble in the way I think many people would when given bad news like this. Instead, she sits tall and says, "Right, so that's where we are. How do we get from here to where I want to be?"

Hayden looks at her with respect. "Good question. The answer relies on my determination of a few things first."

"What things?" Maddie asks like she expects this question to be easy to answer. The way Hayden takes a moment to reply, and the way he doesn't rush his words, tells me this isn't going to be the case. In fact, he appears quite hesitant about it all.

"You have a few options," he starts with. "This exercise could cost you millions if you just want to pay the penalty to terminate, or you could choose legal action to challenge the contract in court, which would likely be lengthy and expensive . . . or it could cost you a lot less. It just depends on how aggressively you want me to negotiate on your behalf."

Maddie appears confused. "Well, I guess I just assumed you'd be as aggressive as needed. Am I wrong?"

Fuck, I know where he's going with this and what it tells me is that he really does understand that I have strong feelings for Maddie. He wouldn't be about to offer what he is if he thought she was just casual sex to me.

"You're not wrong," Hayden says. "But there are varying levels of aggressive." He pauses before finally revealing his cards. "It's come to my attention that Darren and Tucker are heavily into illegal gambling. They've made a lot of money from it that they've funneled into offshore accounts. I imagine Darren would be amenable to terminating his contract with you if I were to mention this, and that we could negotiate a better contract with Tucker for your royalties."

Maddie stares at him, stunned. "You want to blackmail them?"

Hayden holds her stare without so much as a blink. I've watched many people underestimate my brother over the years simply because he's a nice guy. The thing is, underneath that niceness is a ruthless and calculating lawyer who doesn't hesitate to act when the situation calls for it. Most people think Gage is the Black brother not to be fucked with, but I know better. Hayden is the one not to be crossed. And when it comes to his family, and by extension, the people his family care about, he will do whatever it takes to help them when they're crossed.

He doesn't answer her question. All he says is, "It's your call, Madeline."

Hayden would never make this offer to a client, only to family, and I communicate my gratitude to him with a nod when he glances at me while Maddie thinks about what he's said.

"I need a minute," she says before leaving us to go into the bedroom.

When the door closes behind her and a second later she commences screaming, my lips pull up in a grin. And when Hayden looks at me with an arch of his brows, I shrug and say, "I guess she's got feelings about this."

A couple of minutes later, she yanks the bedroom door open, strides back out into the living room, and with fierceness that I've sensed in her from the day I met her, she says, "I want you to go in guns fucking blazing."

When she shifts her gaze from Hayden to me, still fierce, but also now a little *the fuck am I doing*, I nod my support for her choice.

Hayden's phone rings and after glancing at it, he says, "It's my assistant. I won't be a minute." With that, he leaves us to step outside and take the call.

As the door closes behind him, I close the distance between Maddie and me, and pull her in close. "You okay?"

She grips my shirt as she inhales a long, steadying breath. "Yes."

"But?"

"But I want to kill Tucker." Her eyes widen. "Like, for real. Fuck screaming, I'm ready to get a shotgun."

"Well, he is the dickiest dick of all dicks, after all. He probably deserves death."

Her eyes remain wide for a moment longer before her lips kick up slightly, and amusement creeps into those beautiful eyes I think I may never want to stop staring into. Her grip tightens on my shirt and I feel the tug as she tries to drag me closer even though that's impossible. "I like that you do that," she says softly.

"Do what?"

"You calm me down without telling me to calm down. But I know you'd listen to me if I needed to talk it out. And you'd be serious if I wanted that." Her smile is as soft as she is right now. "I don't know what magic you weave, but it works and I appreciate it."

My phone rings in my pocket and I ignore it because I don't want this moment to be broken.

After it stops ringing and starts again almost immediately, Maddie lets me go, pulls my phone from my pocket, and presses it to my chest. "Because I know you like to ignore your phone," she says at the arch of my brows. Then, pushing up onto her toes, she brushes her lips over mine. "Take the call. I'm going to finish getting ready."

I watch her as I put the phone to my ear. "What's up?" I checked caller ID, so I know it's Gage.

"I couldn't get through to Hayden. Can you let him know I'm running about ten minutes late?"

I frown. "Late for what? He's here in Nashville with me."

"I'm late for my meeting with Madeline's manager."

My brain connects the pieces of the puzzle. "Hayden got the gambling info from you . . . and you're the one who'll ensure the manager agrees to whatever Hayden wants from him." This makes sense. Hayden doesn't deal in dirty work like this. Not when his job demands he remains clean. *But Gage* . . . Gage is the keeper of secrets and is more than happy to get his hands dirty when needed.

"You didn't think Hayden would walk in there and extort them, did you?"

"Fuck." I release a breath, staggered that my brothers are doing this for me. Because that's what this is; Hayden may have taken Madeline on as a client, but he's going to these lengths for *me*. And Gage is right there by his side. *For me*. "Thank you."

"Yeah, well, you owe me. The next time you decide Europe's a better option than home, you'll be sending me a weekly check-in text."

"I'm getting the impression you guys missed me." I'm keeping shit light but I'm filled with massive regret for the second time today.

"I hope you're getting the impression we were worried about you."

"Loud and clear. I'm sorry, Gage. I fucked up."

"Yeah, little brother, you did."

The door to the suite opens and Hayden walks back in with a woman in tow.

"Hayden's here," I say to Gage as I take in the woman. Leigh, Madeline's assistant who I met the night she brought Maddie's belongings to my condo. She's tiny, barely five feet tall, and walks with a confident stride like she's here to handle business. Exactly how she walked into my condo that night. "Do you want to speak with him?"

"No, just pass on my message. I've gotta go. Shayla's blowing up my fucking phone."

We end the call and I let Hayden know about Gage's

delay before eyeing Leigh who has taken up residence on the sofa and is tapping and swiping all over her phone with a speed my fingers could never achieve.

She glances up. "Is Madeline ready?" She checks her phone. "We have to leave in ten minutes and I imagine you've slowed her down this morning."

I smirk. "Are you always this stern?"

"She is," Maddie says, joining us while fastening a watch around her wrist.

As I watch Madeline, I'm struck by her beauty all over again. She's wearing her hair up in a ponytail now with some strands falling around her face. And while I prefer less makeup on her, she's glowing with pink cheeks and lips while her big blue eyes are accentuated by the makeup.

"Pfft," Leigh says, drawing my attention back to the conversation. "Wait till you meet Judy."

"Who's Judy?" I ask.

"The sternest one on the team," Leigh says, not really answering my question. Then to Maddie, she says, "Tell me you're ready. We've got a lot to go over this morning and I want to cover it all before Tucker gets in your face."

I frown at Maddie. "You're seeing him today?"

She nods. "We're performing at a thing."

"Together? You're singing with him?" It can't be denied how tense I feel over just the thought of this. The last thing Madeline needs is to be anywhere near her ex.

"No. Not together."

"If I have anything to do with it," Leigh says with conviction, "they won't come into contact."

Hayden interrupts before I can throw out all kinds of demands of Leigh to make sure Tucker is kept away.

Demands that aren't my place to be making but that I want to be making. Looking at Maddie, Hayden says, "I'll be in touch."

"Thank you." Her gratitude for what he's doing is clear in her tone and all over her face.

After he leaves, Leigh eyes the time again before looking at Maddie and me. "You two have five minutes. I'll wait outside." Then, giving me what I think must be one of her signature bossy looks, she says, "If Madeline is late today, you will regret it."

"I like her," I say to Maddie once we're alone and I'm reaching for her, bringing her in close. "I like that she looks out for you."

When my hands find her ass, she wraps her arms around me and hits me with a sexy look that I know I'll still be feeling long after she's gone. "Are you going to make me late, Black?"

I grin down at her, enjoying the hell out of having my hands on her. "Can you tell me what Leigh's idea of making me regret that would be?"

"You wouldn't like it, but I'd be worth it, right?" She's still got sex in her eyes and she's still slaying me with that look.

I press her ass, pushing her into my erection. "Possibly."

"Seriously? Only possibly?" She's bantering and I'm finding it fucking hard not to throw her over my shoulder, take her into the bedroom, and forbid her from leaving this suite today.

I drop my gaze to her lips. "That depends on what filthy things you'd do with this mouth."

She brings one hand to my neck and pulls my face

down to hers so she can kiss me. It's a quick kiss and I'm nowhere near satisfied with it. "You should spend the day coming up with ideas for me and my mouth."

Fuck.

"Jesus. There goes all the work I'd planned on getting through today." I pull her face back to mine, and turning serious, I say, "My first idea for your mouth is a kiss that's longer than the one you just gave me. And if it makes you late, it'll be worth anything Leigh does to make me regret it." With that, I take what I want. A kiss that I give my soul to. A kiss that demands her soul too.

She's breathless by the time I'm finished with her. And a little overwhelmed, which at first, I assume is caused by the kiss, however, it turns out to be something else entirely. Holding me close, she says, "I'm sorry you got dragged into that video of me."

I'm confused as to why she's mentioning the video again. "I didn't get dragged into it, Miller. I was the cause of it."

"No, not that video. The one that went viral yesterday." She stops, her brows furrowing at my blank look. "You haven't seen it, have you?"

"I try to avoid social media unless I'm stalking you." When she doesn't smile at that, I realize we're dealing with something big for her. "What's in the video?"

She bites her bottom lip. "It's not good and I really hope you don't go looking for it now."

"I won't if that's what you want, but talk to me. Tell me why it's got you apologizing to me."

"It's not really a sex video but it may as well be." She grimaces and I get the impression that she hates having to tell me about this. "Tucker made the video last year. I was practically naked and he filmed me talking dirty to him. He's shared it from an anonymous account and the caption is written to make everyone think you made the video. I'm so sorry."

It's undeniable how much I hate thinking about her with Tucker. Hell, with any other man. What I hate more, though, is that she's dealing with this shit.

"You've got nothing to be sorry for," I say, making sure she's listening to every word. "This is the chaos, Miller. You hold your head high and you just keep going. And, baby, let them drag me into it. I don't care. I was made for chaos."

She grips my shirt tightly, fusing our bodies. "I really think you were," she breathes. "And if you keep calling me baby, you and Leigh are gonna have problems because I'm going to be late to everything."

"Fuck it," I growl. And then, without having the first fuck to give about her being late, I throw her over my shoulder.

22

MADELINE

"HOTTIE MCHOTTIE IS GOING to be a problem, isn't he?" Leigh says while we walk into the Nashville International Airport where I'm playing a set today as part of the airport's live music program.

I think about what Ethan did to me this morning after he carried me into the bedroom. By the Ethan Black standard, the sex was quick; by anyone else's, especially Leigh's, it was anything but quick. I have no doubt she will do her best to make him regret that decision, but I don't think he will. I certainly don't. Not even the fact that it caused me to miss my first interview of the day made me regret it.

I grin at her as my security team of four cages us in to keep the crowd that is forming away. "I kinda hope so. I'd like to live a life filled with Hottie-McHottie problems."

She rolls her eyes. "I think you like making my life difficult. Judy reamed me out over the missed interview this morning. Next time, I'm sending her your way. I thought I was all here for this new phase of our working life but now I wonder if I actually prefer the Madeline who always showed up on time and never made waves."

I know she's joking, and since I'm enjoying our new fun working relationship, I play along. "So, you think I should bow down for Tucker today? I could try. I'll smile like a good girl and ignore anything assholey that he says to me."

She lifts a brow. "Well, you always were so good at it. Let's see if you've still got it in you."

I laugh, not even the slightest bit offended because I know Leigh has my back all the way from here to wherever I take us. "I like this side of you. Keep it up."

"Keep what up? Saying offensive things to you?"

I shrug. "You're right. I was always good at letting people get away with this kind of shit. I've probably still got it in me."

Now, she laughs. And then she exhales a long breath before shooting me one of her stern looks. "Seriously, though, no more quickies when we've got a schedule to stick to."

God, I love her. More every day. "I promise, so long as you promise to make Ethan regret this morning. I'd have fun watching that."

"Ooh, I like this side of you. But how do you think I should do that? I mean, I know I said I would make him regret it, but I never imagined having to make good on my threat."

"Start talking to him in acronyms. Better still, I'll give you his number and you can text him all day long with acronyms and slang. He can't stand any of that and he hates his phone. That should do the trick."

She blinks at me. "Wow. If this is how you treat a guy

you're falling for, I'd hate to see what you do when you don't like a guy."

"Get ready, then. We may run into a guy I hate today. Should be fun, don't you think?"

"If you start screaming, I'm outta here."

I laugh, feeling the lightness of it through my body. "I'll keep that in mind."

We make our way toward Concourse C where I'll perform a thirty-minute set after Tucker finishes his. This has been booked for months and we were supposed to perform together. Darren sent me a terse email two days ago letting me know we'd each do thirty minutes. There's a twenty-minute break in between, which is due to start any minute, so we should miss Tucker with any luck.

However, as we draw closer, I hear him. He's not singing but rather talking with his audience. Laughing and being the charismatic performer his fans adore. And since I know him so well, and know how he operates, it doesn't sound like he's anywhere near close to finishing up.

When he comes into view, Leigh eyes me. "You okay?"

I nod right as Tucker spots me. God knows how. A crowd separates us, but still, his eyes are now glued to mine and I'm stuck in a moment I wished to avoid.

I've thought about this moment, the first time we'd see each other after the disaster of our non-wedding. I mean, we work in the same industry, there was never going to be a way for us to avoid each other forever. I just thought it would be a long way off and that I'd have had more time to move through the mindfuck of it all.

My hand goes to my stomach, trying to ease the nerves that have sprung to life.

Shit.

I'm so not ready for this.

I feel sick.

"Maddie," Leigh says, bringing me back to her. She's looking at me with compassion that is so appreciated. "We can leave. You don't have to do anything you don't want to."

I manage a grim smile. "Judy will ream you out again if we do that."

"Let her. I can take it."

I reach for her hand, needing the physical connection, and squeeze it. "I'm so grateful to have you by my side." Glancing back at Tucker who is still watching me intently, I remove my hand from my stomach, push my shoulders back, and say, "I'm not going anywhere. I deserve to be here."

"Damn right you do," Leigh says. "But you also deserve peace in your life. Whatever you choose, I've got you."

Tucker, the asshole, lets the crowd know I've arrived. He does it in such a way that it puts me on the spot, unable to do anything but what he wants me to. "Friends," he says to the hundreds of people hanging off his every word, "my time here has come to an end, but I've just spotted Madeline, and since I know you're all eager to see us together again, to know that we're okay regardless of our relationship ending, I'd love to invite her up here to sing one of our songs with me before I leave."

That fucker.

I paste a smile on my face as all eyes come to me and I do what I'm really fucking good at: I perform. But this time, I don't follow any rule set down by Tucker or Darren. I follow my own rules.

My security guys get me through the throng and then I'm face-to-face with my ex who is watching me with a smile that doesn't quite reach his eyes, his mask of public charm barely concealing the fury simmering beneath. Tucker is a highly strategic person, coldly calculating at times, and I see that in him now. He's already plotted his next move and I'm the prey caught in his sights with no escape route.

I don't think he got my memo though. The one I posted on Instagram in which I made it clear I'm no longer willing to play his games.

"Madeline," he greets me so smoothly, like he's not currently engaging in a campaign to have me canceled. "You're looking beautiful today."

The crowd is deathly silent. Probably holding their breath, waiting to see if this will all crash and burn.

"Thank you." I remove the spare microphone from the mic stand and look out at our audience. "Unfortunately, Tucker and I won't be singing together today. If you've ever gone through a break-up, which I imagine you all have, you'll know how hard the aftermath is. It wouldn't be fair to you if you had to sit through a love song from us when neither of us are feeling what we did when we sang it originally. I think it's best if Tucker finishes up his set, giving you what you love from him, and then I give you what you love from me." I smile genuinely as I add, "I'm really excited to have a new song for you today and can't wait to share it with you." I look at Tucker, ignoring the furious scowl in his eyes that's just for me but that I think anyone with a bullshit detector wouldn't miss, and say, with not one ounce of sweetness, "I'll let you finish up."

Without waiting for his response, I leave the makeshift stage and walk back to where Leigh's staring at me with admiration.

"I like that there was no screaming involved," she says, her lips twitching a little while she aims for a straight face. "Also"—she hands me my phone—"check your messages. The hot lawyer called and when I told him you were busy, he sent a text. He also said he'll try to catch you tonight after you're finished work for the day."

As Tucker's voice drones on in the background, I check my messages.

HAYDEN

Good news, Madeline. Darren has agreed to terminate your contract with no penalty, effective immediately. You're free to hire your new manager and I'm happy to handle that contract for you. Also, we spoke with Tucker earlier and he's agreed to a new contract to split your royalties equally. There will also be a lump sum payment for the royalties you should have been paid to date. I pushed him hard and got him to agree to more than he wanted to give, so I'd prepare for a clash the next time you see him. I'll call you tonight to go over the details as this isn't something I want to put in a text.

I stare at the message for longer than necessary, processing every word of it and every emotion it brings up for me. There's a sense of victory but mostly it feels right and fair. These men took advantage of me for too long, and I let them, but now I'm standing up for myself and that feels like the best damn thing in the world.

"Maddie," Leigh says, "Tucker's finished."

I glance up in time to catch his death stare as he walks away. Wow, yeah, he's *pissed*. I can feel his hatred all the way from here. And he's not even trying to hide it from his fans, which is unusual for him. That shows me the level of his emotion and it makes me suck in a breath.

This is the chaos, Miller.

Yes, yes it is, and while it has me feeling a bit bewildered, I'm running to it, not from it. Getting loud. Grabbing life by the horns.

A few minutes later, I'm standing in front of the same audience Tucker had. No, scratch that. Some guys walked away after he left, so it's not the same audience. But more have stopped by and everyone appears ready to hear from me.

Blasting a smile their way, I strum my guitar and lean into the mic. "Who's ready to hear something new?"

They cheer me on, whistling and yelling their excitement, and I then spend half an hour singing my heart out, not holding back any of myself.

Every second is exhilarating.

I'm wearing what I want.

I'm singing what I want.

I'm saying what I want.

By the time I sing my last song, everyone is singing with me. They're in this special moment with me. Heart and soul. And I know, without a shadow of a doubt, that I am exactly where I should be.

23

MADELINE

"HOLY FUCK, THAT WAS AMAZING!" Leigh is buzzing in a way I've never seen, her entire body filled with excited energy as we make our way out of the airport.

I'm glad to have four security guys guiding us because it's *hectic* in here. It's taken us probably ten times as long as it should have to get through the airport, but that's because I want to stop and talk with the people who enjoy my music and support me. This is important to me. I wouldn't get to do what I love if not for them.

I slide my sunglasses in place as we step outside into the sun. "It really was," I agree with Leigh. "That was my favorite concert to date."

She smiles. "I truly love that you just called half an hour singing in an airport a concert. I'm not sure there are many singers who would do that."

"Any time I get to sing for people is a concert to me. I will never take any opportunity for granted."

"And that is why I will continue putting up with your Hottie McHottie's shenanigans that get me into trouble with Judy. I never want to work for anyone who doesn't care about people the way you do."

God, I adore her and wish we hadn't taken so long getting to this place in our working relationship. "I never imagined you ever using the word 'shenanigans.'"

"Well, the definition of shenanigans is playful and reckless behavior not intended to cause harm, so it's not really the correct word in this scenario since it caused *me* harm. Possibly, high jinks would work better."

I do my best to keep a straight face. I'm actually not sure if she's being deadly serious or if she's fucking with me. "Have you memorized the dictionary? Like, do we know the definition of high jinks?"

I'm treated to one of her stern looks. "We do, but *your* high jinks discourage me from wanting to share it with you."

I can't keep my laughter in a second longer, and while Leigh tries to hold her stern look, she fails and is soon smiling and rolling her eyes at me.

She quickly gets back to business though, always the one to keep me focused when I get distracted. We wait at the curb outside the airport for our car and go over the interviews I have scheduled for this afternoon. My security team stand behind us while we talk. Leigh is in the middle of telling me that Judy isn't feeling well and may not be meeting us at the next interview as planned when I spy Tucker's yellow Mercedes Maybach driving our way.

When it pulls up at the curb and Tucker steps out, I armor up, recalling Hayden's advice. From the feral expression on my ex's face, I think my lawyer was right.

"Get in the car," he snarls. "We need to talk."

"It truly is lovely the way you boss me around, Tucker,

but those days have come to an end. I'm not getting in your car. If you want to talk, we can do that here."

He rips his sunglasses off and I'm hit with his ferocious glare. "You're a piece of work, Madeline, that's for damn sure. You flashed your tits and legs at me all those years ago, and here I am, being taken for a fucking ride by your lawyer after giving you the world." He stops talking, his glare intensifying, turning into something truly menacing before he continues. "You'd do well to rethink all of this because if we get as far as me signing that contract and giving you millions, you will wish you never met me."

"I already wish I never met you, Tucker."

He sneers. "You'd still be writing shitty songs in a trailer park if you'd never met me. And if you steal my money, that's exactly where I'll fucking send you. Back to the hovel I found you in."

"*Your* money?" The violence I felt when I told Darren to never call me sweetheart again the other day rages to life under my skin. "It's half mine, and if my songs were so shitty, you would never have put your name to them." I move closer to him at the same moment I sense Ethan's presence. I'm too far gone on this violent energy though to turn and see if I'm correct that he's now standing near me. Getting in Tucker's face, I allow the storm of anger consuming me to run wild. "You will sign that contract and you will give me *my* money that *you* stole from me. And go ahead and do your best to screw with my career, I'm not going anywhere."

When his nostrils flare and his hand flicks out to squeeze tightly, painfully, around my arm, Ethan's protective streak is unleashed and I realize I wasn't imagining him here. He's on Tucker in an instant, wrenching his hand away and shoving him back. He puts himself squarely between us and growls, "Don't ever put your fucking hands on her again."

Tucker turns his fury toward Ethan as a crowd mills around us. "Keep the fuck out of this. You might be sticking your dick in her but this shit is between Madeline and me."

Every muscle in Ethan's body locks and his voice drops to a low, dangerous rumble that vibrates along my skin when he says, "This *shit* is done, Brandt. There's nothing left between you and Madeline. If you have anything to say to her again, you'll do that through her lawyer. And you'd do well to never say anything like that about her again." He jerks his chin at Tucker. "Now, get out of my sight before I'm tempted to punch the fuck out of you."

Before I see it coming, Tucker takes a swing at Ethan. He's unsuccessful, though, because Ethan blocks the punch in time, stopping Tucker's fist from connecting with his jaw. Ethan slams both his hands to Tucker's chest and pushes him back again, hard enough this time that Tucker crashes into his car with a heavy thud. Ethan then closes the gap between the two of them and says something to Tucker that I can't hear.

When he steps away from him, he looks down at me, his expression furious but his eyes gentle for me, grips my hand firmly, and says, "We're going." His tone implies that no argument I make will dissuade him.

I don't have any reason to argue, and when I walk away from Tucker, I do that without so much as one final glance. Ethan's right: there's nothing left between Tucker and me. If I never see him again, I'll be a happy woman.

Ethan ushers me and Leigh into our waiting car that's parked behind Tucker's and climbs in after us.

"Wow." Leigh's the first to speak as the car starts moving. "Just wow." Her eyes are wide. "I knew Tucker could be an asshole, but I never knew he could be that much of one."

Ethan's watching me closely, his body still strained, his face still tense.

"He never spoke to me like that while we were together," I say to Leigh, but I'm also getting this out there because I don't want Ethan to think I would be so stupid as to stay with a man who treated me like that.

Leigh's phone sounds with a text, then another, and another. She pulls a face. "I imagine you're about to have another video go viral. And I think I want to withdraw my earlier statement about being okay with Hottie's high jinks."

When she shifts her attention to her phone, Ethan places his hand on my thigh and leans in to ask me quietly, "You okay, Miller?"

I look down at his hand. I like it there. I like it a lot. It makes me feel safe for some reason. Like he won't allow any harm to come to me.

Meeting his gaze, I nod. "Yeah. I'm holding my head high and keeping on going."

His eyes search mine for a beat, like he's making sure for himself that I really am okay. "Good."

With that, the tension eases from his shoulders, from his face, and his mood lightens a little. Not fully, though. I think Tucker really got to him and that it may take him some time to rid his system of that.

"Why are you here?" I cock my head. "And did you actually give up your grandpa ways and go on social media to find me?"

This earns me a smirk. And then his hand comes to the nape of my neck to hold me while he bends his mouth to mine for a very un-Ethan-like quick graze of our lips. "I checked out your Instagram. Found a little thing called Stories." Another smirk before another brush of his lips over mine. "I had a gut feeling about your ex running into you today."

His reason for coming is short and sweet but there are a thousand unsaid words sitting between us, along with a million butterflies.

"If we were alone," I say just loud enough for him to hear, "I would be on your lap right now."

His grip on my neck tightens. "I'll take a raincheck on that."

My gaze drops to his mouth and I think about all the things I want him to do with that mouth tonight.

"Miller," he growls softly, "Don't look at me like that."

I pull my bottom lip between my teeth and smile as I lift my eyes back to his. "Did I tell you I'm expecting a parcel to arrive today?"

"No." He keeps watching me, waiting for me to elaborate because he knows I'm going somewhere with this.

I turn into him and place a hand to his chest. "It'll be filled with panties I know you have a fetish for."

The lines that crinkle around his eyes are lines I'm beginning to live for. "Red ones?"

"I got you all the colors, Black. We can start with red."

"Fuck," he groans. "It's gonna be a long afternoon thinking about that."

I pat his chest. "You could distract yourself by learning the meaning of some acronyms. I'll have Leigh text you a list of the most commonly used ones. It'll help you keep up in life."

"Smart-ass." But this gets me his mouth again.

When he gives it to me for nowhere near long enough, *again*, I grumble, "What's with the quickies? I am not here for them."

He chuckles. "I kinda like this whiny version of you."

"Well?"

"Babe," he says and I *melt*, "you're working. I'm trying to respect that."

Leigh takes this moment to interject her thoughts. "You could have tried to respect that this morning."

I laugh and angle my body back to face the front of the car as Ethan looks around me at her.

"When should I expect to start regretting that?" he asks, his tone light and fun, making me think he's moved on from the Tucker encounter.

"Oh, Hottie, you have no idea," she says before glancing out the window and announcing, "Okay, you two, we're here. You've got five minutes." She looks at Ethan. "If you decide to get all handsy, or dicky, I won't hesitate to get back in the car with you and make things real awkward between the three of us."

"Dicky?" Ethan's amused. "Do you two sit around daily and come up with as many outlandish concepts as you can?"

I grin, knowing that he's referring to my talk of the FBI listening in on his phone calls, but Leigh just gives him her best scary look and says, "No sex, Hottie. Keep your dick to yourself."

Once we're alone, he pulls me onto his lap. "We need to introduce our assistants to each other. Troy is just as in my face with shit as Leigh is. They'll be fucking in no time and then I'll have your filthy mouth whenever I want without being ordered to stop." His hands are up under my T-shirt by the time he finishes talking and he's got them all over my breasts.

"Are you seriously groping me like a teenager right now, Black?" It's a good thing there's a screen between us and my driver.

"Fuck, yes." He bunches my shirt up so he can get his eyes on my boobs. "You try being me and see how long you can go without touching these tits."

"You went days without doing that when we met."

His eyes find mine as he slows everything down. "If we'd met under different circumstances, it wouldn't have been days."

I stare at him. There's so much to say but only minutes before I have to go. I press my body to his. "How long are you staying in Nashville?"

"I have to leave tomorrow. Callan's coming home from his honeymoon and I want to spend some time with him over the weekend before he gets busy again with work and life."

"I like that you told me why, but you didn't have to."

"I told you I'm in this with you, Maddie." He gently sweeps a strand of my hair away from my eyes. "For me, that means sharing things about my life like this with you. I don't know what you've had before with guys, but I'm into transparency. No secrets, no lies."

"No games," I say softly, threading my fingers up into his hair at the nape of his neck, loving every word coming out of his mouth.

He nods. "No fucking games."

I hold his gaze for a long moment before saying, "I want all of that too. And I also want a proper Ethan kiss. I'm not letting you go until you give me one."

"An Ethan kiss?" His lips quirk.

"You don't do anything fast when it comes to kissing or sex. I've decided this must be your trademark."

His eyes show how entertained he is by me. "Your mind is fucking fascinating with the shit you come up with."

"Jesus, Black." I grow impatient. "Are you gonna hurry up and kiss me before Leigh gets back in the car and starts—"

His mouth cuts me off and he finally, *finally*, gives me the kiss I want.

24

@THETEA_GASP

BESTIE, strap in for story time about our girl @madelinemontana. Remember when we said, "Tucker who?" because @ethanblack hit our radar? Well, it turns out we may now be backing the right man. @tuckerbrandt went full feral on Maddie today at the Nashville Airport, stunning the crowd when he grabbed her menacingly. We haven't found a video that shows what happened before he did this, but he clearly appeared to be threatening her. Giving the full ick. And then, our new king Ethan stepped into the fray, protector mode activated. Again. And he seriously ate that. He just brings main character energy with him. We're in a frenzy searching high and low for more, more, more of Ethan & Maddie. This relationship is a credit card slam for us. Take our money and let us binge-watch their life. It would be the hottest reality TV. We've noticed though that they aren't moots on Insta. What does that meeeeean? We need to know everything!

25

MADELINE

After a marathon night on Friday of sex and long conversations about some of the things we've done in life, Ethan leaves Nashville early Saturday. We exchange many texts over the weekend and he calls me both nights for more long conversations.

Monday morning rolls around and I wake at five a.m. to a string of texts from him.

> **ETHAN**
>
> Miller, I'm gonna need a photo today.

> **ETHAN**
>
> Scratch that. I need a video.

> **ETHAN**
>
> Fuck it, we need to Facetime sometime today. {Preferably when you've got enough time to say filthy stuff to me and show me your tits.}

If this isn't the second-best way to wake up, I don't

know what is. The first being waking up with Ethan's arms wrapped around me.

> ME
>
> Proud of you, Black. You're finally getting the hang of secret messages.

I snap a photo of myself before leaving my bed and send it to him. He told me last night how much he loves me without makeup. I'm taking that to mean he's into natural beauty, which my first-thing-in-the-morning look is, so I figure he may enjoy this photo.

I'm still on my way to the bathroom when his reply text comes through. The giddy feeling I always get at the sound of his text notifications is a feeling I hope to keep experiencing every time I receive one of his texts.

> ETHAN
>
> Fuck, you're beautiful.

One simple text and my knees go weak and butterflies take over my stomach.

> ME
>
> What are you doing?

It's six a.m. in New York, so I'm thinking he's maybe in his gym.

> ETHAN
>
> Staring at your photo.

Holy god, I don't think I can go on with this living in separate cities thing.

ME

Is it leg day?

He switches to a call, which, of course he does because he really kinda hates texting, and I love this.

"Just an FYI," I say with a grin he can't see, "I don't have time now to show you my tits and say filthy things to you."

"I have no doubt." His voice is deliciously gruff. "What time is Bossy McBossy due to arrive?"

I burst out laughing. "She will love that. She'll be here in an hour."

I hear his smile when he says, "You sound happy."

"I am. I woke to grumbly texts from you telling me you miss me without telling me you miss me. And now you're making up fun nicknames for my assistant. That's everything a girl needs to be happy."

"Grumbly is inaccurate."

"It really isn't." I lean against the bathroom vanity. "Are you happy today?"

The phone goes silent, and while I don't think we've lost our connection, the silence has me wondering. "Ethan? Are you still there?"

"Yeah. I was just thinking that I've never had a woman ask me that."

"Well, this woman is."

I hear another smile when he says, "I'm happy." And then some more grumbling that I am so here for, "But I'll be happier when you give me a time for when we can talk longer."

"Oh, I didn't realize there'd be talking on that call. I thought it was gonna be all about tits."

"Dirty talk, Miller. Keep up."

I could talk to him for the entire day and it still wouldn't be long enough. "You didn't tell me if it's leg day."

"It is. I've just finished in the gym."

"Are you still wearing your hot-quad shorts?" Thinking about those shorts and his quads makes me even happier.

"Yeah, and I could be convinced to send you a photo of them if you give me a time for our call tonight."

Oh my. My man really wants to spend time with me.

"I won't get home until around eight tonight. I'll call you then."

"Eat dinner first and take your bath. I'll be up late."

"I could call you from the bath."

"No, I'm gonna need to see all of you, spread out on your bed. Call me after your bath."

His desire for me is intoxicating and I'm all breathy when I say, "You're looking for a show?"

"Baby, I'm always looking for a show. But what I don't think you realize is that you smiling at me through the phone is a show to me."

I'm going to need so many stolen moments throughout today to revisit this conversation and the way he's making me feel. "Right," I gather myself, "what I'm taking from this is that I don't really need to show you my tits tonight or talk dirty to you. I just have to show up and smile at you."

"That's all you ever have to do, Maddie. The rest is a bonus."

This man.

He has no idea how good I'm going to make it for him tonight.

TUESDAY MORNING IS AN EARLIER START for me than Monday. Four thirty a.m. to be precise, and I hate that I agreed to wake up at such a hideous time for a work thing. Ethan's waiting text helps shift my grumpy mood.

> **ETHAN**
>
> I'm canceling my dinner plans tonight. I need another FaceTime.

I reply before taking a shower.

> **ME**
>
> You can't cancel. It's a charity gala and you're a guest of honor.

I take my shower, checking my phone pretty much as soon as I step out of it to see if he's replied. That's how much I crave him.

> **ETHAN**
>
> I fucking hate galas.

> **ME**
>
> I see you're grumbly again today.

> **ETHAN**
>
> I'm not looking at you, Miller. That makes me grumbly.

> **ME**
>
> I feel the same way. I'm not sure about long-distance relationships.

ETHAN

I'm sure about them. They shouldn't exist.

ME

I can try to rearrange my schedule. I may be able to free up a day early next week if that works for you. I'll come to you this time.

ETHAN

No, don't fuck with your schedule. I've just gotta get through this week of work here. The company is messing me around, wanting me to commit to more than I agreed to when I sold to them. I should be free by next Monday. Tuesday at the latest.

ME

It's not fair to you to be the only one to change your life for us.

ETHAN

I don't give a shit about fairness. You're flat out with work at the moment, so it makes sense for me to travel if I can.

ME

I really got lucky when I met you. Thank you for being so cool about my work.

ME

I'll miss you tonight.

Our FaceTime call lasted for two hours last night. There was no dirty talk or boobs involved. We talked about ourselves and our lives for the entire two hours.

ETHAN

> The gala planners will wish they never
> invited me by the time I'm finished there.

I GET to sleep in on Wednesday. Well, to six a.m. I also get a phone call from Ethan, which is what wakes me because my alarm was actually set for seven.

"You should know up front that I'm not a morning person, Black." I answer his call still half asleep and a tiny bit grumpy about being woken. But let's face it, I'd take a call from this man at any time of the day and be happy about it.

"We're long past the up-front stage of this relationship, Miller. I feel like I've been duped here."

I laugh and sit up in my bed. "You've known me a week. When exactly did the up-front stage end?"

"I've known you eleven days and anything before the first time you begged me to fuck you was the up-front period."

"Begged is an exaggeration."

"You're the unreliable narrator in this relationship, not me. Begged is entirely accurate."

I laugh again. "I am so not the unreliable narrator."

"You told me you're not a morning person, yet you've laughed twice already. I've also known you to wake ready to wrap that filthy mouth of yours around my cock. I'd say you're good in the morning and that your version of events cannot always be trusted."

I have never met a man who did banter so well. "Okay, so let me state the facts again. Before I met you, I was not a morning person. You make mornings fun." He makes everything fun.

"Fuck, I wish I was there with you."

"I do too. How was the gala?"

"It was long. I gave them some cash and bought my way out of there early."

"Oh my god, you did not!"

"I did. I would have given it to them earlier in the night so I could have made it home in time to call you before you fell asleep but Kristen talked my ear off and I couldn't leave."

Ethan's told me about his new sister-in-law and I know it's important to him to get to know her and build a relationship. I love that he chose to talk with her rather than leave the gala early to talk to me. I like that family is his priority. "Who knew you could be such a grumble-bum. I know you would have welcomed every minute of that conversation with her."

"A grumblebum? I see you and Leigh have been sitting around making up new words."

"It's an Aussie word. I picked it up when I was there on tour. It's pretty much perfect for you this week. You're being very cantankerous."

"Tell me we're FaceTiming tonight."

"I'll be finished with my bath by seven."

"Thank fuck. And Miller?"

"Yeah?"

"Put a pair of those granny undies on for me tonight."

∼

ME

I hate today.

ETHAN

It's 5am, Miller. How can you already hate today?

ME

Because I won't get to talk with you on the phone today.

ME

I also hate my publicist for making today such a long day.

ME

And I hate Leigh for conspiring against me with Judy to make today happen.

ETHAN

Anything else on that hate list?

ME

I hate running.

ME

I hate the gym.

ME

I hate my trainer.

ME

I hate that pizza is bad for me.

ME

And I hate that tomorrow is Friday.

ETHAN

What have you got against Fridays?

ME

Nothing.

ETHAN

Is this part of the conversation going to make sense anytime soon, baby?

ME

It should be Tuesday tomorrow. Next Tuesday to be exact.

ETHAN CAN'T GET HERE until then and it feels like a thousand years away.

ETHAN

I'll be on a plane tonight.

ME

No, don't do that. I won't get home until around midnight and then I have to be back up at four tomorrow morning. And you've got work tomorrow too.

ME

Shit, I have to go. Bossy McBossy has arrived xx

I DRAG MYSELF THROUGH THURSDAY. A breakfast, six interviews, a lunch, and a dinner later, I arrive back at my hotel at 11:45 p.m. I kick my heels off before the door of my suite even closes behind me, muttering, "I hate you," as I fling them far and wide. They killed my feet today; tomorrow, I plan to buy ten pairs of flat shoes. Once I've got the heels off, I yank my dress over my head and discard it while muttering, "I hate you too."

I'm halfway into the living room of my suite, wearing

only my panties and bra, when Ethan's deep voice startles me. "I don't know, Miller, I really fucking like that dress."

I jump, my hand going immediately to my heart as I look at him. "Jesus, Ethan. You just shaved years off my life." He's sprawled on the sofa watching me intently and *damn*, even in my exhausted state, I swoon at how sexy he is. "Why are you here?"

He gets up and comes my way, all swagger and hotness, and I wish I looked as good as he does at this time of night after a long-ass day. "You told me you needed me."

I frown. "I told you not to come."

He snakes his arm around my waist, his eyes still firmly on mine rather than my half-naked body, and pulls me to him. "Before that, you told me what you needed."

Still frowning, I grasp his shirt while leaning in close to inhale his scent. God, he feels good, smells good. "I'm pretty sure that before that, I just spent a whole lot of time complaining."

His eyes are *still* on mine. Intensely focused on me. "I read between the lines."

I stare up at him, blinking as my brain finally gets her shit together and figures out what he's saying. As she does this, my heart starts getting her shit together too, and I suddenly feel a whole lot breathless.

Ethan read between my lines.

I grip his shirt harder. "I know you weren't finishing work until seven tonight, so that means you must have gone straight to the airport, and I also know that you have to start work tomorrow at eight, which means you'll have to be up early for that flight." My heart is being so extra right now, racing so fast I'm sure she's skipping a lot of beats. "And I'm so exhausted that I will pass out the second I find my bed, so pretty much, we're gonna spend our time together asleep. This was a lot of effort for that." No one besides my mother has ever gone to this much effort for me.

He grazes his thumb along my jaw. "It really wasn't, and I'm not sure why I didn't think of it sooner."

My eyes go wide. "You say that like you would do it again."

His gaze has dropped to my lips. "I will." His eyes meet mine again as his hand slides into my hair. "I'll be back tomorrow night."

"Oh my god, Ethan, this is crazy talk."

"Why? I want to see you and I can make that happen."

"You can see me on your phone."

"I can't get my hands on you that way." He bends his mouth to my neck to press a kiss there before saying, "I like sleeping next to you, Miller. Let me."

I'm stunned that he would do this, but more than that, I'm happy he's here. Giddily, stupidly happy. And if I thought I'd already fallen for him, I had no idea I could fall further, but I have. I am so deep in this with him.

26

ETHAN

ON THE THURSDAY four weeks after meeting Madeline, I'm at my place while she's in Los Angeles to perform at a charity concert. I've spent the last three weeks going between New York and Nashville, often flying in for just the night because work has been keeping us both busy and we can't spare longer than the night.

We woke together today but she had to leave for California early and I had to come home to attend a photography exhibition. I had less than forty minutes with her this morning, and most of that time was spent talking to her while she showered and got ready for the day. Due to our commitments, we haven't been able to connect all day with a call or text; it's safe to say I don't recall much of the exhibition or of anything I did today because my mind has been on Maddie.

I've just walked in the door of my condo Thursday night when Callan texts.

CALLAN

You home?

ME

Yeah.

CALLAN

You got any beer?

ME

Yeah.

CALLAN

Put the game on. I'll be there soon.

He arrives ten minutes later. I've got the beer ready and the football on the television and we spend half an hour watching the game before I ask, "Where's Liv tonight?"

"She's at some yoga thing with Blair."

I look at him. "On a Thursday night?"

"Yeah."

"Since when did Liv stop watching the Thursday night game with you?"

"Since now."

Thursday night football used to be our thing before I fucked shit up between Callan and me. The three of us always watched the game together and sometimes we invited our brothers.

"She told me they'll be doing this every Thursday for four weeks," he says. "And that I should find someone to watch football with because she doesn't wanna hear me complain about her not being available."

I reach for my phone and send our group chat a message.

ME

Liv. This is some rough shit you're pulling on your husband just weeks after you married his ass. Ditching him for yoga every Thursday night.

She comes right back.

OLIVIA

I just fell off my yoga mat. Since when does Ethan Black engage in a group chat willingly?

ME

Are you actually at a yoga class? Surely they don't condone texting while yogaing.

GAGE

Yogaing? Is that a word now?

BRADFORD

It is when you've got a woman teaching you words.

OLIVIA

Spoken from experience, I imagine, Bradford.

CALLAN

Liv, get your ass over to Ethan's if you're not yogaing.

HAYDEN

It's clearly a word now.

GAGE

Are you two watching the game?

CALLAN

Yeah. You should come over if you're not busy.

OLIVIA

Liv is absolutely yogaing and now I'm confiscating her phone. I have no idea why she would even think it okay to text while down-dogging. If we get barred from this class, Callan, you better run the next time I see you. Not love, Blair.

CALLAN

Fuck, I just worked out why I'm a single guy again for four Thursdays. You're there for a dude, aren't you, Blair?

KRISTEN

OMG WHY WASN'T I INVITED FOR YOGAING?

A text comes in from Madeline and I can't get out of this group chat fast enough to check it.

MILLER

{My filthy mouth wants to do nasty things to you, Black. Let a girl up to your condo.}

I frown.

ME

You're here?

MILLER

Yes, this is not a test to see how you react to a spontaneous visit from your girlfriend.

ME

I'm hard now that you just called yourself
that and fuck me, my entire fucking
family is about to arrive.

MILLER

laughs I can't wait to see how you
handle that.

MILLER

Hurry up! It's been too many hours since
I've checked out that ass of yours.

Callan eyes me questioningly when I move off the
sofa.

"Madeline's here," I say, "So it's on you to entertain if
every fucker in our family shows up here." With that, I go
and let my girlfriend in.

She steps off the elevator into my condo and moves
straight into me, her arms coming around me, her body
pressing hard to mine, and her face angling up for my
mouth that's instantly on hers.

"Fuck," I growl after I kiss her for longer than I've ever
kissed her. "I needed that."

Her eyes are filled with heat. Her arms tighten around
me. "Me too."

I hold her face, running my thumb along her jaw.
"Why aren't you in LA singing songs?"

"Well, it seems I have an ex who really doesn't want
me to sing songs anymore. He had me removed from the
concert lineup."

"The fuck?" The fury I always feel over this dickhead
thunders to life. "I didn't think he was a part of this
concert."

"He isn't, but still, his reach is far and wide."

"Why don't you sound angry about this?"

"Oh, I'm angry. I screamed. I shouted at some people. I threw a tantrum that you'd be proud of. And then, after Leigh dragged me away from those people, I got on a plane and came to see you." She pulls my face down to hers. "I'm looking at you, Black, so that's why I'm smiling now."

"Callan's here. We're watching a game. I'd kick him out, but he's invited Gage over, and I'm pretty sure Liv will arrive at some point too."

"So, what you're saying is that there'll be no filthy mouth for you tonight."

"No, what I'm saying is that I'll have to wait for that filthy mouth."

Mischief flashes in her eyes. "I don't know . . . I may be too tired later."

"You could be asleep for all I care. I'm having that mouth and you'll wake up if you have to."

Her fingers dig into my neck as she grips me harder. "There is something seriously wrong with me. I liked that arrogant bossiness far too much."

I've never spoken to a woman the way I just spoke to Madeline, but hell if I could stop myself. I want her so damn much; in ways I've never wanted anyone. Mind, body, and soul. I want all of it from her and I've had to stop myself so many times from making demands of her. I'm unable to do that anymore, so it's a good thing she likes my bossiness because I suspect she's going to experience it a hell of a lot going forward.

I take hold of her hand. "Come watch the game." I stop as I realize I don't know if she likes football. "Do you like football?"

"I was raised on football. My dad was glued to the television for like half a year." She pauses before asking, "How much do you love it?"

The elevator opens as she says all this and Gage joins us. Looking at Madeline, he says, "You'll fight for his attention during football season."

That statement right there should tell her how addicted I am to her. The season started weeks ago and I've missed more games this year than I've watched.

The way she's looking at me says she fully grasps this and the way she grips my hand a little harder and gives me those soft eyes of hers says she likes it a lot.

I get her a beer when she asks for one and sit next to her on the sofa as Callan and Gage get into a conversation about our team with her. Maddie joins in easily as we alternate watching the game and talking about our week in between plays.

We move onto discussing Gage's current frustration with his ex-wife over the fact she's started violating their joint custody agreement, often changing plans at the last minute. Gage was supposed to have Luna this weekend but Shayla called him at four this afternoon and said she'd decided, just this morning, to take Luna to Florida to see her parents.

"She can't do that." Olivia's voice sounds from behind us as she walks into the room. "I hope you're documenting these violations."

"Yeah, Liv, I am," Gage says.

Olivia is one of the sharpest lawyers out there, and while she isn't officially Gage's counsel because family law isn't her specialty, she fiercely guards his interests, especially when it comes to navigating the minefield that is his relationship with Shayla.

Her best friend, Blair, comes in after her, and if someone asked me the definition of a shark lawyer, I'd tell them it's Blair. She's a high-powered attorney who is well known for the complex cases she handles with ease and a very aggressive approach.

She narrows her eyes at Gage. "You need a new attorney, Gage. I've told you that. Your guy is useless."

A look of *not this shit again* crosses Gage's face. He has little time for Blair, mostly, I think, because they're too similar. They butt heads every time they're in the same room because neither will back down on anything. "If I wanted your opinion, Blair, I'd ask for it," he says.

She shrugs. "Suit yourself, but if you were my client, she'd be killing herself to never violate your agreement."

"Yes," he grunts. "As you've mentioned before. And as *I've* mentioned before, I'm not looking to completely fucking alienate the mother of my child."

"Okay," Liv says, her attention focused on Gage, "Let's not get into this tonight. But please make sure you mention this to Brett." His lawyer.

Gage nods. "He's aware."

Callan reaches for his wife and pulls her onto his lap. "How was yoga?" He eyes Blair. "And did you achieve your goal?"

"I'm unsure why you're giving me grief over stealing Liv on a Thursday night," Blair says, gesturing at the game on the television. "It's not like she'd be getting any attention from you if she stayed home."

"Has she told you how many games I've watched this season?" he asks.

Now, she rolls her eyes. "We need to send you back to school so you can re-learn the definition of 'watch' because having the game on in the bedroom while you pretend to talk to her is in fact still watching the game. As is taking her on a date to a sports bar where a thousand screens have the game playing."

Callan grins. He loves Blair almost as much as his wife does, and he particularly enjoys her saltiness. "I let her do filthy things to me last Thursday night, no game in sight. Surely that counts for something."

Olivia's lips quirk and she shakes her head at him. "You are such a shit-stirrer."

I lean into Maddie as they all get into a conversation about how much time football season steals from couples. "We could sneak out now and no one would notice."

She angles her face my way as her hand comes to rest on my thigh, and I'm suddenly wondering why the fuck it wasn't already there. "I see why you and Callan are so close. You two are the wicked brothers, right?"

"I would say that's an incorrect conclusion. Gage is the wicked one."

"Okay, so when I said wicked, I didn't mean morally grey. I meant mischievous."

"I'll accept that." I smirk. "It beats the other words I've been called."

Now, she twists her entire body my way and shifts her hand further up my thigh. "What words have you been called?"

The conversation around us stops as everyone watches the game again. I ignore the television and stay right in this moment with Maddie. "It's not in my best interests to share that information with a woman I'm trying to impress."

Her eyes sparkle with enjoyment. "We're way past the up-front stage of this relationship, Black. Are you telling me I've been deceived?"

"You use such harsh words, Miller."

"Well?" She tilts her head, waiting, doing her damnedest to appear serious.

I reach a hand along her leg, up to her waist, and try like fuck not to slip it under the hem of her shirt but fail. My fingertips meet bare skin as I say, "Asshole is a firm favorite of some when it comes to me. Bastard comes in a close second. Jerk might have been mentioned a time or two."

"Give me their names," she breathes, leaning closer. So close that it's an effort for me to form thoughts of any use. "I'll set them all straight."

"Fuck," I growl, and then I'm standing and dragging her up with me and looking at the people in my media room who I wish to fuck were not here. "We're leaving. Do not come looking for us."

I catch Liv's grin on my way out. I also catch Madeline's hesitation, the way her hand doesn't feel quite sure of holding mine. It's this that causes my steps to falter as we exit the room.

After I turn and give her a questioning look, she pulls her hand from mine and says softly, "We can't just leave everyone. It's your home. They're here to see you."

"They're here to see the game."

She gives me a look and from that alone, I know I'm not going to win here. "Ethan."

"Fuck," I groan. "We're going back in there, aren't we?"

"Yeah, baby"—she puts her hand to my chest, no clue how affected I am by that 'baby'—"we're going back in there. But you know I live for this grumpiness of yours, so just know that once everyone leaves, you're in for a good time."

"Not helping," I mutter.

Her laughter leads the way back into the room and as I follow her to the sofa, my brothers both arch their brows knowingly at me.

Yeah, I'm so fucking gone on this woman.

27

MADELINE

"WE'RE NOT LEAVING this bed today," Ethan says on Saturday morning as he spoons me and cups my breast. His voice is so husky that I'm almost tempted to let him do whatever he wants to me and forget the work commitment he has today.

"Has dementia set in already, grandpa?" I roll to face him, loving the way he groans when I press the front of my body to his. "You're busy today."

"Smart-ass." He reaches for my ass before sliding his hand down the back of my leg and pulling it over his. Then, after not kissing me, even though I know he's desperate to but won't because he knows I'm not a fan of kissing before teeth brushing in the morning, he says, "I'll rephrase. I don't *want* to leave this bed today."

"I've got something to tell you that may make you happier."

"Nothing will make me happy about leaving this bed, Miller."

"How about if I told you I'm moving to New York?"

That slows his roll.

"What?" he finally says. "When? Why? Fuck, why am I only hearing about this now?"

"You're cute when you're in a tizzy."

His only response to that is to give me a look, and *holy heck*, this look makes my core want to seize control of all my decisions today.

Ethan has some feelings over me moving here and he doesn't want to wait a second longer to hear about it.

"I bought a condo yesterday. Hayden's pushing for it to close in a couple of weeks, but I'm going to fly home tomorrow, pack some things, and stay in a hotel until I can move in."

"What about your work? Aren't you better off based in Nashville?"

I snake an arm around him. "Okay, your first girl-friend lesson is this: when she tells you she's moving to the city where you live, which means you'll no longer have to drag your ass to her city every night, you should tell her this makes you very happy."

He's amused but mostly holding it in as he grips my leg possessively, bringing me in closer to him. "If we're handing out lessons here, babe, a woman should keep her man in the loop at all times. She should also know that when her man has a perfectly acceptable bed at his place, staying in a hotel isn't something that's gonna happen."

I bite my lip. I thought he might say this. "That feels very much like jumping fast." At his frown, I glance down at the tattoo on his chest and remind him, "You told me you don't want to jump so fucking fast anymore."

"Jumping fast would be moving you in. All I'm

suggesting is that you rest your head on a pillow in my place each night until you can do that in your own place."

I laugh. "You have a way with words, Black. *Rest my head on a pillow*." I give him a flirty look. "Does that mean that's all I'll be doing in your perfectly acceptable bed?"

"So long as you put those granny undies of yours on while you're in my bed, I don't care what else you do."

"That's because you know those undies always come off so easily. I'm onto you. You're a very strategic thinker."

"Are you going to tell me how this will affect your work? I'm more than happy that you're moving here, but if it's going to put you at a disadvantage in any way, that will cancel out my happiness."

I roll so that I'm on top of him, bringing our faces close. "Those women that called you those names never even knew you, Ethan." My tone is soft but my energy is intense because I'm deeply affected by the way he cares for me and wants nothing but the best for me. "If they did, they'd have used words like gentleman, one in a million, a good man, a *king*." I pause and all we do in this moment is watch each other, taking the other in, processing so many feelings. "Moving to New York will work well for my career. I've signed with the new label, and my new manager and I have found a songwriter and producer to work with here. Judy's pulling back on my PR commitments so I can get back to writing. Things are going to quieten down a bit now." I rest all my weight on him and grind a little, getting the exact reaction I'm looking for when he groans. "We'll have more time for you to practice your orgasm-delivering skills."

His hand is on my ass. His brows are arched. His eyes are so heated. "You're saying my skills are lacking?"

I grind some more. "I believe in personal growth, Black."

He squeezes my butt before smacking it. "Get this ass up, Miller, and into the bathroom. We're going to brush our teeth and then I'm going to practice my bossy skills and order you into doing some truly filthy shit. After that, I'll think about practicing other skills."

ETHAN'S WORK commitment today is a charity gala lunch that Kristen's foundation is hosting. He agreed to be the official photographer even though this isn't the kind of photographic work he usually does. After he has a call with Kristen to double check a few things, he tells me that I now have an invitation to attend. I absolutely want to go, especially since he told me that Kristen's foundation is focused on helping women rise, however, it's a black-tie event and with just over an hour until the lunch starts, I'm not sure I can pull it off. I don't have anything to wear. Ethan texts Kristen to ask if she has a dress, and within seconds she's texting me.

KRISTEN

Can I give your number to my sister?
She's a stylist and is sure to have
something for you.

ME

That would be great. Thank you!

KRISTEN

I'm excited you're coming but also disappointed that I won't have a lot of time to spare to chat with you. Promise me we'll get together another time when you're back in New York.

ME

Well, since I'm moving here, I hope we'll get to know each other.

KRISTEN

Bradford is so dead for not telling me this information.

ME

LOL. Ethan only just found out today. Spare Bradford's life.

KRISTEN

See you later xx

I eye Ethan who's looking hotter than ever as he fastens his cufflinks on his white dress shirt. That shirt isn't done up all the way and I, for one, hope he doesn't bother with those top few buttons. I like them exactly how they are.

"Don't look at me like that, Miller." He finishes with the cufflinks and snags his jacket from the bed. "I don't have even five minutes to spare for that filthy mouth of yours."

As my phone sounds with a text, he leans in for a kiss. "I'm sorry I can't wait for you." He needs to get to the hotel where the lunch is taking place so he can see what he's working with there.

I wave him off. "Go. Don't even think about me."

"You'll arrange security, right?" That concerned,

protective glint in his eyes always hits me low in my stomach.

"Yes. I've texted Leigh to ask her to handle it for me. She's on it. I won't step outside this condo without a big, strong man by my side."

"Good." With one last kiss that he seems very reluctant to walk away from, he's gone.

I check my texts.

UNKNOWN NUMBER

> Hi Madeline, I'm Jenna, Kristen's sister. She's sent me a brief of what you need for the lunch. I'm attaching some photos of dresses I have on hand. Let me know if any would work and I can have them to you in fifteen minutes. I can also have hair and makeup people to you in about twenty minutes if you need that. They work super fast, so you'd make the lunch in time because we both know these things never begin on time.

ME

> Wow. This is amazing. Thank you, Jenna!

I'm so impressed with her from just this one text. And when I check out the dress options, I decide I need her on my team if she's got any openings. She's sent through three options and I know instantly that they are all perfect for my shape. The one I love the most is a timeless and romantic navy gown with an asymmetric neckline, a built-in corset to snatch the waist, gathered detailing, and a slit up one thigh. The bias-cut silk cinches the figure and drapes beautifully.

ME

It has to be the navy gown. It's stunning.

JENNA

That would be my choice too. Would you like me to arrange hair and makeup also?

ME

Yes, please. Thank you. I appreciate all of this.

JENNA

I'm really happy to do it. I'll see you soon.

True to her word, Jenna arrives fifteen minutes later with the gown. Hair and makeup arrive shortly after, and then two security guys turn up. I walk into the lunch almost on time, catching Ethan's eye as I make my way to his family's table where only two seats remain empty. Mine and his.

Ethan's busy with Kristen but the way I distract him enough that she has to snap her fingers in his face to regain his attention helps me center myself and shift some of my nerves over seeing his parents today. I met them at Callan's wedding, but today, I'm spending time with them as Ethan's girlfriend and I would have rather done that with him by my side.

"Madeline," Gage welcomes me as I take the seat next to him.

I smile at Ethan's brother. "Gage. How are you?" I enjoyed his company last night. He's an interesting guy. Enigmatic with a darker edge than his brothers, from what I've picked up so far. Ethan told me that Gage was the one who found the illegal gambling information about Tucker and Darren for Hayden, so that's made me curious about him. Like, how did he find all of that info? Did he hire someone? Or did he search himself? And why would he do that for me? I would have asked Ethan these questions, but we got sidetracked and I forgot to return to the conversation.

Gage lacks the playful and fun side that Ethan and Callan have, and instead has a dry sense of humor that I like. And there's an intensity about him that's like a steady hum of *don't fuck with me and we'll be good*. I get the impression that Gage sees everything in this world. It's like he's always watching and waiting, and I wonder what made him that way.

"Better now that you're here," he answers my question.

I'm surprised at his response and before I can stop myself, I say, "That's totally not what I expected you to say."

"What were you expecting?" He's watching me intently like he's looking for clues about me.

"Honestly, I've no idea, but I wouldn't have thought that."

He lifts a glass of whiskey to his mouth and eyes me over the rim after swallowing some of the amber liquid. "These galas bore me to tears. You'll distract me from that boredom."

"So, you're using me."

"That sounds accurate."

I laugh because that statement reminds me so much of Ethan. "Is this a thing all the Black brothers do, or just you and Ethan?"

"What?"

"He's always saying things like 'that's highly inaccurate' and 'I would say that's an incorrect conclusion.' Did he learn this from you?"

Before Gage can answer, Hayden meets my gaze from the other side of his brother and says, "Any bad behavior of Ethan's and Callan's can be directly attributed to Gage."

My smile is big as I really settle into this conversation. "You're the one who taught Ethan to break as many rules as possible?" I say to Gage.

"Guilty as charged," he admits freely.

"What about his propensity for having no safeguards in life?"

"No, that's not on me."

"I would agree with that," Hayden says. "Gage has safeguards all over the place."

"Hmm, what about before you became a father?" I ask. "Were you more relaxed back then?"

"Relaxed isn't a word anyone has ever used to describe Gage," Hayden says.

"I've always made sure I'm protected and my family's protected," Gage says.

"Well," I say, "you need to get onto Ethan about putting a password on his phone. That man is out there playing fast and loose with his phone and it worries me to no end."

Gage's eyes flicker with an emotion I can't quite pick. It's like he's made some kind of decision and feels certain about something. After he sips some more of his drink, he says, "Has Ethan mentioned Luna's birthday party to you yet?"

I frown, confused at the change in conversation. "No, why? And why are we not still discussing how you're going to get a password onto your brother's phone. I'm being deadly serious about that."

"I know you are," he says, a new intensity blazing from him. "And I fucking like that. Not one woman Ethan has been with has ever worried about the fact he's out there playing fast and loose with shit in his life. And while they've sat around our family table and spent the entire time trying to get him the fuck out of there as fast as they could, you've spent one night with us so far and you dragged him back *in* to be with his family. My daughter is turning six in a couple of weeks and I'd like you to meet her because you're the kind of woman I want her to look up to. *And* because I suspect my brother intends on making you the only woman he ever brings to our family dinners again."

I'm lost for words. But not for feelings. I'm overwhelmed by those. And if I'm not mistaken, I think I may shed tears if I don't get a handle on these feelings, which isn't something I really want to do right now.

But goodness, I haven't experienced true family since my mother passed away, and now I've had it twice in twenty-four hours. And on top of that, it's one of Ethan's brothers who is saying things to me I didn't even realize I needed to hear.

Gathering myself, I say as steadily as I can, "That's the nicest thing someone has said about me for a long time. After the last few weeks of being judged as an immoral woman, it means a great deal for you to say I'm the kind of woman you want your daughter to look up to." My voice cracks with emotion as I add, "Thank you for saying it."

A darker mood moves into Gage's eyes. "I have no

idea how you endure it. I'd be out there silencing the fuck out of everyone, no matter what it took, like Ethan is."

I don't know what he means by that but before I get the chance to ask him, Bradford motions to Gage from across the table as he pushes his chair back and stands. Gage immediately stands, as does Hayden, and the three of them leave together, deep in conversation.

I'm watching them walk away when Ethan's mouth brushes against the shell of my ear and he murmurs, "You good, Miller?"

I almost jump out of my skin, not expecting him. Turning, I meet his beautiful eyes. They hold none of his usual playfulness. Instead, he appears serious and I can tell that this is him checking in on me. "I'm good. I've just fallen for your brother a little."

He takes Gage's seat. "Which one? I'll be sure to keep you two apart from now on."

I smile and lean in for a kiss while sliding my hand under his suit jacket and curving it over his abs. "Gage, and there is no chance of me ever forgetting that you're the Black brother who owns this filthy mouth of mine, so please don't keep him from me. I enjoy his company too much for that."

"Fuck," he curses softly. "I really like seeing you with my family."

My hand is still on his body and I'm unsure how I'll let him go. "You say that like it's something new for you." I'm recalling what Gage said about the women Ethan has brought home before.

"It is new for me," he confides. "Connecting my family with my girlfriends has always been difficult. For a number of reasons, the least of which was me and the emotional place I was in. With you, it feels easy."

Ethan's told me about his relationship with his parents, in particular his father, so I know that would have played a part in this. We haven't really talked about the women he's dated, so I have no knowledge of that, but Gage has me thinking that those women maybe didn't support Ethan the way he needed. And while Ethan's saying that connecting me with his family feels easy, I know that's not all on me because he's told me about the work he did on himself while he was away in Europe.

"I'm glad," I say. "And just so you know, being with your family feels easy for me too."

He rests his hand on my thigh. "I'm going to introduce you to my parents now. Are you ready for that?"

"Yes. Let's hope they can forget that the first time they met me I was running away from my wedding."

His eyes search mine. "You're worried about that?"

"Yes." I take a deep breath. "Our meet-cute really isn't the kind that I think any parent would imagine for their child. Your dad gave me some looks at Callan's wedding and I don't blame him. And before you go all protector over that on my behalf, I think it's a very reasonable response to seeing his son arrive at his other son's wedding with a woman wearing the wedding dress she put on for another man."

He takes that all in and is quiet for a moment while thinking about it. Then, he says, "What the fuck is a meet-cute? Did you and Leigh make that shit up?"

I pull my hand from his abs and pat his chest. "Contrary to what you think, Leigh and I do actual work all day. We're very busy women. I suggest you use those thumbs of yours and spend some time on Google, grandpa, so you can keep up with us."

His lips twitch. Then, he looks at his mom who's sitting three seats away from me and says, "Mom, I'd like you to meet Madeline. And if you know what a meet-cute is, you two are bound to become fast friends."

The warm smile his mother gives me can only be classified as the best thing that's happened to me today. "It's lovely to meet you, Madeline." Her smile grows and her eyes twinkle as she glances at her son and then back at me. "I do know what a meet-cute is and I hope my son is right that we will become fast friends."

I take back what I said about her warm smile being the best thing of today. What she just said has taken its place.

"I hope so too, Ingrid. And honestly"—I grin at her son—"how do these men survive in the world when they don't know things such as meet-cutes and acronyms and slang?"

Ingrid laughs. "That's why they need us, honey. To help them get through life."

"I absolutely agree," I say, enjoying her son's full attention as he gives me a fun shake of his head.

Then, he looks at his dad. When he speaks this time, he's more reserved. Far less relaxed than when he spoke to his mother. "Dad, Madeline."

Edmund's eyes have been glued to me since the moment Ethan introduced me to his mother. Not that I've been staring at him all that time, but much like Gage, his father has an intensity about him that can't help but be sensed. "It's good to meet you, Madeline." He's not as reserved as Ethan, but his tone and body language show he's holding himself back. Watching. Waiting. Just like Gage. And like I told Ethan, I don't blame him.

"You too, Edmund. Do you know what a meet-cute is?"

He blinks. Sits back a little. Appears surprised. He doesn't smile but there's a subtle easing of his expression. "I do not. I hope you'll enlighten me."

Ethan chuckles. "You and me both."

Ingrid leans into her husband as she waits for me to share this information with her husband and son. I'm struck by the way Edmund's body magnetizes to hers as she does this. Ethan has told me a lot about their marriage and I'm not sure I would have expected this display of affection.

"Okay, you two," I say, playfully stern, "listen closely. A meet-cute is a cute, charming, or amusing first encounter between two people that leads to a romantic relationship. Like the first encounter that Ethan and I had." I look at Edmund. "Has he told you about how we met?"

"He has not."

With a quick smile at Ethan, I launch into a story that's important for me to share with his dad because if I know anything about the way men interact, I don't think Edmund would ever get this full story from his son, and I want him to know all of it.

I begin with a quick explanation of why I was running from the hotel that day, so he can understand why I couldn't go through with my wedding. Then, I share how his son was the one person in the traffic that day who came to my rescue, and how he then cared for me.

"I know how it must have looked to you when Ethan

arrived at Callan's wedding with a runaway bride on his arm," I say to both his parents, "but I want you to know that my actions on the day we met were out of character. I'm not flighty and I never break commitments like I did then. However, right now, sitting here with your son, I'm so glad I broke that commitment and I can't be sorry about that."

Ingrid's the first to speak. "Thank you for sharing that with us, Madeline, and I want you to know there's no judgment here. Like I told Ethan recently, the only people who know what goes on in a relationship are the people in it. I can see how happy my son is with you and that's all that matters to me."

"Thank you." I think I'm going to really like Ethan's mom.

Edmund is still watching and waiting. I can see that in him, but I also see respect in his eyes. "I appreciate your candor," he says. And that's all he says, but then, I probably didn't expect more. I think he needs to watch and wait a while longer before he'll give me more.

Ethan gets back to work and his brothers return to the table. I spend a fun afternoon with the Black family and we all get to know each other a little more. Ingrid comes to sit with me for a bit and we talk about my parents, my childhood, and how I got started in my career. She's so different to what I imagined after learning about her from Ethan's perspective, but then, I know it to be true that no two people have the same point of view on anything because we all carry different baggage in life that frames how we see things.

As Ethan guides me out of the hotel after the lunch, I say, "Gage said something odd to me today."

He looks down at me. "Yeah?"

"He said that if he had to endure lies being posted about him on social media, he'd silence everyone like you are. What did he mean by that?"

Ethan stops walking, his gaze resting on me for the longest moment before he says, "He put me in touch with someone who digs into people's lives. Finds the shit they're trying to hide. We used that to get those assholes to take down those videos of us from Louisville. I also had Hayden hit them with lawsuits that'll go nowhere but scare them a little, and rightfully fucking so. And we've done it with some other videos too." At my wide eyes, he says with determination, "I won't sit back and watch this shit, Miller. I get it that this is just how the world works now, and I'm not going after every video or story that's posted about you, but fuck, everyone's entitled to quiet enjoyment of their lives. If people get in your face while you're off the clock and post nasty shit about that, you better believe I'll go after it."

I grip his jacket with both hands and pull him close. "You are absolutely the best man I know." I'm so overwhelmed that he has done this for me that I can't even figure out exactly what I want to say. All I come up with is, "I'm so glad I found myself a grandpa who refuses to just accept the way of the world now."

His hand slides around my body to my ass. "At some point in this relationship, you're gonna have to stop calling me grandpa. It's fucking creepy when you think about it."

"It's entirely accurate, Black. I mean, you still haven't figured out what that text of mine from yesterday meant."

"Babe, give a man a break. I'm over here trying to

wrap my head around secret message brackets, talking in capital letters, and asterisking words all over the damn place. Then you start talking about flag situations and it's like my fucking mind explodes. Beige flags, red flags, green flags . . . How a guy's supposed to make sense of any of this shit is beyond me."

"This conversation is fast becoming a beige flag situation, just FYI."

"Great to know, and if I ever figure that flag shit out, that statement will make so much more sense to me."

I let his jacket go. "Are you going to be a grumblebum all night or are you going to do something useful with that mouth of yours?"

He takes hold of my hand, very firmly. "I'm going to do something useful with my hands, and hopefully I'll be able to wait until we get home to do that." He runs his eyes over my body. "This dress has been fucking with my dick all afternoon."

"You say the sweetest things to me, Black." It can't be denied, though; I *really* like his crude way of saying some things.

"I told you up-front that I wasn't the guy for you if you wanted flowery."

"Ah, no," I say as I try to keep up with his long, fast strides out of the hotel, "you told me that *after* you fucked me, which was after the up-front stage apparently."

He gives me a look and we then proceed to banter our way to his condo at which point, he tells me to spread my legs because we're spending the rest of the day working on his orgasm-delivering skills.

Screw flowery; I'm all about Blackery now.

28

MADELINE

LIFE MOVES at a much slower pace after I pack some of my belongings and move them to New York. After weeks of hectic back-to-back interviews and appearances to help build my new brand that Judy and I are creating, that all eases. Tucker is out there being a dick and I think a lot of people are starting to see him in a new light, which means the negative publicity I was enduring has decreased. And Judy was right: people find other scandals to get invested in and they move on, forgetting the one they were just fixated on.

Once I'm in New York, I divide my time between songwriting, doing some PR, and spending time with Ethan, learning so much more about him and enjoying the kind of domestic life I've never had with a man. We do everyday couple things like taking in a movie, having date nights, enjoying lazy reading afternoons together, cooking together, and laughing a lot. Ethan snaps a million photos of me and I start writing songs that have pieces of him in them.

I also spend Tuesday nights having dinner with the Black family and it's becoming a favorite part of my week.

Two weeks after I make the move, I wake on a Tuesday morning to Ethan cursing as he checks the time. "Fuck, I'm gonna be late for my shoot." He throws the bed covers off and strides into the bathroom.

Ethan has gone back to doing what he loves for work: photography. He's still consulting for the company he sold his app to, but after spending a lot of time with them initially, he now only has to work a few days a month with them. Last week, he opened his books for portrait photography for the first time in years and people are excited he's back.

By the time I wander into the bathroom, he's in the shower. I brush my teeth and then step into the shower, moving behind him and wrapping my arms around his body.

"Miller," he growls, "I haven't got time."

I kiss his back, keeping my arms around him but letting one hand glide down his body toward his cock. "You have got time."

He grasps my hand and stops it moving any lower. "Baby, I can't afford to be late." He turns in my embrace, looking down at me with both lust and frustration. "You need to get out of the shower."

"Wow. I never imagined the day you'd boss me into leaving you alone."

He groans and I see just how much he wishes he could say, "fuck it all" and push me back against the tiled wall.

"You absolutely have time," I say and when he opens his mouth to argue, I silence him with a finger to his lips.

"I don't know what time you think your shoot is, but if you fuck me fast, you definitely have time."

"Babe, my shoot is at nine. I don't even have time for a five-minute fuck."

"Without touching the idea of a five-minute fuck, which, you should make note of, I never want, your shoot is at ten."

He looks truly frustrated with me now and it's the first time he's ever clenched his jaw with me. "Maddie, I think I know my own schedule."

"Okay, Black, here's your next girlfriend lesson: women know their man's schedule better than their man does. We memorize that shit like it's our own schedule. There's this little thing you can do where you share your digital calendar with someone else, which I've done with yours. Every night, I note what you've got on the next day, so I know that your shoot does not start until ten today."

He's stopped clenching his jaw and is eyeing me questioningly. "How the fuck do you share a calendar with someone?"

"Well, I mean, it's hard to do if they have a password on their phone, but since you refuse to have any kind of security on your device and are more than happy for me to access it, I sent it to myself." I pat his chest. "And look at this, you get two girlfriend lessons in one morning. Put a damn password on your phone."

Before I can take another breath, he's got me up against the tiled wall and his mouth on mine, and he's kissing me with everything in him.

Our hands are everywhere.

Desperate.

Possessive.

Claiming.

Ethan brands me with his touch, and when he tears his mouth from mine, the searing hunger in his eyes continues to mark me as his. "Your smart mouth will get you in trouble one day, Miller."

I dig my fingers into his skin. "Promise?"

Without answering me, he roughly grabs my hips and spins me to face the wall. His breath is hot on the back of my neck when he rasps, "I'm gonna do my best to make this longer than five minutes, but here's *your* lesson for today: you wanna speak to me like that, you're gonna get fucked fast and hard."

It's like my pussy has never met a man before with the way she reacts to that. At this point, I don't care if he only fucks me for *one* minute, I just need him inside me. *Now*.

With my cheek pressed hard against the tiles, I moan. I couldn't even stop myself from doing that if I wanted to.

"*Fuck*." It's practically a grunt that falls from his lips after my moan fills the bathroom. He reaches one hand down to my clit while his other one comes to my breast, and not in a gentle, loving way. His touch is as crude as his mouth is at times. "Do you have any idea what you do to me?" He kisses my neck, biting and sucking me in such a way that he may as well just stamp his name there, all the while rubbing my clit and continuing to be indecent with my breast.

I rock my hips and grind my pussy against his hand, which causes him to make obscenely masculine sounds as he bites me and presses his dick against my ass.

I vaguely think about reaching for his cock but the pleasure he's delivering has my brain so scattered that I think I may have forgotten how to move my arm in order to do that. My body has completely taken over and I'm moving to the beat of Ethan, unable to focus on anything but that beat.

By the time he takes hold of my hips and thrusts inside me, I'm so high on pleasure that it seems impossible to feel a greater high. I should know better, though, because there is nothing in this world that feels better than having Ethan deep inside me.

He fucks me like he can't get what he wants fast enough.

I'm not sure we've had sex this intense. This wild. This *reckless*.

It's like Ethan's lost his mind and is just taking, taking, *taking*.

And it may be the greatest sex of my life.

I want him to take everything from me that he wants.

Ravage me, wreck me, ruin me.

He can have it all.

His thrusts speed up and his breathing turns ragged.

"Fuck, Maddie," he grunts as the sounds of our skin slapping together fills the bathroom. "*Fuck.*" His fingers dig into my skin painfully and *oh so* rudely, and my cheek gets forced harder against the wall.

In amongst all of that, I make so many filthy noises that are almost pornographic.

By the time we come, I'm a hot panting mess, desperate for release. Ethan leans into me afterward, resting against my back while he catches his breath.

"You should clench your jaw at me more often," I say.

"What?" He kisses the nape of my neck, staying right where he is.

"You fuck me real good after you clench your jaw all angry like."

I can't see him, but by the way his body gently shakes, I think he's shaking his head at me and silently laughing. Which kinda was my goal with the words I chose to string together for him.

He pulls out and turns me to face him, and yep, his eyes have that amused look in them. "I wasn't angry."

"Well, you were definitely frustrated with me. And you did clench your jaw."

He swoops in and steals a rough kiss as his hand settles on my stomach. "And you had a smart mouth." He traces his finger over my lips. "What time today do our calendars get in sync?"

My body arches into his. "Twelve thirty."

"Can you edit my calendar from your phone?"

"Yes."

"Add lunch in at twelve thirty. Pick a place. Let me know."

I pull his mouth to mine again, taking the kiss I need before letting him go.

"And babe?" he says.

"Yeah?"

His hand on my stomach presses against it a little harder, a lot more possessively. "I'm never adding a password to my phone."

ETHAN ARRIVES five minutes late for lunch, brushing a kiss across my lips before taking the seat across from me, pulling his sunglasses off, and saying, "I'm sorry I'm late. I just got off a call about a conference I've been invited to. It took longer than I predicted."

I rest my elbows on the table and lean forward as I swoon over so many things about this moment. The absolute domesticity of it. Having lunch with my partner on a weekday. Him arriving wearing quad-hugging jeans, a casual black T-shirt, and the kind of facial scruff I die for. The middle-of-the-day kiss that couples sneak when they have the chance. Being able to catch up during the day and share things that we now won't have to wait until the end of the day to share.

"What conference?" I ask.

He grabs the menu. "It's an international conference for photography and theory. I've always thought it a bit pretentious, but the team behind it changed a few years ago and it's become a prestigious event to the point where receiving an invite is a huge thing now. I haven't been able to accept their invites, though, because work kept me too busy." He pauses while perusing the menu. "What are you gonna eat?"

Ethan likes to share food. I learned this after the up-front stage of things with us. He's always eyeing my plate, reaching across to steal food, and happily sharing his. I've never done this with anyone, so it took me a hot minute to get used to it, but now I'm well-versed and know what to expect.

I tell him what I've decided on and then say, "Are you going to accept the invitation?"

He nods as the waitress comes to us. He then rattles off our order, stopping to ask what I want to drink. Once we're alone again, he says, "Yeah. They want me to run a workshop too, so I said yes to that. The timing is great now that I've decided to go back to photography and am looking to rebuild my profile."

He shares more about the workshop and I see the fire in him. Ethan loves the craft of photography as much as I love the craft of singing. And while I think it's taken him a lot of introspection and soul searching to get to the place where he is, ready to go back to doing what he loves the most, he's all in now.

"When's the conference?" I ask, sipping some water.

"The same week you'll be in London for your PR week there. And since the conference is also in London, I figured we could stay a few days afterward and play tourist." His eyes crinkle with a playful smile. "Unless you've got shit on your calendar I don't know about because I don't have access to it."

I motion at him. "Give me your phone and I'll put my calendar on it. And yeah, I have some free time then."

I'm in the middle of adding my calendar to his phone when a text notification arrives. The sender's name is Melanie and I swear I stop breathing for a second. My fingers still as I read the lines of the text that I can see.

> MELANIE
>
> Miss you, Ethan. When can we hook up again? I'm in New York in a couple of weeks. We should grab a drink and . . .

"Miller," Ethan says. "What's wrong?"

I tell myself not to jump to any conclusions, not to suspect the worse. I mean, this is *Ethan*. The guy who lets me into his phone whenever I want; the guy who got on a plane almost every night to come see me; the guy who protects me at all costs; the guy who values transparency and hates playing games.

But, holy hell, the baggage I'm carrying over Tucker that I didn't even realize I was carrying has my mind racing down some crazy paths.

"Babe," Ethan says again. "What is it?"

I slide his phone across the table and meet his gaze. "You just received a text from Melanie." I hate that I watch him so closely right now, looking for any little sign that Melanie is more than a friend to him.

"Okay." He gives me nothing. Either he has no tells or she really is only a friend.

I really, really, *really* don't want to ask him who she is. Jealousy isn't something I've ever had a problem with, but here I am, my entire body blazing with that emotion.

Shit.

Ethan narrows his eyes at me. "Maddie, what's going on?"

I inhale a breath.

Transparency.

No secrets.

No lies.

No fucking games.

Those were the things Ethan told me are important to him, and they are to me too. Asking him a simple question is my right as his girlfriend. And fuck Tucker for making me think it wasn't a right I had.

"Who's Melanie?"

Ethan's a smart, intuitive man, and he quickly connects the dots. "She's a friend I've known for about five years. No benefits. We met through Callan who worked with her for a while. She's been living in Hong

Kong for two years. I imagine her text is either telling me she's coming back to the States and wants to catch up, or that she's finally divorcing her dickhead husband."

"Fuck," I breathe, my legs feeling wobbly even though I'm not standing. "I'm sorry for asking that."

His eyes remain fixed to mine. "You have nothing to apologize for. That was a reasonable question to ask a guy you've been dating for seven weeks. And I'm glad you asked it because not asking that kind of stuff is what leads to games and bullshit."

"I know you're right. I think I just have some work to do after Tucker, you know?"

His eyes are so intense right now. "I've dated five women and slept with two others. I told you I hate one-night stands and I meant it. Sex is meaningless to me without the connection." He leans forward. "This"—he motions a finger back and forth between us—"is what turns me on. Sitting here telling you about a conference I feel privileged to be invited to while we discuss what we want to eat together for lunch. Knowing I'll see you at my parents' place tonight where at least one of my brothers is sure to piss me off while you make that bearable. Knowing I'll get to sleep next to you tonight. I fucking love sex, but *this* is what I love more. And Miller?"

"Yeah?" I manage to croak out, all up in my feels over what he just said.

"I hadn't had sex for fifteen months before you. I was trying not to fuck you that first time because I wanted to wait for you to be ready for me. And I would have waited because this connection we have is something I've *never* had with anyone."

If I could crawl across the table and curl up on his lap,

I would. I'd sit there and try to untangle all my thoughts and all my feelings, and I'd tell him every single one. I'd maybe even tell him I love him. Because I do. This man has practically removed my heart from my body and taken ownership of it.

Since I can't crawl across this table, and since I don't know that either of us are ready for the "L" word yet, I say, "Thank you for telling me all of that." I'm interrupted by the waitress bringing us our meals. Once she's finished delivering them, I find his eyes again. "I've never had a connection like ours either."

"I have nothing to hide from you, Maddie."

I reach for his hand, needing his touch. "I know this. I just had a moment."

He watches me for another few moments before appearing settled over this. Then, eyeing my plate, he leans across to steal some of my chicken. "Tell me about your morning. Did you finish that song you were working on?"

Ethan's right: *this* is what turns me on too. Having a man's heart in this way.

29

MADELINE

A Black family party is rowdy. Having five brothers in the one place ensures this, I guess, but still, it's loud and they're rambunctious. It doesn't help that there are twenty six-year-olds in attendance too.

It's Luna's birthday today, and all family members have taken the mid-week afternoon off work for the party, which I think says a lot about the Blacks.

"Thoughts and feelings?" Olivia asks, coming to stand next to me while I watch Gage and Callan try to wrangle the six-year-olds into some kind of order that will allow them to take part in karaoke. Ethan's photographing all the fun. Bradford's in charge of the food with Kristen. Hayden's busy taking care of one of the little boys who scraped his knee. Ingrid and Edmund are finishing the set-up for the karaoke. And Shayla, Luna's mother, is currently on her phone. Her fiancé is nowhere in sight.

I glance at Olivia. "I have way too many to narrow them down."

She laughs. "Give me the first that comes to mind."

"Are all the Black parties this boisterous?"

"Honestly, this is nothing. Wait till there are no kids around." Her brows arch. "That's when it gets really boisterous."

"Wow. I can't even imagine it."

"Surely you had some wild parties down there in Nashville."

"I never really had anything to do with them. And now that I know my ex was cheating on me the entire time, I know why I never got invited."

Olivia blinks. "He didn't invite you? At all?"

"No. I attended official work things, but not his private parties with his boys. And I didn't care because that kind of party isn't my thing." I gaze out at the Blacks doing their thing. "This is more my style. Family get-togethers." I look at her again. "My family was tiny, though, so this noise is all new to me."

"You'll get used to it."

That thought feels good. Getting used to it means I'll have come to many of these get-togethers, and that's something I'm hoping for.

A few minutes later, karaoke begins and two hours pass in a blur of kids singing, adults laughing, and hearts connecting.

Luna is the sweetest little girl who captures my attention easily. The way she has her father and all her uncles wrapped around her little finger is lovely to watch. These are the guys I've watched tease each other, dish out hard truths to each other, bicker and disagree over all kinds of things, get annoyed with each other, and at times had to walk away to blow off steam. *Now*? They're like saints, loving on this little girl like she's the most precious thing in their world. They're also doting on her best friend, Sarah, because they know how special she is to Luna.

As the party gets closer to ending, Ethan finds his way to me. "I feel like I just did a triathlon. I'm fucking exhausted."

"It was a lot. Imagine having to do that every year for your kid." My eyes go wide. "Imagine having to do that for *five* boys like your mom did. Wow. Did you guys have a party like this for each birthday?"

"Yeah." He turns quiet, thinking, probably remembering. "It *was* a lot, wasn't it? A lot of work for parents to do."

During the last month while I've been living in New York, Ethan has started spending more time with his mom. He's told me they're finally having the sort of conversations he's wanted with her his entire life. There are also the weekly Tuesday night dinners with the entire family; Monday Night Football, which is fast becoming a tradition in Ethan's home; Thursday nights with Callan watching the game while I go to yoga with Olivia and Blair; and the occasional Sunday spent with the family for football and food. His father comes to as many of the football gatherings as he can swing.

One of my favorite things about these get-togethers is watching Ethan slowly find his way with his family, especially his father. I know they haven't talked yet about what went down between them before Ethan left for Europe, but all these pockets of time spent together will hopefully lead to that conversation as they add shared-hour upon shared-hour to their relationship.

It's funny how the stories we believe about our parents and our childhood can change and morph into stories that aren't quite accurate. Or that are accurate but have their origins in a bigger picture we don't know about. Like the story Ethan has always believed about his mother not loving him as much as she loved his brothers.

"Do you know," he says slowly, turning into me so that we're in our own little bubble amongst the hum of the party, "when I turned twelve, Mom and Dad let me invite about twenty friends camping and fishing for an entire weekend. I'd forgotten about this."

"Holy fuck, how? How did they manage that many boys on a weekend away all by themselves? It sounds like hell to me."

He chuckles. "No, Dad asked some of the other fathers to come too. They had help, but shit ... that's a lot compared to this party. Fuck, I can't believe I'd forgotten about that weekend. It was one of the best weekends of my childhood."

I give him the space to reminisce, the moment only broken by Luna who races over to us and grabs her uncle's hand, begging, "Uncle Ethan! Sarah and me want to do karaoke with you."

He's immediately crouching to get down to her level. "Yeah? What song will we sing?"

Her eyes light up. "We want "Shake It Off" this time."

"*This* time?" he asks and I have to contain my laughter.

"Yes, silly." She yanks his hand, pulling him up out of his crouch. "Her mom's running late, so we can sing *all* the songs until then! And you *have* to twerk. And you're in charge of the rap. We've got pom poms for you!"

By the time Luna and Sarah get Ethan up onto the makeshift stage Gage built for the karaoke part of the party, I've almost got tears running down my cheeks thinking about him twerking that gorgeous ass of his all over the place and performing a rap with pom poms.

Luna, looking super cute in the unicorn tutu her father got her, hands her uncle a mic and bosses him and Sarah to stand in a line with her. As she motions at her grandfather to start the music, Ethan winks at me and grins. He then proceeds to thoroughly entertain me, and everyone else. This man has no fucks to give when it comes to putting himself out there. He sings his heart out, twerks his ass off, and raps like a pro while shaking his pom poms. He doesn't care that by the time the song's finished, he's got a captive audience of parents who've arrived to collect their kids. All he cares about is making this birthday and this party the best it can be for his niece.

Luna convinces him to sing two more songs, and during those, Sarah's mother arrives to collect her. My attention is pulled from Ethan for two reasons. Firstly, Sarah's mother is drop-dead beautiful. With her long brunette hair, high cheekbones, flawless porcelain skin, and toned figure, this woman must stop traffic. Like, literally.

Interestingly, she's unlike every other woman I've seen come to pick up their child. There are no designer clothes here, no Botox or filler, no cool detachment. There's a mother dressed in jeans and a simple white T-shirt, her long wavy hair a little messy like she quickly brushed it this morning and called that enough, long bangs that look like she maybe missed her last hair appointment, and lipstick that's barely still there. And instead of cool distance, she greets Ingrid with a warm smile and waves at her daughter to let her know she's arrived.

The second reason my attention stays with Sarah's mom? I catch Gage's reaction when he sees her and then I see *her* reaction when he walks over to her. He's talking with Bradford close to where she enters from and I swear he checks out of the conversation. Bradford's still talking but Gage's eyes are firmly on Sarah's mother. When he goes to her, she's suddenly all cool detachment. She doesn't ignore him. I mean, their daughters are best friends, so that would be impossible. But she certainly seems immune to the Black effect. Gage has the kind of charisma and sexy looks that I've witnessed in action while Ethan and I have been out with him. He's the kind of man who only has to walk into a room and his presence alone has women fighting over him. Sarah's mom? She looks like she wishes he'd go away.

She doesn't have to stay long. Sarah finishes singing a few minutes after her arrival and they leave soon after that. And Gage? He stares at her until she's in his elevator and on her way downstairs.

"Have you met Sarah's mom?" I ask Ethan when he joins me after he's finished with the karaoke.

He's got his camera with him again and is fiddling with it while I ask him this. Glancing up at me, he says, "Amelia? Yeah. Why?"

"What's the story with her and Gage?"

His brows pull together. "Huh? What story?"

"Seriously, do men miss everything?"

He finishes with his camera and gives me his full attention. "You're gonna have to elaborate, Miller."

"Have you ever known Gage to stare at a woman?"

"No." He frowns again. "Why?"

"Okay, so Amelia came in and was all sunshine-y and warm. She's a Heather. Gage's eyeballs are glued to her from the second he sees her. When he approaches her, she's no longer a Heather and treats him like he's one big red flag. I seriously hope you can give me the scoop on their story."

"Right, so if I knew what the fuck you just said, I could maybe help you out, but since I'm confused as to whether or not there are one or two women in this story, and about how a human can be a flag, you're gonna have to hit up someone else in the family for this scoop."

I grin because how can I not. Then, I pull his face down to mine so I can have his lips for a few seconds.

After I let him go, he looks confused by everything that's just occurred and mutters, "One of these days, women will make sense to me, but I don't think that's going to be this day."

I move into him and rest a hand on his hip. "Don't ever change, Black. You're too much fun exactly how you are. Now, I do have another question for you."

"Jesus, is it one I'll understand?"

"How the heck did I end up with the only Black brother who can't sing?"

Amusement fills his eyes and then I've got a possessive, demanding hand around my waist, pulling me tightly against him. His mouth comes to my ear and his voice is so fucking hot when he growls, "Did I, or did I not, tell you that your smart mouth would get you into trouble one day?"

I grip his shirt, my core feeling every word he just uttered. "Will that day be today?" I'm leaving to catch a flight to London soon but we could be quick. God knows Gage has enough floors in this condo that we could find a private spot far away from everyone.

He looks at me, his eyes heated. "Since you've got places to be, and since my niece has begged for another photo shoot, it won't be today." His voice still holds sexy gravel. "But next week when I see you will be another story."

My phone sounds with a text, interrupting us. I try to ignore it, but when two more come in straight away, I know I can't. I've got a team working in the background, ensuring my week in London goes off without a hitch. I can't ignore them.

"Shit," I murmur.

"Yeah," Ethan agrees roughly. I know he's feeling my impending five-day absence as much as I am. "Okay"— he lifts his chin at me—"go handle your business, Miller, and I'll go handle a six-year-old."

"Kiss me first."

His eyes crinkle and then I've got his hand in my hair and he's giving me what I want.

I turn back to him as I walk away and say, "One last question, baby. Do you even know what the word 'hella' means? You rapped it so good while shaking your pom poms with the girls, but is hella actually in the Ethan-Black dictionary?"

He holds his grin on the inside but I see it. "You should be hella concerned about your ass being so red next week that you won't be able to sit on it."

I stand rooted to the spot for way longer than I should, and we both just watch each other. Communicating so much without saying a word. When I finally turn from him and go in search of a quiet spot to check my texts, I already miss him.

The messages are all from Leigh who has also moved to New York. She packed herself up and moved here last week, and she's flying to London with me today while the rest of my team will meet us there. I lock myself in one of Gage's bathrooms and read her texts.

LEIGH

We need to delay this entire trip.

LEIGH

I just got my period.

LEIGH

I hate flying with my period.

This girl never fails to make me smile.

ME

Me too. I'll leave now and go home and collect my period kit for you.

LEIGH

I have a period kit I'm packing.

ME

Right, but what's in it because mine might have more things.

LEIGH

Pads in all various absorbencies, tampons in the same, period underwear, wipes, pain relief, heating pad, essential oils, big granny undies like the pair I gave you, dark chocolate, herbal tea, a face mask, foot mask, hand sanitizer, stain remover wipes, small trash bags, five romance novels to choose from, a deck of positive affirmations, a "Do Not Disturb - Uterus on Fire" sign for the restrooms that I am not afraid to use, fuzzy socks that say "Don't Talk To Me", my inflatable uterus punching bag, and my copy of "How To Be A Functional Adult When Your Uterus Is Trying To Escape."

ME

Wow. Will all that even fit in your suitcase?

LEIGH

Yes. Do you have anything not on my list? I feel like I don't have everything I could.

I actually laugh out loud while reading her last text. Leigh is always the take-charge one of us. The one who is scared by nothing. Except periods, it seems.

ME

I think you're covered, babe.

LEIGH

WHY MUST WOMEN HAVE TO TAKE PERIODS FOR THE TEAM?

LEIGH

I hate my period app for letting me down
this month. I wasn't supposed to start
bleeding my lifeblood away today.

At her mention of the period app, a thought teases my
mind. I can't quite catch it, but there's something there.

ME

Is your period clockwork?

LEIGH

No. Maybe I need a better period app. Is
yours clockwork? I'm always jealous of
women who have regular periods.

Yes, my period is regular as heck.

Always.

Holy. Fuck.

I catch that thread of a thought floating around in my
mind and quickly find my period app on my phone. I'm
not sure I've ever tapped my phone faster for anything.

My heart starts beating so fast and hard I swear I can
hear it in my ears.

Fuck.

I'm late.

Two weeks if the app is to be believed.

I collapse onto the toilet seat lid.

This can't be happening.

No, no, no.

I tap out a fast text to Leigh.

ME

Do you know the reliability rates of these
period apps?

My brain races, trying to figure out when exactly I had my last period. The problem is that the past nine weeks have been a whirlwind and my memory is hazy.

ME

> Like, your app fucked up, right? Mine could have too.

LEIGH

OMG

LEIGH

You're late, aren't you?

LEIGH

I knew I should never have left you alone with Hottie McHottie. I bet that man has super sperm.

ME

> I swear I never missed a pill.

LEIGH

How late?

ME

> 2 weeks.

LEIGH

Shit.

LEIGH

Do NOT go and buy a pregnancy test. I'll do it for you. God knows you don't want that shared on social media.

It's at this point that I realize it's not my career that I'm even thinking about right now. It's Ethan. Being pregnant at the nine-week mark in a relationship must surely be categorized as jumping too fast.

Oh, god.

I feel sick.

Everything was going so well for us. *Everything.* And now it's going to be all fucked up.

He's a guy who doesn't want to jump too fucking fast anymore and I'm a girl who won't ever abort another baby.

My stomach cramps, I feel dizzy, and I quickly stand and vomit into the sink.

This *cannot* be happening.

"ETHAN."

I turn at my father's voice on my way to the terrace where Luna's waiting, not so patiently, for me to take more photos of her. "Yeah?"

"Can you give me a minute?" He gestures toward Gage's library.

I grimace. Not because I don't want to give him the time, but because my niece is waiting and I'm aware that Gage doesn't want her to stay up too late tonight, so every second I delay pushes her bedtime.

At the face I pull, Dad says, "Please, son. This is important."

It's his tone that causes me to agree because I hear warmth and vulnerability I've never heard from him. "Okay."

When we're alone, he indicates for me to sit with him, his expression earnest, leaving me wondering what we're about to discuss.

"Ethan," he starts, "I love you, son." I wait for the but

that always follows those words, however it never comes. Instead, Dad continues. "And this is a conversation that should have happened a very long time ago. That, I am sorry for. You'll never know just how sorry." He swallows hard and I'm stunned. My father is feeling emotional, which is something I have never seen.

His shoulders hunch a little, the complete opposite to his usual straight back, and he glances down at his hands briefly before meeting my gaze again. His words are measured when he speaks. "Being a father is the hardest thing I've ever done in life, and my mistakes are a testament to that. I failed often and, at times, I failed terribly. I also had my share of failures when it came to my marriage. The thing I didn't understand for a very long time was that being a husband and being a father aren't always separate things. You're aware of how my marriage to your mother came about, so I won't go over that, but I entered our relationship thinking that being a father had nothing to do with being a husband. I was very wrong.

Cheating on your mother not only hurt her, it hurt you boys. The difference was that she knew why she was hurting, but you did not. You had a mother hurting deeply during your formative years, unable to bond with you because of that hurt. And you had a father who couldn't express his emotions or connect on an emotional level. I didn't give you what you needed as a child, Ethan, which I have deep regret over. I didn't understand just how profoundly my actions would affect my entire family."

He stops talking when his voice wavers and I sit in shock while I wait for him to continue. It's jarring to experience Dad's strict and emotionally guarded demeanor give way to vulnerability. It's also unexpected and disorienting.

"I made your teenage and early adult years harder than they needed to be, son. I watched you get lost in high school, drinking and taking drugs. I watched you make friends with boys who concerned me and girls who distracted you. Your school attendance dropped. Your grades dropped. And you were never happy from what I could work out. I didn't understand why, because your brothers didn't struggle in the same ways, and I thought that because you were all raised under the same roof, you should all have the same experience. I was harder on you than the others because I was scared. I didn't know how to help you, and I just kept pushing, hoping you would do what I told you to and that together we could make everything right.

Son, I'm sorry it's taken me until now to grasp that I was wrong. I'm sorry that when I found you that day, in your condo, high and paranoid after taking those drugs, clearly hurting and needing help, that I didn't do everything in my power to help you. That I didn't stop trying to fix you by force and that I didn't see what you really needed from me. I won't ever treat you that way again. I want you to know that, but more than anything, Ethan, I want you to know I love you and I'm proud of you. What you've achieved in your life is beyond anything I could have ever hoped for, and I know you may find that hard to believe from me, but it's the truth. You were right when you said it's wrong of a parent to expect their child's happiness and life to look a certain way. I had it mixed up and I tried to force my ideas onto you, and I won't do that again."

I'm frozen, staring at this man I don't recognize, listening to him say words to me I don't think he's uttered to anyone in his lifetime. Dad being so raw and open in this way has shattered the familiar landscape of our relationship, and where I've always had go-to defenses at the ready for him, I now have nothing.

I knew something was shifting between us. He's spent more time with me over the past month than he's spent with me in years. He's initiated conversations, albeit stilted ones at time, but still, he's made an effort to talk, to find out what I've been doing with my time, and to find out about my relationship with Madeline. But *this*? I never saw this coming.

Blowing out a long breath, I say, "This is a lot to process, Dad."

He nods. "Yes. And I imagine that will take you a while. I don't expect anything tonight, Ethan. In fact, if it takes you the rest of your life to process this, I understand. I wanted you to know my feelings. And I want you to know I will always be here, ready with whatever you need, son. I also want to say that I was very wrong to judge Madeline that first night I met her at Callan's wedding. She's an amazing young woman and I have great respect for her. Mostly, though, I like seeing how happy she's making you."

Dad has always been the epitome of stoicism. He was an impenetrable figure to me. And I have always been the opposite. This is why we always clashed. Now, seeing him admit mistakes and flaws, experiencing regret, and talking about his emotions, is stirring hope that I gave up on long ago. I also feel empathy for him, something I've always easily felt for anyone but my father. And for some reason, feeling this for him helps ease some long-carried tension from my body, which is a mindfuck all on its own.

"Growing up with you as a father *was* hard, Dad. That's no secret for any of us. But I always desperately wanted your approval." Fuck, talking about this shit with him is way harder than fighting about it. I grip the back of my neck and rub my hand over it. "I always felt like the son you and Mom never wanted. She ignored me. You punished me for not measuring up. And then you presented all us boys to the world as your pride and joy. It was confusing and painful, and every day chipped away another tiny piece of me." I exhale a breath. "I never knew how or where I fitted. That's why I went in search of things to make me feel better. I know, sure as fuck, it's why I kept ending up in dysfunctional relationships with women who were wrong for me but who looked all kinds of right to begin with. And the app I made with Bradford? Sure, I enjoyed building it, but running an actual company? That was never going to be for me.

I did that for your approval, not that I knew that at the time, but it's true. Honestly, you finding me that day, wiped out on all that coke, was the best thing that could have happened. It forced me into action. Europe changed me, Dad. I put the work in. I learned about myself, figured my shit out. Coming home and meeting Madeline has been lifechanging too. She's good for me. She actually gives a fuck about me, which isn't something I've ever had in a relationship before. I don't need your approval anymore, and that may be hard to hear, but I don't. I have my own approval. But I do want your love"—my throat clogs with so many fucking feelings—"so it means a lot to me to have had this conversation with you."

Dad has tears in his eyes and I'm not convinced I won't soon too. He places his hand on my arm and it's such a foreign thing for us that we both look away for a beat. I think his hand hovers after that, but he doesn't pull it away and that fucking speaks volumes. "I'm honored to be your father, Ethan. I hope we can find our way to a place where talking is easy between us and where spending time together is the most natural thing to do. I'm committing to you now that I will put the work in to make this happen."

I swallow down my rising emotions. I'll let them come later, but for now, I need to get through this conversation. "Maddie and I were talking about birthday parties today . . . about how much work they are for parents. I've never stopped to think about what it must be like to be a father. To really think about every little thing fathers have to do. I know none of us are perfect, Dad, and I know they sure as shit don't hand out parenting manuals." I smile and it might be the first time I've given him one of those since I was a kid. "Mom asked me to think about how you were as a father rather than as a husband, because your cheating hasn't been something I've been able to forget. I've been thinking about what she said and I will keep thinking about it."

Dad stands and I quickly follow suit. I think we both know we're at our limit for this kind of conversation. He puts his hand on my shoulder. I think he wants to hug me, but he hesitates and so do I. That might really be pushing it for us today.

In the end, he nods in the way he does, and then we go our separate ways. I'm heading for Luna on the terrace so I can get these photos taken, my mind all over the place and my emotions heightened in a way they've never been, when I run into Maddie.

She appears to be in a daze as we collide and I grab her biceps to steady her. "Miller." I frown as she looks up at me with a range of emotions plastered to her face that look equal parts nervous, worried, and queasy. "What's wrong?"

"We need to talk." The words breathe out of her anxiously, triggering my protective streak.

"What about?" Fuck, if her ex has done something else to her, I will lose my shit.

She shakes her head. "No, not here. Somewhere more private."

I guide her into the library where I've just come from and once we're away from everyone else, I ask, "What is it? Has Tucker done something else?"

Staring at me like she's maybe changed her mind about this conversation, she puts her hand to her stomach. "Shit." Then, she bends at the waist, still with her hand on her stomach, and releases a long breath.

I'm concerned she's about to pass out, so I take hold of her and try to get her to sit. She doesn't want that, though, and pushes my hands away. That's the moment I realize that whatever this is, it's fucking bad. Maddie has never pushed my hands away like that.

"Okay," I say, my chest filling with dread, "Please tell me whatever it is, Maddie, and then we can deal with it together. You're worrying me."

Her big blue eyes bore into mine and I take note of how her breathing has sped up. She doesn't say anything for what feels like fucking hours but is less than a minute. When she finally speaks, her words rush out of her. "I think I'm pregnant, Ethan, and I swear I took all my pills. And I know this is jumping too fucking fast and that you don't do that anymore, so this is probably going to ruin everything between us, but"—her entire face twists with fear—"I really hope it doesn't."

It's not often I'm lost for words and I hate that this is the moment when my brain fails me. I've got a head full of thoughts over the conversation I just had with my father about being a parent, about how hard it is, and now . . . *I might be a father.* And I am so fucking unprepared for that. If Dad fucked shit up, why would I think I wouldn't? I never want to fail a child . . . and I don't know the first thing about how to not do that.

When the only thing that comes out of my mouth is, "Fuck," I want to kick my damn self. That is not what Maddie needs to hear right now. *It's not what she needs from me.*

Her eyes go wide and all she does is stare at me.

Fuck.

I'm fucking this up.

I grip the back of my neck. "You took a test?"

She blinks. "No. Not yet."

Her phone sounds with a text, which she ignores.

"Okay," I say, blowing out a relieved breath, "so maybe you're not."

The library door opens and Luna comes in, jumping in front of me. "Found you!" She appears happy with herself. "Come on, Uncle Ethan. You promised more photos!"

I glance between Luna and Maddie who looks like she's going to be sick. Then, quickly moving to my niece, I crouch down and take her hands in mine. "Can you give me five minutes, sweetheart? Maddie really needs my help with something. I promise I'll be out once I've helped her." I tap her nose. "I'll see if I can convince your dad to let you stay up later, okay?" Gage will kill me for this, but Maddie's my top priority.

Luna's face lights all the way up and she starts bouncing on the spot, clapping her hands. "Yes! Yes! Yes! This is the best birthday ever!" She runs out of the library and I shut the door again before going back to Madeline.

"Let's not rush into assuming anything," I say. "Let's get a test and make sure before we go any further."

Another text comes in for her and she gets cranky with her phone, roughly swiping and tapping to read the texts. Then, she says, "Shit!"

"What?"

"My car's outside. I have to go."

Fuck, that's right. She's flying out tonight.

"I'll come with you. We'll get a test on the way."

Maddie glances at the door. "No, you have to stay and take the photos you promised Luna."

My brain does mental acrobatics, trying to figure out in half a second flat how to do two things at once, how to be in two places at the same time. It feels like I'm screaming down a highway at 200 mph with a bend in the road coming up and no brakes to save myself.

"I'll—"

I'm cut off by Luna who has opened the door again. "Uncle Ethan!"

Maddie's phone rings at the same time and I think my brain might fucking explode.

I'm frozen for the second time in an hour, unable to work my way through my crowded thoughts.

Maddie's eyes are on mine and then they're not. She's putting her phone to her ear and she's walking away from me to take the call.

I have no idea how to be a father.

"Uncle Ethan!"

Maddie finishes her call and looks at me from across the room. "I have to go."

Why is she standing all the way over there?

"I'm coming with you."

Luna's face falls. It crumbles so fast it kills me. "You promised photos," she cries.

I don't know anything about being a father. Not a fucking thing.

"Ethan," Maddie says, already halfway out the door, "I'll call you when I land."

"Wait," I say, but she's already out of the room. I scrub a hand down my face. "*Fuck.*"

I glance between the door and Luna who's sobbing on the floor. And then I make a decision that I fear may haunt me for the rest of my life.

I bend down and scoop my niece up into my arms. "It's okay, baby. We're going to take photos and then we're having ice cream."

31

MADELINE

LEIGH and I arrive in London at around 8 a.m. London time and we're both wrecked. Not from the flight so much as from hormones and emotions. She spent the flight coping with period pain and the emotional abuse of periods. I spent it panicking that my relationship may be over.

I've spent seven hours replaying my conversation with Ethan in my head, dissecting every word, every inflection of his voice, every micro-expression. Over and over. *And over.*

The first thing he said was, "Fuck." I don't know what the standard is of what to expect from a man when you tell him you're pregnant, but I've now told two men at different times that I was pregnant and they both pretty much responded the same way. Tucker said a few more choice words than Ethan, but the general gist was the same.

This doesn't give me confidence that this time around is going better than my first time. Ethan is *Ethan*, though, so that gives me some confidence. But then, he didn't say much except he wanted us to get a test. And while I agree that a test is important, I was looking for so much more reassurance than what he gave me. Which was none. He said nothing to make me believe we would be okay, that our relationship would survive. In fact, I think I felt worse after speaking to him than before.

I brought up the *jumping too fast* thing and he didn't respond to that either.

I'm thinking about all of this after Leigh and I exit the private jet we flew here on, and when I get to the *jumping too fast* thing, it all feels too much and so I throw my head back and scream.

We're crossing the tarmac to the car waiting for us and Leigh jumps in fright when I scream. Then, she turns and practically yells in my face, "You can't do that without telling me you're going to do it! Especially not when my lifeblood is draining from me." Then, she throws her head back and screams too.

She's right in my face.

Screaming like a banshee.

With her lifeblood draining from her.

And suddenly, all I can do is laugh.

God bless the driver of our car. He stands at the back door of the car waiting for us with a perfectly straight face. He shows not one sign of recognition that we're screaming and laughing like we've been possessed.

Well, I mean, I think *I've* been possessed.

By a baby.

And then, at that thought, the air whooshes out of me and I have to grab Leigh to steady myself because I think I might fall otherwise.

I'm going to be a mother.

"Maddie," Leigh says with concern. "Are you okay? What's happening? Talk to me."

At that, tears leak from my eyes and within seconds, they're streaming down my cheeks and I'm blubbering, "You sound like Ethan. He says stuff like that."

Leigh's eyes are wide. "I don't think we need a pregnancy test. Not when you've just gone from zero to one hundred, screaming, laughing, and then crying, all in the space of like, two minutes." She nods like she's just solved the greatest mystery of the world. "Yup, I think you are most definitely a raging, hormonal, pregnant woman."

"Okay," I agree. "We don't need a test."

She blinks like I just said the dumbest thing she's ever heard. "Of course, you need a test."

"You just said I don't and I agree with you."

"Why would you listen to anything that a woman who is currently taking one for the team says?"

"Taking one for what team?" I frown.

"Oh my god, keep up. Remember in our texts, I said that?"

I commence crying again and at Leigh's furrowed brows, I say in between sobs, "Ethan can never understand my texts."

Leigh takes a deep, deep breath and looks to the heavens before looking back at me. "It's going to be a long nine months, isn't it?"

I'm still sobbing. "You have to be nice to me."

She throws her head back like she's going to scream again, but instead she yells out, "I can't be nice when I'm running on half my lifeblood!"

It's at this point that my phone sounds with text notifications and I don't think I've ever checked my texts faster.

> ETHAN
>
> Maddie, I fucked up. I'm sorry. Please call me.

That one came in while I was still in New York, sitting on the plane waiting for it to take off. I'd switched my phone off, though. That was after I ignored Ethan's phone call.

I don't feel good about ignoring his call, but I had nothing inside me to give to a conversation, so I decided it would be best to turn my phone off and wait until after the flight when I'd had time to think. Well, it's after the flight now and I still don't know what to say to him.

I read the texts he sent after that one.

> ETHAN
>
> Okay, so you're on the flight now and waiting to talk with you is excruciatingly painful.

> ETHAN
>
> I wish I could have a do-over of that conversation, Miller. You caught me at a bad time and my head was all fucked up over stuff Dad said to me. I know that I let you down in a moment when you really needed me. Please call me when you land in London. I'll stay up and wait for your call.

I read his last two texts a few times, trying to figure out whether I think he's going to end our relationship or not. It's one thing to apologize and admit he let me down, but nowhere in his messages has he said anything about his feelings over a pregnancy. Over a baby.

Ethan is such a good man, so I know he won't avoid his responsibilities toward a child, and that's what I think he's saying in those texts. He would never want to let me down, but that doesn't mean he would want to *jump fucking fast* with me.

"Is that Ethan?" Leigh asks.

I nod but I don't drag my attention from my phone.

"What did he say?"

I show her his messages. "What do you think he means?"

She reads the three messages before looking at me like I have ten heads. "What do you mean? It's pretty obvious what he's saying."

I snatch the phone back and re-read the texts. "No, it's not."

The look she gives me can only be described as woman-draining-all-her-life-blood-cranky. "What do you *think* it means?"

"That he wants to tell me he won't walk away from his responsibility."

She gapes. "That is so *not* what I took from those texts. Maddie, come on, stop letting your brain mess with you. Call him. Everything's going to be okay."

The idea of calling Ethan fills me with panic. "I'm tired, Leigh. It's like three a.m. our time. I'll text and let him know I'll call after we've both had some sleep."

I tap out a text quickly before I can overthink this.

> We've just landed. I'm exhausted and you must be too. I don't think this is a conversation to have when we're not at our best. I'll call you tomorrow. I hope you're okay after what your Dad said to you.

I switch my phone off again and slip it into my purse, ignoring the look Leigh gives me. She wasn't the one who told him she was pregnant. She doesn't know how he responded. She has no idea how it made me feel.

All he kept saying was that we needed to take a test.

That we shouldn't jump to conclusions yet.

Let's get a test and make sure before we go any further.

Leigh doesn't know that these were almost exactly the same words Tucker said to me before he made me get an abortion.

I can't call Ethan back now because I'm not ready to have my heart broken if all he wants to talk about is getting a damn test.

32

ETHAN

GAGE

Have you heard from her?

ME

She sent a text an hour ago when she arrived in London telling me she'd call today.

ME

Why are you awake? It's 4am. I thought you were doing better with your insomnia.

GAGE

Not while Shayla's fucking with me.

ME

Sorry, man. Maybe it's time to take Blair's advice?

GAGE

There would have to be no other option before I'd hire her.

GAGE

What are you going to do?

ME

I'm about to board a plane.

ME

I've really fucked this up, Gage.

GAGE

Yeah, you did, but it's not the end of the world. You'll get face-to-face with her and fix it.

ME

It fucking feels like I've ruined everything.

GAGE

That's because you love her. Everything feels a million times worse when you love her.

I HAVEN'T TOLD Gage that I'm in love with Maddie, but it doesn't surprise me that he's already figured it out.

ME

Sorry about the ice cream and late night with Luna. I had to bribe her with something.

GAGE

Payback will be a bitch.

Thank fuck for my brother. Gage is the one who talked me off the ledge last night when I was losing my shit over becoming a father. He shared that he also had doubts before Luna was born, not confident that he'd make a good father. That stunned me because he's a great dad. We talked for a few hours and that conversation really helped put my mind at ease.

I imagine that Maddie thinks I don't want the baby. I certainly didn't say anything yesterday to indicate that's not the truth. If we'd had that conversation at any other time, away from distractions, it would have gone down very differently.

We would have talked the way we always do, openly sharing our fears and concerns, as well as our hopes. I would have been able to express where I was coming from, which was a valid place of doubt over my ability to be a good parent. And she would have been able to tell me why she was so anxious over telling me about the pregnancy.

But, we didn't have those opportunities and where we've ended is a murky pit of misunderstandings.

I've thought deeply about what Dad said to me last night about parenting and marriage. I think what he was essentially saying was that parenting is teamwork and a team can't show up and get the job done well if they aren't *together*.

I think communication, trust, and respect are some key qualities of a great team. And when it comes to being a great father, a husband needs to show up in his marriage first by taking into consideration his wife's needs, because if her needs aren't met, the communication, trust, and respect are out the window. And vice versa. The trickle-down effect to their children comes from that, which is exactly what happened in my family.

I did not show up well as Madeline's partner yesterday in the way she needed and that is what I need to do now.

My flight leaves just after 4 a.m. and I try to catch some sleep once we're in the air. I manage a couple of broken hours at the most. When I land in London, I check for a missed call or text from Maddie and find both, which helps settle my gut a little. At least she's not completely shutting me out.

> MILLER
>
> I'm sorry I missed you. I won't get a chance to try again until tonight.

She has never not been able to find even just a few minutes for me in the midst of her busy work schedule. I think she's avoiding me and I need to know why because it's unusual for her to stop communicating with me.

I don't call her. I text Leigh.

> ME
>
> Hey, it's Ethan. How's Madeline? Is she doing okay?

She comes straight back to me.

> LEIGH
>
> Holy fuck, Hottie, you have screwed up!

> ME
>
> Yeah, I know. What are the chances of getting a ticket or pass or whatever I need to get into the studio to see Maddie before the show is filmed this afternoon? I'm assuming you're already there.

> LEIGH
>
> You're here? In London?

ME

Yeah.

LEIGH

If my lifeblood wasn't draining from me, I
would be way more enthusiastic right
now, but that was a good decision.

ME

So, a pass?

LEIGH

Leave it with me. I'll get you in.

ME

Thanks.

LEIGH

And Hottie?

ME

Yeah?

LEIGH

Don't fuck this up again.

ME

You didn't tell me how Madeline is.

LEIGH

At the risk of breaking girl code rules,
your girl is struggling big time. IDK what's
going on in her head but she's refusing to
take a pregnancy test. She keeps crying
and then there's the occasional bout of
screaming. Whatever you did to her, you
did it well and good. And if you tell her I
told you all this, I will deny it until the day
I die. And I will make you hurt. But for the
love of god, Ethan, FIX THIS.

I will forever regret the way I handled that conversation, but since I can't change it now, all I can do is fix my mistake.

After I leave the airport, I gather supplies and head to the TV studios where Madeline is recording an episode of a live talk show. I receive a text from the photography conference organizers on my way.

IPTC

Ethan, we received your email advising of your inability to attend the conference tomorrow. We're disappointed you can't make it but hope all is okay with you. It's quite unfortunate you had to withdraw. We know you would have received the kind of work opportunities from the conference that would be invaluable to your career. We will endeavor to send people your way where we can. Best, Janie.

She's right that I'll miss a lot of work opportunities after withdrawing, but I can't find it in me to care. Not when the only thing I care about is making sure Madeline is okay and then doing everything I can to convince her that I'm the man she wants to raise a child with.

After I read that text, I tap one out to Madeline.

ME

> ILY, Miller. I'm on my way to you rn and
> we're going to talk this out. I think you're
> avoiding me because I didn't give you
> the support you needed. And that's okay.
> I'd probably do the same thing if I told a
> guy I was pregnant and the first thing he
> said was, "Fuck". That's a massive red
> flag. I'll save the rest of what I want to
> say to you for when I'm looking at you,
> but I have two urgent questions that I
> really hope you choose to send a reply
> to. 1. I know I hurt you and you aren't
> okay but are you feeling okay pregnancy-
> wise? and 2. Do you prefer lavender or
> chamomile?

I hit send and wait, hoping to fuck that she reads it
and replies.

A reply comes through within three minutes.

MILLER

> You did not just tell me that you love me
> via text!

Fuck, I have never felt relief the way I feel it now. I feel
winded.

ME

> Shit. I thought that meant I like you.

MILLER

> Smart-ass.

MILLER

> And you're already in London?

ME

Yes. I won't ever wait to fix things between us.

MILLER

How did you know where I was?

ME

There's this little thing called my girlfriend's calendar that's on my phone.

MILLER

Your smart mouth is going to get you into trouble, Black.

ME

Are you going to answer my questions?

MILLER

I don't feel sick or anything. But apparently, I'm a raging, hormonal, pregnant woman.

ME

That all seems pretty standard from what I've been reading.

MILLER

You've been reading up on pregnancy?

ME

Yes. There's a fuckload to learn and only a very short window of time.

MILLER

You are such a nerd.

ME

The other answer?

MILLER

I can't decide. I love both.

ME

That's good enough for me.

MILLER

This is a lot of texting for you.

ME

You're telling me I could have called?

She calls me and I fumble with my fucking phone in my haste to answer the call.

"I was thinking of baby names on the flight over," I say.

"Did you come up with any that you like?" she asks and I hate the tentativeness I can hear in her voice.

"I'm still thinking, but what I realized is that I don't know your middle name."

"It's Wren. That was my mother's middle name and her mother's too."

"So, our kid's middle name will be Wren."

"Well, I mean, if we have a girl."

"I just googled it. It's gender neutral, but regardless, there are no rules, Miller. We can give our kid whatever name we want."

"Okay, *no*," she says, quite bossy, and *there's* my girl. All that tentativeness has disappeared. "I know you're all fast and loose with your 'no rules' thing, but there is no way I'm sending our child out into the world with a weird name. A friend of mine in school had a weird name and she was picked on all the time for it. We are not doing that to our child, Black."

Fuck, I love her.

"Two things. Firstly, thank you for telling Gage all your thoughts on the fact I don't have a password on my phone. He gave me a lecture about that last night, and at the time I didn't realize it came from you, but he used the term 'fast and loose', which I thought was fucking odd for him, and now I see it was your term, which makes much more sense."

"You're very welcome," she says so sweetly it makes me grin. "But you didn't listen to him, did you?"

"Fuck no."

She sighs like she's highly frustrated with me and I decide that I want a lifetime of those sighs. "What's the other thing you wanted to tell me?"

"With this weird name shit, is there a list of weird names? Like, who makes that ruling?"

"I do love you, Ethan Black, but honestly, trust me, some names are weird and I will tell you if you choose one."

She just told me she loves me like it's old news to her. It's not old to me, though, and I'm taking a moment to sit with it, to enjoy how fucking good it feels to know that the woman I love feels the same way.

When I don't speak, she prods, "Ethan?"

"You just told me that you love me, Miller. I'm taking a moment here."

The line goes silent for a few moments before she says quietly, "It feels like we're doing everything the wrong way in this relationship."

"What's the right way?"

More silence for a beat. "Well, not meeting the love of your life in the middle of New York traffic while running away from your ex-fiancé for a start." She releases a breath. "And not making the man you love jump really fucking fast when he doesn't want to. And I really hate that we're having this conversation over the phone. It's not how things should be done."

"Baby, the way we should do things is however we decide. Would I prefer to be in the same room as you right now having this conversation? Fuck yes. But I'll take a phone call over no conversation at all. And let's address the jumping fast thing. That's not an issue for me and I regret making you think it was."

"You were pretty adamant about it when we talked about your tattoo."

"And then I got to know you, and honestly, Miller, it wouldn't have been jumping too fast for me if you'd moved into my condo rather than buying your own. I should have told you that at the time. I don't even want you to move into yours next week when it closes."

The silence is deafening after I say that.

"Maddie, talk to me. Tell me why you showed up with fear in your eyes yesterday when you came to tell me you were pregnant."

Her voice shakes like tears are close when she says, "I didn't think you would want the baby. I thought you would leave me."

"Have I done something or said something to make you think that?"

"I thought you would think it was too soon . . . but I also know that everything that happened with Tucker and my abortion played into my faulty thinking." Her voice wobbles again. "I'm sorry I ran away from this rather than talking to you."

"Well, you didn't technically run away. You had to leave for work."

"You're giving me an out, Ethan, that I don't deserve."

"Okay, here's what I think. I've told you before that I don't fuck about with fairness in relationships. I think that at different times in our lives, we'll need varying degrees of support, of love, of grace. We're gonna have misunderstandings and hard times. That's a given. What we don't know yet is who will need more grace in which difficulty, or who will need more support, or love. There are no rules about that shit as far as I'm concerned. We fly by the seat of our pants on all that. The only rule I will ever follow is to love you with everything inside of me, even in the middle of a misunderstanding. Even when you're frustrating the hell out of me. Even when you're picking a fight with me that doesn't need to be picked. Even when you're throwing so much fucking slang my way I can't follow a word of what you're saying. I will love you and adore you, and I will always fight for you. The rest will take care of itself if I follow that one rule."

Silence greets me again, but this time it's closely followed by crying. "I love you, Ethan Black," she gets out in between sobs. "And you went and learned about flags." More sobbing. "And you did all that texting for me even though you hate texting." The sobs increase as she splutters, "You found ILY." After that, it's a good thing I've arrived at the studio because she can't stop crying.

"Babe, where's Leigh?" I get out of the car and load my arms up with the things I bought her.

She answers my question but I can't make out a single word she says and I wonder if these tears are in response to what I said to her or from her hormones.

"Okay, I'm here," I say, "so I'm going to hang up and find my way inside."

"Okay."

I call Leigh and hear Madeline crying in the background while I find out where to go to be let in. Ten minutes later, I walk into Madeline's dressing room and every muscle in my body relaxes when I see her. How that can happen, I have no idea, but it always does when I'm with her.

She's sitting in the makeup chair while a woman paints her face. Her hair is hanging in loose waves over her shoulders. And she's wearing torn jeans with a white T-shirt. She's fucking beautiful and I need every other fucker in this room to get out.

I eye Leigh and while this chick is great at everything she does, she's exceptional at reading my mind when it comes to Madeline. She takes one look at me and is instantly rounding everyone up and herding them out of the room.

She's the last one to leave, and as she walks through the door, I say, "Thank you."

"You owe me, Hottie, and I *will* be collecting."

"Whatever you want, it's yours." My attention has already shifted to Madeline who has moved off her stool and is looking at me like I'm a fucking king. If I don't get to see another sunrise it won't matter because what she's giving me in this moment is the only thing a man needs to die happy.

My arms are around her before the door clicks closed and then I'm lifting a hand to slide into her hair so I can pull her mouth to mine. When she gives me what I want,

I vow to myself to do whatever it takes to never lose this, to never lose *her.*

Her body sways into mine and she moans into our kiss, and *fuck.*

When we draw apart, I keep her close and study her face, taking in the puffiness around her eyes. Sweeping my thumb over her cheek lightly, I say, "I can't promise I won't ever make you cry again, but I'm gonna do my damnedest not to."

She grips my shirt tightly and breathes, "Stop talking right now, Black."

"That's gonna make having a conversation with you real hard."

"We don't have a lot of time to talk now. I only have fifteen minutes until I have to do this interview, which means we've got about five minutes before I have to finish doing hair and makeup."

"Your hair is perfect."

"Yes, to you, but not for TV."

I run my eyes down her body, stopping on the white T-shirt that says, "Girls Can Do Anything." "We're gonna need that shirt in every size."

She frowns. "Do you mean for when I put on weight while I'm pregnant?"

"No, I mean for our daughter."

"We might have a son."

"This time, yeah."

She blinks. Grips my shirt harder. "How many children do you want?"

"However many you wanna give me."

"Ethan." My name whispers out of her as her eyes

shine and I think I've just failed at my pledge to not make her cry.

The door to the room opens and Judy strides in with an air of command. Meeting my gaze, she says, "Madeline needs to finish getting ready."

"No, we've still got stuff to discuss."

The way Judy gapes at me makes me think not many people say no to her. The next nine months are gonna be a rude wake-up call for her. "I don't think you understand, Ethan," she starts, but I cut her off.

"Yeah, I get it, but you're gonna have to give me about ten more minutes with her."

Madeline looks at her. "Give us a minute, Judy. I won't be long."

Judy looks anything but pleased. "Graham won't be happy if you hold his show up."

When Madeline simply nods to let her know she heard, Judy leaves, but not before throwing me a dirty look.

Maddie's expression is part chastising, part I-love-you-anyway. "Is this your new plan of attack with my team? You're gonna try bossing them around like you boss me?"

"There's not going to be any trying about it, Miller. It's my job to protect you and our child, and that's what I'm gonna do."

"I still haven't taken a test," she says softly.

"Do you want to do that now?" Leigh already told me this and I think there's something I'm missing here.

"Yes, but first, I want to tell you why I was hurt yesterday."

"I assumed it was because of my reaction and lack of support."

"That didn't help, but no, it was the fact you kept focusing on getting a test before we went any further." Her voice holds a deep ache that I hate having contributed to. "That was exactly what Tucker told me. It brought up a lot of feelings over my abortion and the way he treated me. I think it triggered my brain into making me believe that you would do the same thing. And while I kept trying to talk myself down from thinking that, because I know you would never do that, I just couldn't get past those irrational thoughts." She looks at me sadly. "I'm so sorry, Ethan. I hate that past stuff you had nothing to do with came between us."

"Well, I froze because of my past, so you're not alone. I'd just had a conversation with Dad and had a million thoughts running around my brain about being a father. When you told me I was going to be one, all I could think was that I wasn't fit to be a father, because what do I know about raising a child. My self-doubt shut me down."

"Was it a good conversation with your dad?"

"It was fucking unexpected. He gave me an insight into his parenting choices and he told me he was sorry for a lot of things. It'll take a bit to process."

She smiles. "I've liked watching you two growing closer."

"Yeah," I say gruffly because the conversation with Dad is still affecting me.

With one last smile, she eyes the massive shopping bag I brought in with me. "What's in the bag?"

I turn and reach for it. "I picked up a few things that I thought you might like." I start unpacking the bag. "I did some research on what kinds of things pregnant women could use for self-care. I don't know that you'll use all of it, but I grabbed what I thought seemed useful or that I thought you'd like."

Madeline watches as I fill a table with things like belly butter, a silk pillowcase, a pregnancy support pillow, a soft plush robe that I thought could be good for lounging around in at home, a foot massager, a heated eye mask, a lavender moisturizer and a chamomile one, and a pregnancy journal. "Oh my god, Ethan." She picks up the journal and flicks through it. "I love all of this."

I reach for her hand and pull her in close again. "I bought some pregnancy tests too. I thought we could do it together."

"As in you pee on a stick while I pee on another?" She manages to keep a straight face but there's a fun sparkle in her eyes.

"Yeah, baby, that's exactly what I was thinking."

Her grin is so fucking beautiful.

She grabs one of the tests and goes into the bathroom. I wait outside but she keeps the door open while she pees on the stick.

"You have to pee on it for five seconds, Miller," I say as I lean against the doorjamb. "And keep the tip pointing down."

"You're so cute, knowing that. Did you do thorough research on every brand of test? You know, to make sure we got only the best."

I arch my brows at her smart-assery. "You know I fucking did."

She grins as she puts the lid back on the stick and lays

it flat on the vanity. "For a fast-and-loose guy, you're so pedantic about some things."

"Are you gonna complain about that when it benefits you?" I set the timer on my phone.

"I'm not complaining, Black. Just making an observation."

I drag her in close to me, resting my hand on the curve of her ass. "You know, we never did finish ordering the songs on our playlist."

"Oh, I did."

"What? Without my input?"

"Well, I mean, you can rearrange them, but we're not changing the #1 song."

"That sounds like a rule I wouldn't care to follow."

She gives me a look. I imagine it's the same look she'll give our kids one day when she's making it clear she's to be obeyed. "You break that rule, there will be consequences."

"What's your #1 song?"

She glances down at my phone that's sitting next to the pregnancy test. "Take a look for yourself. And it's *our* #1 song."

The timer goes off on my phone as I open up our playlist and find the song she chose, smiling when I see her choice, fucking *loving* her choice. My attention is immediately shifted to the stick sitting on the vanity that will tell us if we really are going to be parents.

Maddie's hand finds mine while we both read the result.

Two lines.

Two lines that represent an entire life that will be lived because Madeline Miller let me join her on a recklessly, wild adventure and stole my heart without even trying.

She brings her beautiful blue eyes to mine. "It had to be that song."

I trace my gaze over every curve, every line, every inch of her face, wondering if our baby will have those same lines and curves or if they'll have mine. "Tell me your reason."

Her hand comes to my abs. I hope it always does. "There are so many reasons."

"You're gonna have to spell them out for me, Miller."

"I mean, firstly, it's a great song."

"Agreed."

She turns into me, presses her body to mine, keeping her hand right there on my abs. "Second, life really is a highway." She gives me her mouth. I will never have enough time with her mouth. "And you taught me that the bumps along the road make life interesting."

"They do." I only ever want to ride those bumps with her.

"And lastly." She grips my neck with her other hand and if I can't have an eternity of her claiming my neck, I don't want that eternity. "When we listened to that song, it was the first time you looked at me like I was everything you ever wanted to see."

EPILOGUE

@THETEA_GASP

BESTIE, we are dead after spotting our girl @madelinemontana at a football game yesterday with @ethanblack and his family. Never have we seen her so happy. She laughed and cheered her way through the game while her bae struggled to take his eyes off her #sigh But wait for it . . . WAIT. FOR. IT. After the game, these lovebirds were sharing a private moment (ahem, word to the wise Mr. Black, there are no private moments for you anymore) when bae leaned in to kiss her and put his hand on Maddie's stomach very daddy-possessively like, and shee-eesh, holy mother of little baby bows, we think they're expecting a little #MontanaBlack of their own #gasp Whatever will her ex think of this? Wait, what was his name again? Thinking, thinking, thinking. Nope, we're drawing a blank and we know you are too, because no one cares about him anymore. Seriously, @tuckerbrandt has shown us who he really is and all we can say is no wonder Maddie ran wildly into her new bae's arms. It's time to get your riding boots back out, girlfriend. We're in full cowgirl era now. And one other thing, whoever dreamed up the idea of bringing FIVE of those Black brothers into this world should be given a gold medal. Forget subscribing to RedZone. Take our money and give us BlackZone.

Thank you so much for reading Ethan & Maddie's story. I hope you loved it as much as I do!

Want more?
Scan the QR code to download their bonus epilogue!

The next book is...

Yours Until Forever

NOTE FROM NINA ABOUT THIS SERIES

Dear Reader,

One of my favourite things about this series is the family dynamics woven throughout each book. I love getting to know the brothers a little bit more as we go deeper into the Black family with each book that's written.

I want you to know that I plan to write a series epilogue once all the brothers have their story. In that epilogue, we'll get to catch up with each couple and get more of their HEA.

So, if, after reading Ethan & Maddie's book, you're feeling a little like "but I wanna know more about their baby and their life together as a family", never fear, I'll continue to weave their story into the rest of the series.

To be honest, I fell so hard for this couple that I really would love to write their pregnancy novella! If that's something you'd love to read, please let me know! Either on social media or send me an email:

nina@ninalevinebooks.com

Nina x

ALSO BY NINA LEVINE

Escape With a Billionaire Series

Ashton Scott

Jack Kingsley

Beckett Pearce

Jameson Fox

Owen North

Only Yours Series

(The Black Brothers Billionaire Romance)

Accidentally, Scandalously Yours

Yours Actually

Recklessly, Wildly Yours

Storm MC Series

Storm (Storm MC #1)

Fierce (Storm MC #2)

Blaze (Storm MC #3)

Revive (Storm MC #4)

Slay (Storm MC #5)

Sassy Christmas (Storm MC #5.5)

Illusive (Storm MC #6)

Command (Storm MC #7)

Havoc (Storm MC #8)

Gunnar (Storm MC #9)

Wilder (Storm MC #10)

Colt (Storm MC #11)

Sydney Storm MC Series

Relent (#1)

Nitro's Torment (#2)

Devil's Vengeance (#3)

Hyde's Absolution (#4)

King's Wrath (#5)

King's Reign (#6)

King: The Epilogue (#7)

Storm MC Reloaded Series

Hurricane Hearts (#1)

War of Hearts (#2)

Christmas Hearts (#3)

Battle Hearts (#4)

The Hardy Family Series

Steal My Breath (single dad romance)

Crave Series

Be The One (rockstar romance)

www.ninalevinebooks.com

ABOUT THE AUTHOR

Nina Levine

Nina Levine is a *USA Today* and *Wall Street Journal* bestselling author of over thirty books, including the Escape With A Billionaire series and the bestselling Storm MC series. She's known for protective alphas and women who don't hand their hearts over easily.

She lives in Australia and when she isn't creating with words, she's busy trying to be a Pilates goddess, a Peloton Queen, or drinking one too many gins with friends. Often though, she can be found curled up in the sun with a good book.

www.ninalevineromance.com

Scan the QR code on the next page to join my reader group on Facebook:

PLAYLIST

"Comeback" by Carly Rae Jensen, Bleachers
"this is how you fall in love" by Jeremy Tucker, Chelsea Cutler
"As You Are" by Daughtry
"Wild Horses" by Alicia Keys, Adam Levine
"Horses" by Keith Urban
"What My World Spins Around" by Jordan Davis
"The Good Ones" by Gabby Barrett
"Starlight" by Taylor Swift
"Everything Has Changed" by Taylor Swift, Ed Sheeran
"A Lot More Free" by Max McNown